LET'S TALK ABOUT IT

ANGEL AVERETTE – POWELL

Let's Talk About It is a work of fiction. Names, characters, places and incidents are products of the author's imagination. Any resemblance to actual events or locales or person, living or dead, is entirely coincidental.

Copyright © 2021 Angel Averette-Powell

LIBRARY OF CONGRESS CATALOGING-IN-PUBLICATION DATA
Averette-Powell, Angel
Let's Talk About It / Angel Averette-Powell.
p. cm.

ISBN: 978-0-578-96692-2 (print)

Publisher: Crown Yourself Production Publishing LLC

Cover design by: Keni Aryani

Editor: Tiffany McCain and Morshe D. Araujo

Printed in the United States of America.

DEDICATION

This book is dedicated to my mother, Odell Averette. My aunts Loventrice Averette, Roberta Ann Williams, Faye Alice Porch, Sarah Wilson, Bobbi King, and Lucille Huntley. My beloved grandmother, Christine McElrath. My big sister, Michelle Ratliff. My daughters – Mioria Averette and Chrisette Powell. My husband, Christopher Powell. My cousins – Christina William, Charlene William, and Faye William. Kacey Heard, my best-friend. And my beloved wonderful friend, Lenette R. McElderry, may you rest in eternal peace dear friend, but I also dedicate this to you, and all women and men around the world. May this book help us remove skeletons, reveal secrets, and heal.

"The truth shall set you free…"
Jenny

Table of Contents

ACKNOWLEDGMENTS

First, I got to give big thanks to the head king of my life and that's God. He blessed me with a gift, that I had been carrying for years, but I didn't know I had till I picked up a special authors book. Ms. Lurlene McDaniel. Her books were real, and that's what attracted me to her. "Garden Full Of Angels," was the book, that made me get to the computer and start typing. So, I thank God for placing this woman's books into my life, and for awakening the writer within me.

Secondly, I want to thank my family. My Husband, Christopher Powell. For believing in my dream and buying me the laptop to type up all these amazing stories, that I'm about to flood my readers with. Thank you, Hubby. Next is my daughters for being patient with me, while I worked on this story. Mommy loves you girls and thanks you for understanding her dream. Thirdly, I want to thank my cover designer Keni Aryani, for and awesome cover design. My editors, Tiffany McCain and Morshe D. Araujo, thank you ladies for your hard and honest work.

Lastly, I want to thank you. Dear Reader, I want to thank you for taking out the time to purchase and read my book. It's because of you, that us authors are able to do a craft that we love. I hoped this book motivates, inspire, change and heal you. 'Cause this is what it has done for me. Thank you.

Sincerely,
Angel Averette-Powell
Queen of Storytelling

CHAPTER 1
~BREWED COFFEE~

Life is filled with so many wonders. Wonders of, how did I get to this point in my life where I'm working three jobs to support myself and my son. Where did I go wrong? How did I allow this? There were so many things I wanted to do and be in this life, but I had to give them up. My son is not the reason for the delayed dreams – just me. It was always me. I'm a black woman – not light or brown, just dark – and I don't feel beautiful. I think that I am so dark that my beauty is hidden somewhere underneath all this darkness – and no one sees me. They don't see the soul of Valarie, just the angry black woman. They assume I'm angry because I don't carry a smile everywhere I go. They assume I have no personality because I'm not chirpy like the white girl Jenny, but honestly, who the hell is really that happy everywhere they go. It's a front, and I'm not the type to front. I'm too real and black for that, but they see my body. It's not as tone and perfect as Nina or slender like Stephanie, but they see it. My big, oversized breasts, out of waxed hips, big and wide flabby ass is enough for me to be seen. I still wonder though. Can God see and hear me? If so, could he come on down from the heavens and save a wretch like me? I guess you can't save what's lost. I'm still lost and waiting to be rescued. Don't look like it's happening today. I'm just brewed coffee – waiting to be poured out of this glass prison.

"Valarie! Valarie!" Gerald Coleman shouted angrily as he impatiently waits for his coffee.

"Hold on, Mr. Coleman. I'm coming with your coffee." Valarie was exasperated with this man. Gerald Coleman was the kind of man who you didn't want coming into your coffee shop. He was bad-mannered, grumpy, and crippled and loved giving Valarie a tough time. She never understood what Gerald Coleman's issue was with her. She always prepared his coffee how he asked, and every time, he would make her remake it. She hated having him as a customer. Gerald was a short, bright-skinned man with freckles. He had lost his leg fighting in the Gulf War, so he walked with a cane. He and his son, Harp, owned a furniture store across the street called Colemans. Every Monday morning, Gerald would come in for a cup of coffee. He and the owner, Betty, were friends. They served in the military together. Gerald was a sweet man – when he wanted to be. He had his picks when it came to who served him coffee. Valarie wasn't one of those picks.

"Speed it up! I got a doctor's appointment at ten!" he shouted.

"You'll make it; it's just eight-thirty." Staring at the clock on the wall, Valarie rushed to finish preparing the coffee. She placed the mug on a small white plate and grabbed a spoon and napkin before quickly walking to Gerald's table.

"Here's your coffee." She tried to hand the mug and plate to him, but he snatched the cup from her hand and gently placed the rim against his lips, shaking as if he would drop the mug. He drank the coffee. Valarie was relieved. *Finally, I made a cup of coffee he liked.* After a few more sips, Gerald spat out the coffee with a disgusted look on his face.

"What the hell is this?" he asked.

"It's what you ordered," Valarie replied. She walked away from the table to the counter and grabbed a damp rag from the dish bucket. She squeezed the excess water out, wishing she were squeezing Gerald's neck. *How could he act like he was enjoying the coffee and spit it out?* She was pissed. This was the same routine every Monday with him.

"I didn't order this!" Gerald continued complaining. "You must've mixed up my order!" Valarie inhaled and exhaled as she walked back to Gerald's table with the damp cloth in her hand. She wanted to slap him across the face with the rag as if she were Pooty Tang.

"With whom? You the first one in here every Monday. Ain't nobody been in here but you!" Valarie wiped his table. "And you order the same thing every Monday," she added, annoyed by Gerald at this point.

"This not the coffee I had last Monday – it tastes different!"

Valarie finished wiping the table. "Mr. Coleman, that's the same coffee you have every Monday – roasted, with three sugars, two milks, and four punches of cream," she announced as she left his table to place the rag back into the bucket before going to stand behind the register at the counter. She had had it with him.

"Now, look! I don't have all morning to argue with you. I got other things to tend to," Valarie stated.

"Tend to making me some more coffee! How you going to give me this nasty shit! And make it right this time!" Gerald didn't like Valarie. He felt she always had an attitude when he would come into the café. She wouldn't laugh or joke with him like the others. She just always looked angry. Like she was never having a good day. *Why did Betty put this woman as the face of her company? Making her a shift leader? Valarie's look is too black. Her face isn't relaxed like most women. It looked vicious and ready to explode. She need to put someone up here like that light-skinned girl, Nina. She's the best face and complexion for this place.*

She's at it again. Valarie is always running off the customers. Nina was in the back, stocking the shelves with the freight that had just come in that morning. Nina had opened the café and was hoping she could get her work done in the backroom before Ms. Betty came in from her doctor's appointment. But some days, that was impossible, especially when Valarie stayed arguing with customers. Nina had stood back and listened to Valarie and Gerald throw shots at each other for far too long. She placed the last of the freight on the shelf. She wasn't feeling up to working upfront with Valarie or saving her ass from another customer, but she loved Ms. Betty, and she wanted to see her business thrive. So, she remained, cleaning up Valarie's mess. Nina headed through the double doors, where she immediately saw Valarie and Mr. Coleman exchanging words. Nina walked to Gerald's table, hoping to diffuse his tension toward Valarie.

"Mr. C, I figured that was you I heard up here. What's the problem?"

Gerald pointed his finger at Valarie. "That damn girl over there… made me this nasty coffee!" He raised his mug and showed Nina. "This ain't what I ordered. I need another cup! I'm not drinking this nasty shit," he added.

"Nina," Valarie said, "that's the same coffee he orders every Monday when he comes in here, and every time I fix it, he spits it out."

Nina could see the defeat in Valarie's face. *Gerald Coleman has given her a run for her money today.* "Mr. C," Nina replied. "Do you want me to fix you some coffee?"

"Hell, yeah! I paid my money. I better be getting some coffee!"

"No need to worry. I got you, Mr. C." Nina grabbed the coffee mug and made her way toward the counter to prepare Gerald's coffee.

Gerald watched her as she walked away. To him, Nina was beautiful. She had big, honey-blond, curly hair styled in an afro, like how the women wore their hair in the seventies. She wore long, pretty eyelashes that curled up like cat claws. Her skin glowed as if the sun followed her everywhere she went. She had a tattoo on her right chest that read: *With Pain Comes Strength*. Gerald could tell the tattoo meant something to her. Every day she would come to work, she made sure she wore a shirt underneath her apron to reveal the message. She exposed the tattoo like a badge of honor, and everyone needed to see it.

As Nina prepared Gerald's coffee, Valarie watched, wondering would he spit out the coffee Nina prepared, like he did hers. Valarie, in some ways, was envious of Nina. The woman was pretty to Valarie. Her body was perfect from top to bottom. Nothing was out of proportion like Valarie's body. As Nina finished up with the coffee, Valarie stated, "I made his coffee the same way."

"Let's just see what happens," Nina replied and walked back over to Gerald.

He wet his pants, watching her draw closer to his table. She was like a walking gelatin. Every step she took caused her breasts, legs, thighs, and ass to jiggle. Nina placed the mug on the table.

"Here you go Mr. C, tell me how it taste." He picked up the mug while flicking his tongue in and out. Touching his lips to the rim, he sipped the coffee.

"How does it taste, Mr. C?" He glanced up at Nina and smiled a warm smile of satisfaction.

"Now that's good coffee. Thank you."

"You're welcome," Nina said with a smile. "If you need anything else, Mr. C, let me know."

He nodded while drinking and enjoying his coffee. The coffee Nina had prepared him was the best mouth orgasm he'd ever had. Nina returned behind the counter where Valarie stood. Valarie shook her head in disbelief.

"You fixed it the same way I did," Valarie said. "I don't get it."

Nina shrugged. She didn't have the answer to why Gerald was giving Valarie such a hard time, but it delighted her to know she had made his day with her coffee.

Ding Dong, the front entrance doorbell chimed.

"Nina, darling!" Peaches said, strutting through the door like the drag vulture she was. Peaches was a woman, but she wasn't a woman. To others, she was a man dressed in women's clothing pretending to be a woman, but to Nina, she was a woman, inside and out.

"Peaches! What's up, girl?" Nina asked as she leaned on the counter to talk with her friend.

"Honey, nothing! I came to get me a latté so I can get ready for this partay. You coming through?"

"If I can get someone to keep an eye on Queenie, I will."

"What about Todd?" Peaches asked.

"Girl, fuck Todd! Till he pays me my child support, he ain't gotta ever worry about seeing Queenie."

"I feel you girl. Mama needs that check."

"Righteously!" Nina responded. She grabbed a cup and began preparing Peaches' latté.

Gerald Coleman couldn't believe his eyes. He knew Peaches and couldn't believe how she was dressed. She wore a yellow sun hat, a floral red and yellow top, cut-out jeans, and red high heels. Gerald knew Peaches as Percy Henderson. He remembered her from when she played football in high school with his son, Harp. Gerald had to get up out of his chair and get closer to make sure his eyes weren't deceiving him. He approached Peaches and stared at her.

Peaches watched Nina fix her drink but could feel Gerald breathing on her neck. She turned around and found him staring at her in disbelief; his mouth gaped open like a frog waiting to catch flies.

"Can I help you with something?" Peaches asked.

"What are you?" Gerald said.

Peaches chuckled and smiled. "What do I look like?"

"A confused motherfucker," Gerald replied.

"Well, no confusion here baby!" Peaches snapped her fingers, pulled out her geisha fan, and snapped it open in Gerald's face. "I know exactly who I am."

"I do too! Your name is Percy Henderson. You played football back in the day with my son, Harp. Yeah. You were a wide receiver."

"I still am one," Peaches replied with a saucy smirk. "'Cause I love to receive it, and I know how to spread it real wide, but you can call me Peaches." She lowered her fan and placed her hand on Gerald's shoulder. "Everyone calls me Peaches."

Gerald quickly removed her hand from his shoulder. He looked her up and down in disgust. "Look here, Percy. I'm not calling you no damn Peaches! If it look like a duck, quack like a duck, walk like a duck, it's a duck. Now, I don't care what you change your name to or how much you try to look like a woman. If your birth certificate says Percy, then your ass is Percy. I'm not calling you no Peaches. Them sissy ass boys you sleep with may call you that, but I ain't. Hell, what I look like calling a grown-ass man Peaches. Sick son of a bitch!" Gerald made his way toward the entrance door. He couldn't continue to stand in the face of something he couldn't understand and didn't care to.

"Bye, Mr. C," Nina shouted out to him. "Here girl." Nina handed the latté to Peaches.

"Thank you baby," Peaches said. Reaching into her bra, she retrieved a few folded bills and handed the money to Nina for her latté.

Nina could tell Peaches was upset with how Gerald talked to her. Nina had to say something to lift Peaches' spirit. "Girl, you got to overlook Mr. C. He ain't nothing but a shit talker."

"Trust me, I know. Why he trying to call me out? He be the same one at the club getting fresh with the trans. Then, when he see somebody he knows, he try and play like he lost. Talking about he thought this was The Palace. Get the fuck out of here!"

Nina laughed. "Girl, shut up. Mr. C got a fantasy!"

"That ain't all he got, but it ain't my tea to spill, and I be damn if sugar don't look like salt. Honey, let me take my latté and finish setting up for this party." She pulled out her keys to crank up her 2019 Mercedes-Benz GLE-Class, that was parked in front of the café and waved by at Nina before leaving. Peaches was an event planner in The Magic City of Birmingham, Alabama. She was renowned for having eye-bulging, mouth-dropping events. If anyone had a bash that needed to be the talk of the town, Peaches was the one to make that happen.

"Okay girl. Do you need your change?" Nina asked.

"No. Keep it as a tip," Peaches insisted.

"Oh, thank you, girl."

"You welcome boo. Just call me if you decide to get out tonight "

"I will," Nina said. "See you later girl." Peaches made her way out the door. Nina faced Valarie, who had been standing in front of the register, watching everything without saying a word.

"Here, I'll let you ring it up," Valarie said. She moved away from the register, allowing Nina to ring up Peaches' order. "So, let me ask you something," Valarie said. "You okay with having a friend like Peaches around your daughter?" Nina looked at Valarie briefly, then focused her eyes back on the register.

"Yeah. Hell, I got people in my family who are like Peaches, and my daughter knows what it is."

"So, you teach your daughter that being someone like Peaches is okay?" Nina closed out the sale, pulled the receipt from the feeder, and placed it in the drawer. She slipped her tip from Peaches into her bra and faced Valarie.

"I teach my daughter that not everyone is going to like the same things as her, and that's okay. Some people are just uniquely made to like what they like, and we can't judge them for that because it's not our place. We should embrace others and their differences. That's how you eliminate hate in this world. We got to teach love to our children. So that they can teach it to theirs and place it in this world."

While Valarie and Nina stood behind the counter discussing Peaches, Ms. Betty, the owner of the café, had arrived outside. She had been going to a shrink to help her battle her depression. The ladies didn't know it, but Betty had a lot of mental trauma she was dealing with. She had lost her husband, then a couple of months back her sister. She just couldn't figure out how to accept their deaths and let go. She hoped that going to the shrink would help, but it didn't. She had to put her emotions behind her, the best she could, so she could run her café and live her life. She approached the door, afraid of what she might walk into. *Here it goes.*

Ding Dong chimed the main entrance doorbell.

"Ladies," Betty said. She walked behind the counter to secure her purse.

"Hey, Ms. Betty," Nina and Valarie replied at the same time.

"I had a doctor's appointment this morning. So, how's everything been running?" Betty glanced around her café, making sure everything was how she left it.

"Smooth like cream," Nina said. "Mr. C came and got his coffee and bounced, and my girl Peaches stopped by too."

"Okay. So, not too bad," Betty said, still looking around her café.

"Not at all," Nina returned, "but since you here, I'm a go take my break."

"Break? It's been two hours already," Betty said, glancing at her watch.

"Yep. I opened up this morning for Valarie."

Betty look at Valarie and notice a sour look on her face.

"I was stuck in the five o'clock traffic on two-eighty. It won't happen again," Valarie said, upset with Nina for snitching.

"Well, if it's that time, go ahead. And twenty minutes, no longer, Miss Simone!"

"Yes, ma'am, Ms. Betty."

Nina walked to the back to take her break. Valarie watched Ms. Betty as she rearranged items on the counter that were out of order. That was just how Ms. Betty was. She liked order. She was a natural beauty. She had salt and pepper hair and wore her do in an afro like Flo on the T.V. show *Good Times*. She was nicely shaped for a woman her age and had a smile that could turn any frown upside down, especially Valarie.

"How'd everything go at the doctor's office?" Valarie asked.

Betty turned her head to face Valarie. She was surprised Valarie even asked about her visit to the doctor. Betty didn't want any of the ladies to know she was going to see a therapist. So, she lied and pretended she was going to her regular family doctor for checkups.

"It went pretty well. He said I'm doing fairly good for my age." Betty swallowed her guilt for fibbing when she saw a broad smile spread across Valarie's face.

"Well, that's good to know, Ms. Betty. You're very blessed. Can't too many people say that at your age."

Betty cracked a smile. "Yeah, the good Lord been watching over this fool."

Ding Dong chimed the main entrance doorbell.

James, a short, stout, light-skinned male, with dreads hanging down his back, and a beard that hid and hugged his mouth and chin like a mask, entered the café. His clothes looked as if he had been rolling in dirt, but after looking at his hands, you could tell he had the hands of a working man.

"Good morning, ladies." Betty's face lit up when she saw him. She stared at him like she was looking at a ghost. She hadn't seen him since he went away to prison for a drug trafficking.

"James!" She walked over to him and hugged him. "Boy, I ain't seen you in forever! How you been?"

"Good, Ms. Betty. I can't complain. God has really blessed me. I got a job driving trucks now."

She smiled. "Really, James! That's awesome."

James replied, "Yes, ma'am." It charmed her ears to hear he wasn't back on the streets selling drugs.

"That's good, and you like it?" she asked.

"I love it," he said, "I get to travel the world and meet a few girls."

"Alright, you better be careful with them girls," Betty said jokingly. "'Cause ain't all of them really girls."

"Oh, Ms. Betty, if I see anything poking out, I'm shooting." She laughed.

"Boy, you sound just like your mama! But I'm happy you're doing so well. You want some coffee?"

"Yes, ma'am. I'll take a cup to go." Betty glanced over at Valarie, who wasn't doing anything but looking busy. "Valarie, this James. James, Valarie. Fix him a cup of coffee. I got to run to the restroom. Excuse me, James. Valarie will help you. I'll be back." Betty left for the restroom, leaving Valarie and James alone.

"What would you like?" Valarie asked. James walked up to the counter and leaned, slowly reviewing the menu. He didn't see anything he wanted on the menu, but he saw everything he wanted in Valarie. She didn't have a supermodel face or body, but he could work with it. He thought Valarie was a nice-looking, dark-skinned woman who would look even cuter if she would just smile.

"Your number," he said to her.

"My number ain't on the menu," Valarie said.

"Well, how do I get it?"

Valarie grabbed a cup and walked over to the coffee machine. *He's trying to flirt with me.* "You like your coffee black or with cream and sugar?" she asked.

"How do you like yours?" he asked her back, trying to make conversation with her.

Valarie smirked. "I like my coffee how I like myself."

"Oh yeah? And how's that?" he asked. The more he talked, the more Valarie noticed how sexy his lips were. They were full, plump, pink and wet; from him licking them every time he spoke. His teeth were aligned like pearls on a string, straight and glossy. His voice was soft, deep and seductive. He had dimples in his cheeks that would form after he finish licking his lips. His whole mouthpiece was sexy to Valarie.

"Simple," she answered, picking up a lid and placing it on the coffee cup. "Dark, bitter, and too hot for you." She pushed the cup in front of him. "That will be three dollars and twenty-eight cents."

James rose off the counter. He dipped his hand into his pocket and gave Valarie the money.

"Thank you." She took the money and rang him up.

James took his coffee off the counter while eying Valarie suspiciously. He couldn't believe Valarie was so mean to him. He wasn't an arrogant man, but he'd never had a problem when it came to flirting. Most women would flirt back, but not Valarie. She didn't crack a smile, blush, or anything. She was just unaffected.

"You always this mean to your customers?" he asked.

"No, just you."

James smiled. "I guess that makes me special."

"Not special enough."

Betty walked back up to the counter. "Valarie, did you get him right?"

"He got his coffee," Valarie said.

"Ms. Betty, where you find her at?" James asked.

"Well, she came in for an open interview and almost jumped on your mama."

Valarie's mouth dropped open as she gazed at Ms. Betty bottle-eyed. This handsome man was the seed of spoiled milk Ruth? Betty's loudmouth friend that Valarie couldn't stand.

"Mama? Hold up. This Ms. Ruth's son?" Valarie asked.

"Yeah, this her baby boy James."

"Oh, you ain't nothing like your mama," Valarie exclaimed.

"Naw, I get the charm from my father," James said.

"Oh, you don't have that either," she quipped. "Excuse me. I gotta run to the ladies' room." Valarie hurried to the bathroom, conscious of James' eyes on her backside. To her, her behind was flabby, but to him, it had the perfect jiggle.

"Man, Ms. Betty. She so mean, put me in the mind of mama."

"Yeah, she does have that mouth like Ruth."

"You know, Ms. Betty, the reason I stopped by is that I wanted to thank you for all those encouraging letters and books you sent me while I was locked up. It really helped me to reevaluate and find myself. I know me and mama ain't always seen eye-to-eye on things, and she got her own demons she dealing with, but you always been there. Even when mama couldn't. I just wanted to say thank you, Ms. Betty, for being there for me and Jason."

Pride swelled inside Ms. Betty's chest, knowing she made an impact on James. She fought back the tears that wanted to flow like a river from her eyes.

"Oh, baby, it was nothing. Back then, we were a village, and the village looked after everybody's child – not just they own. We've gotten away from that now, but you were always like a second son to me."

"Speaking of son, how is Brian?" James asked.

Betty's face went from joyous to dry. Betty didn't like talking about her son, Brian. His girlfriend, Sidney, was the reason Betty kept her distance. Sidney treated Brian like trash, and he was too blinded by love to realize it.

"Child, I don't want to talk about Brian. He a damn fool. Still chasing behind Sidney with her mean ass."

"Well, Ms. Betty, that's what love will do to you."

"You right, 'cause that fool still ain't learnt, that love don't love nobody."

"But it takes a fool to learn," James said.

"That's true too," Betty replied.

"But hey, Ms. Betty, I got to go make this delivery. I just wanted to stop by and thank you, and I hope everything goes well with your cafe."

"Thank you, James, and you be careful out on that road."

"Yes, ma'am."

Valarie returned to the front of the café to see James leaving. He looked back at her before he exited the store.

"See you around, Valarie."

She flashed him a fake smile and waved goodbye as he gifted her with a smile of his that left her insides feeling like puddy. It had been years since Valarie had been with or loved a man. She had so many personal issues going on with herself; that she had given up on love years ago and wasn't hoping to find it any time soon. But that man, with his sexy smile and drop-dead gorgeous looks, made her rethink her sabbatical on love.

"Valarie," Betty said, "why you giving my godson such a hard time? James is a good man."

"What's your definition of a good man, Ms. Betty?" Valarie asked, wanting to hear what she had to say.

"James! He's hardworking, handsome, trying to get his life back together, and he's loyal."

Digesting her employer's words, Valarie knew, somewhere deep down inside, she believed her. But she just couldn't allow herself to fall for anyone. Instead, her focus was on her son. She worked three jobs to secure the bag for her son's future, not hers. Her life could be over any day now.

"Well, if he's that good, I don't want him," Valarie said. "Ain't nobody that good, not even me. But the truth is, I don't want no man."

Betty couldn't believe her ears. Even after losing her husband, she still missed the touch of a man.

"Don't want a man? Then what you want? A woman?" Betty asked sarcastically.

"No ma'am. I don't play them games, Ms. Betty. I'm just content with being by myself. Now don't get it twisted. I like men. I just don't want one at the moment."

Betty could tell Valarie was hiding something, but she couldn't figure out what.

"Well, do you date?" Betty asked.

"I ain't been on a real date in about ten years. Haven't slept with a man in about sixteen years." Valarie spoke before she knew it. She didn't mean for Betty to know that part of her.

"Sixteen years?! Got damn! I mean, good Lord child! What you running from?"

Valarie looked embarrassed, "I'm not running from anything. I'm just not crazy about sex or no man. My focus is my son."

Betty laughed. "Girl bye. I'm sixty years old, and I'm still getting what I want."

Valarie scrunched her nose up at Betty. "You be having sex?"

Betty placed her hands on her hip. "Hell, yeah. I got it this morning and going to get it tonight. See, you got to use Mr. Wrong while you waiting on Mr. Right. Like Peggy Scott-Adams, hell yeah, I'm getting it. That's too long for any woman to go without a man. Damn! No wonder you so angry. You built up and ain't been tore down."

"I'm not trying to get tore down," Valarie admitted.

Betty laughed again. "Trust me. You need to be tore down."

"I don't think so," Valarie said. Somedays, she did yearn to have a man, to wake up next to him every morning and make love. Someone she could go on a date with. She wanted that kind of romance, but who could give her that? Who could love her? She didn't feel she was worthy of being love.

Ding Dong chimed the front entrance doorbell.

"Praise the Lord, Saints! Praise the Lord!" Katrina said. Betty's face lit up once again, except this time like a firework show.

"Well, look at how the Lord is working today," Betty said. "Katrina!"

"Aunt Betty!" They hugged. It felt good for them to see each other. Betty stopped going to Katrina's church when her husband got sick and didn't return after he died. Betty broke out of the hug. She stood back and admired how fantastic Katrina looked. Katrina wore her hair low like Betty, except with curls, and she wore a lot of makeup. She only had big breasts; her hips were wide but no behind. She was still a pretty, light-skinned woman.

"Girl, look at you. You look good," Betty said.

"Thank you, auntie. So do you."

"Well, what can I say. You know this black won't crack. What brings you by?"

"Malaysia's birthday is next month, and I was wondering…."

"You need a cake," Betty guessed.

"You still bake, don't you?"

Betty smiled and nodded her head. "Oh yes. As you can see, I got sweets lined up and down the counter." Betty looked back at Valarie. "Valarie, hand me my appointment book." Valarie turned to retrieve the book from underneath the counter and handed it to Betty. "Oh, and Katrina, this is Valarie, my shift leader. Valarie, this is Katrina, my niece and First Lady of Calling All The Saints Temple." Katrina gave Valarie a friendly smile.

"Nice to meet you," Katrina said.

"Likewise." She raise her hand to produce a slight wave, while looking away from Betty and Katrina with her nose to the air.

"Okay, so let's see here." Betty opened her appointment book to find an empty page. "When do you need it?" she asked.

"The first Saturday of next month," Katrina replied. Betty wrote down what Katrina said.

"What time do you want to pick it up?"

Katrina pauses to consider a good time. "Can I come at eleven?"

Betty nodded. "Eleven is fine," she said as she continued scribbling down the details. "She still like chocolate?"

"Yes, and I need it big enough to serve at least thirty people," Katrina said.

"Thirty people? Y'all having a large crowd, huh." Betty raised her eyes to look at Katrina over her glasses.

"Yes ma'am."

Betty smiled then turned her attention back down to her pad. "What do you want the cake to say?"

"Happy Sweet 16, Malaysia… then put Mommy and Craig Loves You."

Betty gave Katrina an unsure look before continuing to jot down the information. "Okay, then. I will have it ready for you. The first Saturday of next month at eleven o'clock." Betty placed her pen down then snapped her appointment book closed.

"Thanks, Aunt Betty, and we really miss you at the church. You should come by sometime and fellowship with us."

"When I get a chance, I will. But, dang, I can't get over how good you look. You look just like your mother, Carole."

Carole was Betty's older sister who had died from lupus a couple of months before her husband. The bubbly façade Katrina had worn since walking into the café, became sadden after the mentioning of her mother. She lowered her eyes as silence filled the area. Betty hurried to change the subject by drawing Valarie into the conversation.

"Valarie, ain't she pretty?" Betty asked.

Valarie didn't want to answer that. In her mind, all light-skinned women were pretty, even prettier than her. She hated knowing light-skinned women were such a desirable color. Yet, hers was not. Colorism affected her so badly; she couldn't stand the presence of a light-complexion woman. Their hue intimidated her, and she didn't like that. She most definitely didn't want to tell one how pretty she was and boost her self-confidence even more than what it already was.

"Of course, she's light-skinned," Valarie responded. Betty was shocked. She couldn't believe Valarie said that.

"Now, what that got to do with anything?" Betty asked.

"I don't know. Ask society," Valarie said with a shrug. Betty placed her hands on her hips. Before she could get out a word, Katrina's phone rang.

"Oh, it's Craig. I got to take this. I'll see you the first Saturday of next month, Auntie." Katrina made her way toward the front of the main entrance door.

"Okay. It will be ready then," Betty said.

"Thank you and love you!" Katrina said, waving goodbye.

"Love you too," Betty said. She watched Katrina walk out the door. Betty missed her niece. Seeing Katrina reminded Betty of the bond she had with her sister. She wished Katrina could've stayed longer, but she understood that being the First Lady of a church demanded the majority of her time, and when Craig called, Katrina had to go. At least she'll get to see her again in another month. However, Betty didn't forget what Valarie said. She had to address it.

"Girl… you got to learn how to bite your tongue around here. You can't just say whatever comes to your mind all the time, Valarie."

"But, Ms. Betty, I told you, biting my tongue ain't me. I take my freedom of speech very seriously."

"Voice your opinion, be yourself, but choose your words carefully."

"Okay? Whatever you say, Ms. Betty," Valarie said, taking the planner that Ms. Betty handed to her.

Sometimes, Valarie made Betty regret she hired her. Valarie's mouth was just too smart. Every day she came to work, it seemed as if her attitude was getting worse. If it weren't for Ruth, Betty's best-friend, who helped her with the hiring process of picking the right candidates to work in the café, Valarie wouldn't have a job. Betty didn't want to hire Valarie due to all the jobs she worked, and while Betty was using that as a reason not to hire her, Ruth added that 'Valarie had no personality and shouldn't work anywhere in customer service.' Ruth also said, 'she had the look of a person, who needs to be on the assembly line.' And that's when all hell broke loose. Valarie and Ruth, exchange curse words, took off their wigs and removed their earrings, while Betty was stuck in between them, trying to put out the fire. Betty didn't want to hire Valarie after that; even though, Ruth was in the wrong. Betty didn't think Valarie had the right attitude to work in the café. But later that day, after interviewing all the candidates for the positions Betty had open, Ruth admitted she was out of line during Valarie's interview and suggested that Betty give her one more chance. And that she did. Valarie's second interview went well. So well, that Betty gave her the position of shift leader. Betty knew Valarie had some personal issues, but she just couldn't figure out what. Valarie is the only woman, who work in the café, whose life is a mystery. She never shared her personal life or past with any of the ladies, that she worked with. All they knew of Valarie is that she works three jobs to support her son, nothing else. Betty knew Valarie's soul was lost, but she couldn't help her employee discover what's missing by herself. Valarie had to want to be found before Betty or anyone could support her.

Melvin pulled up to the curb. He glanced around for his wife's car but didn't see it. He looked over at Betty's Café, and through the window saw two women in there, but he couldn't quite tell if one of them was his wife. Melvin got out of his car and walked toward the café's entrance. He could smell the beans of coffee as he made his way to the door. *She better be here.*

Ding Dong.

Melvin entered the café, which was nicely decorated with cacti, succulents, and tropical plants spaced throughout the café. The walls were blush pink and green with a border of gold glitter. White linen blanketed tables with a bouquet of pink, blush roses as a centerpiece. Quotes in flowing script and pictures of all the great African-American athletes, musicians, poets, dancers, activists, and movie stars adorned the walls. Each image captioned the tale of the moment the photos were captured. Melvin was impressed by the history displayed in the café.

"Hi sir, can I help you with something." Melvin turned around to see an older, caramel-complexioned woman address him.

"Nah," he said. Betty could sense he wasn't there for coffee.

"Well, are you looking for someone?"

"My wife… she said she worked here. Thought I'd come peep it out."

"Your wife? Is your wife's name Stephanie?"

"I guess she spoke of me." Melvin smiled; his chest puffed out at the idea of his wife mentioning him to her co-works. He could only imagine the glorious things she said about him. Melvin was one of the top-selling real estate agents in Birmingham. He was well known for selling top-dollar homes to all the city's elite.

"No, you did that yourself without saying a word," Betty said. Melvin's smile transformed into a thin line. He didn't have time for foolishness. He needed to know more about Betty's Café.

"How much you paying my wife to work in this café?" he asked.

"Does it matter?" Betty replied.

"Yes, it does. She doesn't need a job. She's already taken care of."

"Well son, maybe she's tired of being taken care of," Betty offered. "Maybe she wants to take care of herself for a change. Make her own money. Feel some independence about herself again."

"You women always trying to wear the man's pants," Melvin said, with a sour grin. "Don't seem to understand your place as a woman."

Betty folded her arms over her chest and gave Melvin a quick look over. *Who the hell does he think he is*, she thought? "Well, help me understand," Betty said. "Tell me. What's our place?"

Melvin was tall, heavy-set, and for anyone else, an intimidating black man with a bald head and a white gold tee. He had a look about him that screamed, I BEAT WOMEN, no matter how much he tried to hide it under the suit and tie. Betty could tell he was full of aggression, but she wasn't scared of him – not by a long shot. Melvin was the personification of the devil she had been running from for years, and in her café, they meet again.

Ding Dong.

Stephanie, a dark, caramel-complexion female with long black braids and glasses, entered the café. She stopped in her tracks when she saw her husband at her job.

"Melvin? What are you doing here?" Stephanie stood frozen, afraid to move, not knowing what to expect from Melvin.

"I thought you said you were at work," Melvin said as he walked toward Stephanie.

"I said I was on my way to work. I stopped and grabbed a bite to eat." Stephanie prayed to herself in her head that Melvin wouldn't slap her in front of Betty and Valarie.

"It was food at the house," he said as he continued to stalk toward her.

"Melvin, can we go outside and talk? Please?" He nodded his head and turned to leave the café. Stephanie followed behind him.

"Stephanie," Betty hissed across the café. Stephanie and Melvin both stopped walking and turned in the direction of Betty. "Is everything okay?" Betty asked in concern.

"Everything is fine," Melvin answered on his wife's behalf.

"I was talking to Stephanie," Betty replied.

"Ms. Betty, everything is fine. I'll be back." Stephanie looked as if she was afraid to walk out the door, and she was happy that Betty called her name and stopped her. Betty wanted to race over and save Stephanie but, she knew, at that moment, it wasn't her place. Stephanie and Melvin exited out the main entrance door. Betty couldn't take her eyes off the door. She could see Stephanie and Melvin talking, which was fine with her as long as he wasn't touching her.

"That boy beating on that girl," Betty said.

"How do you know?" Valarie responded.

"A blind man could see it. I know a controlling man when I see one. I done been there and done that." Betty and Valarie continued to watch them out the window to make sure everything was fine.

"I'm back. What I miss?" Nina asked, coming back from her break that had been over minutes ago.

"Stephanie's husband done popped up," Valarie said.

"What he want?" Nina asked. She stood beside Valarie, who stared out the window. Betty turned her attention from the window to face Nina and Valarie, then walked to the front of the counter.

"Trouble. If he bring his big ass back in here talking about a woman's place—"

Ding Dong chimed the main entrance bell.

"Okay, I'm ready to work," Stephanie said, quickly walking behind the counter to place her things.

"Valarie, Nina, can you two give Stephanie and me a moment?" Betty asked.

"Sure, I'll go to the back and do inventory," Valarie said.

"I'm behind you," Nina added. They both walked to the back of the café, leaving Betty and Stephanie alone in the front. Stephanie knew what Betty wanted to discuss, so she began talking.

"Ms. Betty, I know Melvin can be a bit intimidating, but he means no harm. He just likes to make sure my work environment is okay. You know the world is so crazy now."

Betty moved behind the counter with Stephanie. "Yeah, there are too many demons roaming this world. So, how long he been putting his hands on you?" Betty knew she was out of her place to ask, but she had to ask.

"Excuse me?" Stephanie responded. As her eyes grew big and her bottom lip dropped. She try to respond but her mouth only moves with no sound coming out.

"It's nothing to be ashamed of. Before I met my husband, I was involved in an abusive relationship. So, I know something toxic when I see it."

"He's not beating on me, Ms. Betty. You got this wrong. We are fine. You're reading us wrong. He just wanted to make sure I was all right. That's it."

"If I got it wrong, then I'm sorry. I don't mean to be sticking my nose in your business, but when you're here, in my café, your safety is my concern. So, let Melvin know, in my place, you're safe. I got a gun in the back as long as a pool stick, and I know how to use it. I won't let anything happen to you. Not while you're here."

Ding Dong chimed the main entrance bell.

"Betty! You're not going to believe what just happen." Ruth entered the café talking as if she wanted the whole world to hear. Ruth was Betty's best friend and Valarie's worst nightmare. Ruth was an older, light-skinned woman with long wavey, salt and pepper hair. She wore a lot of rings on her finger, and everything that came out of her mouth was vulgar.

"What happened?" Betty asked. Ruth sat at the center table in front of the counter. Betty walked over and joined her.

"Mildred just caught Paul in bed with a man child," she said as she flicked her hair from her face.

"No!" Betty said, shocked by the news.

"A white man at that! Say he was just wood pecking the hell out of Paul, and Mildred passed out in shock! Say her eyes couldn't take it!" Betty looked down and shook her head, trying her best not to laugh at Ruth, who was imitating Mildred passing out.

"Girl, shut the front door!" Betty said. "But you know what? Peggy Scott-Adams warned them, baby. She shed light in her song Bill. And in these times, gay men ain't just gay men anymore."

"Hell naw!" Ruth said. "They trying to be women, and them the ones I don't like Betty. The motherfuckers that's trying to be me. Out here confusing men, women, and children with their sex changes and hormonal pills. My thing is this. Be happy with you. Like what you like but be happy with you. Don't be out here causing confusion 'cause you wanna be me. It's a reason God made you, who you are, and not me. Just pray for it in the next life, but in this life, be what he made you. A man, if you a man, and a woman if you a woman. Don't give me chlorine and tell me it's water. I want the natural form. Not this mix breeding shit."

Ruth never cared who it hurt when she expressed herself. Ruth spoke her mind. She felt entitled to her expression. She had lived a hard life, and her voice meant something. No one could take that away from her again.

"Girl, I can't deal with you, but you got a point," Betty said.

"I always do. I'm Ruth the Truth."

Stephanie loved to stand by and watch Betty and Ruth gossip about everyone they knew in The Magic City of Birmingham, Alabama. It entertained her to watch older women still act like younger women at heart, regardless of their age. Being in the café and listening to their stories was an escape from her story. Stephanie didn't know how much longer she could continue lying to Betty about Melvin, but she knew she wasn't ready to have that discussion yet.

Ding Dong chimed the main entrance doorbell. "Hey, Grandma," Malaysia said. Malaysia was Betty's great-niece, Katrina's daughter, and Ms. Ruth's deceased son, Jason's daughter. She approached Ruth and hugged her.

"Hey, baby," Ruth said.

"Hi, Aunt Betty." Malaysia made her way around the table to hug Betty, who thought Malaysia looked so cute in her little pink and brown school uniform with her schoolbooks pressed up against her chest.

"Hey pretty lady. Why you not at school?"

"Today was skip day. Mama's not home, and you didn't answer your phone," she said, looking at her grandmother Ruth. "So, I came here."

"Well, you know Grandma can't stay put for long. I'm tired of sitting in the house watching court shows, *Maury*, and all the game shows. Getting old is boring," Ruth proclaimed.

"It seems like the life to me," Malaysia replied.

"Well, keep living, and you'll see, taking medicine every morning for your blood pressure and diabetes ain't no life," Ruth said. Betty pulled out the chair beside her and signaled for Malaysia to sit.

Malaysia placed her books on the table and sat next to Betty.

"So, tell me, great-niece. Have you started thinking about what you want to do after you graduate? You only got one more year left."

Malaysia was such a pretty young lady. She had long, shiny black hair that most would think was weave. She had braces on her teeth that she treated like gold teeth. Every time she talked, she made sure to smile so that you could see her braces. She was tall, slender, and toned.

"To be honest, auntie, I want to be a famous singer because I love to sing," Malaysia admitted.

Betty smiled at her, feeling proud to know that this child at least had a dream when most didn't. "Well, it's nothing wrong with that, but do you really want the fame? Famous people don't get to live normal lives. Paparazzi and bloggers stay in celebrities' business."

Ruth nodded her head, agreeing with what Betty said.

"If that's the case… then I'm already famous. Church people always in our business. I don't know. I guess I just want to sing. I really don't care for the fame."

Betty could sense Malaysia didn't have it all figure out, but she had to keep pushing her to think about her future. "And if being a singer doesn't work out, do you have another plan?" Betty wanted Malaysia to really start thinking about her future. She didn't have but one year left before she graduated.

"I wouldn't mind being my own boss like you," Malaysia said. "Starting me a clothing store or maybe even a hair business. I guess I really haven't thought about all this yet.

"And don't rush yourself. School don't prepare you for the world. They just rush you and push you out into it without a solid plan. No one really knows what they want to be in life until they live life and find out who they are and where they want to be in it," Betty said.

"Some lose their way trying to figure that out," Ruth interjected, "It's life baby. It's a gamble everyone must take."

"I thought about joining the military once," Malaysia said.

"The military? You don't want to do that," Ruth said.

"Well, Ruth, it's not a bad choice. I was in the military. That's how I met your Great Uncle Stan."

Malaysia focused her attention on Betty. "Was it love at first sight, Aunt Betty?"

Betty placed her hand on Malaysia's hand. "Child no! More like hate at first sight! He was such a butt. He was my drill sergeant."

Malaysia's mouth dropped. "Drill sergeant! Uncle Stan was your drill sergeant?"

Betty nodded. "Yeah... I thought you knew that."

"No. I mean, I knew you two had met in the military, but I didn't know he was your Drill Sergeant!"

"Yeah, he was, but we didn't hook up while in the military. It was some years later when we finally got together."

"So, you two had a thing for each other in the military?" Malaysia asked.

"No, afterward. We bumped into each other at a bar in Memphis. I was supposed to re-enlist that year, but I didn't. Stan had just ordered him a shot of Louis XIII. I spotted him at the bar sipping the shot. So, I had to pick with him 'cause in the military, he was this tough, mean, guy, and here he was at the bar sipping a shot. So, I walked over to him, and I said, 'Pass that shot to a real drinker 'cause you playing with it.'"

Malaysia smiled. "What did he say?"

"He said, 'Bald-headed Betty! I never saw you in a dress. Have a seat. Take the shot. And damn, you actually fine outside that uniform.'"

Malaysia laughed as Betty impersonated her Great Uncle Stan.

"That conversation led to a lifetime of happiness. We shared so much, being in the military and all. We knew so much that we could only share it with each other. But one thing most of all, we loved each other very much," Betty said.

Malaysia loved to hear a good love story. "I hope I will find love like you and Uncle Stan one day."

"And you will. The key is not looking for it but letting it find you, and you're young. You got time to find love. The main agenda is focusing on yourself. Love yourself and stay true to yourself. This world is going to constantly try and change you. And if you don't know yourself, it will," Betty said, reaching over to take Malaysia's hand. "You can't love another if you don't love yourself first and if you don't know yourself or your worth. People can mold you into whatever they want you to be. Concentrate on self. I'm going to give you some advice, and I want you to try it. First, write down what you love and hate about yourself. What you love, keep. What you hate, fix. Next, to understand your worth, write down what you will and won't tolerate. Not only from yourself but men, family, friends, people. Whoever you come in contact with day-to-day. Finally, write down what you look for in yourself. Write down in detail the kind of man and career you want. And the people you want to surround yourself with. Jot down your dreams and goals. Go over this templet daily so it can register. And when people try to come at you like you don't know yourself. Then you can show them just how in tuned you are with yourself 'cause you studied yourself. That's something that a school can't teach you. Only you."

Malaysia squeezed her aunt's hand and promised herself that she would hold on to the wisdom her aunt spoke to her. Malaysia had been dealing with and going through so much that she needed that word. She wanted to tell her aunt a lot at that moment, but she didn't know how. She didn't want to cause any more trouble than what she was already facing.

Ding Dong.

A tall, dark-skinned, muscular-built young man entered the cafe. He was dressed in a school uniform similar to Malaysia's. He wore his hair pulled back in a ponytail. Interest piqued; Malaysia admired the young man from head to toe. He was handsome.

"Hi, is my mom here?" Joshua asked.

"Yeah, she in the back. I'll go get her," Betty said. She released her niece's hand and gave it a gentle pat before she rose from the table and walked toward the double doors leading to where Valarie was.

"Well, Betty. I guess we bout to go," Ruth said, calling out to her friend. She got up from the table stiffly as her body adjusted to standing once again. Malaysia placed a hand at her grandmother's elbow to help her. Ruth smiled at her granddaughter then returned her attention to Betty. "I'll come pick you up tomorrow for the funeral."

"Okay girl. Holla at you later," Betty said, waving goodbye to Ruth and Malaysia, then she disappeared out the room.

"Come on, Malaysia," Ruth said, making her way out the main entrance door.

"Let me get my stuff. Here I come." Malaysia gathers all her books. She tries her best to slither past Joshua, but she's so enchanted by his muscular, toned body that she accidentally bumps into him. She drops her books.

"Dang… my bad!" Malaysia said.

"Naw, you fine. I mean, let me help you," Joshua said. He bent over to pick up her books. He caught a peek of her long, toned legs. *Focus.* He stood up to hand the books to her. "Here you go."

Malaysia smiled shyly at him. "Thank you," she said.

Joshua grinned at her. He was so nervous he could feel his forehead sweat. "You're welcome."

Malaysia felt so embarrassed for bumping into him; she felt an overwhelming need to make conversation to cover up her goof. She didn't want him to know how shy she was.

"You're Joshua, right?" she asked.

Joshua was just as nervous as she was. He began to stutter as he responded to her question. "Yeah. I'm... I'm... Joshua. That's my name. Yeah, I'm Joshua."

Malaysia was relieved to see that he was nervous too. She always thought he was cute, but she never tried to approach him due to her issues. "I'm Malaysia."

Josh nodded. "I know who you are. We have chemistry and history together. I sit behind you in both classes."

She was blown away by his voice. It was soft, rasp, and deep, but that was nothing in comparison to the joy that sent her heart racing when he admitted he knew who she was. Malaysia jumped at the sound of her grandmother blowing the car horn, signaling that it was time to leave. Beep... Be-e-e-e-e-e-p. "I better get going," she said breathlessly. "See you around."

"Yeah, I wanna see you too... I mean, see you. See you around."

Malaysia smiled warmly up at Joshua. "Bye Joshua." She inched past him and walked out the door.

"Bye Malaysia." Joshua watched Malaysia exit the café and get into her grandmother's lemon-lime, 1970 Cadillac De Ville with twenty-four-inch, chrome, gold rims. Her grandmother's car looked like a spaceship with those giant rims on it. Malaysia was one of the most popular girls at school. A lot of the students' parents attended her parents' church. Joshua always wanted to talk to her but just didn't feel like he would live up to any expectations that she had for herself or her parents.

Stephanie restocking the front counter, noticed Joshua still watching Malaysia. She leaned over on the counter. "You shy when it comes to girls?"

Joshua tore his gaze from Malaysia and looked at Stephanie.

"No ma'am. Just that one. She's one of the most beautiful girls at school."

Stephanie missed the puppy love phase of her relationship. She and her husband were the same age as Joshua and Malaysia when they first started dating. *We were so happy then.* She wished she could have that part of their marriage back. The happiness, the innocence.

Valarie entered the front with Nina trailing behind her. She approached her son while Nina posted up behind the counter with Stephanie.

"Joshua, what are you doing here. Why aren't you in school?" Valarie asked angrily.

"It's skip day, and I left my keys at the house. I need yours."

She was so sick of Joshua being irresponsible. *What would he do without me always saving him?* She grumbled as she stuck her hand in the pocket of her apron. "Do you have basketball practice today?" she asked, still searching for her key.

"No ma'am," Joshua replied. He regretted leaving his keys at the house. He knew this would be an argument with his mother later about being irresponsible. He would just have to endure it.

Valarie found her keys and handed them to Joshua. "Take these keys and go straight home. I don't want you out in these streets."

Joshua nodded. "Yes ma'am. I got you, mama."

Every day, Valarie hoped her son took to heart the things she was trying to teach him. There was so much going on in the world, as well as Birmingham, with the police gunning down black men. She didn't want her son to be the next black male on the news, getting killed by an officer who supposedly feared for his life.

"I'll see you when I get off. Love you son." She hugged him.

"Love you too, ma." They released their hug, and Joshua exited the café.

Valarie watched her once a baby, now a young man, walk out the café. If it were the Lord's will, she would be everywhere Joshua went, making sure no harm came his way. He was the only thing living that could show that she once existed before she would have to leave this world. Valarie had been waiting for some years to leave this world and was still waiting. She just didn't know when the day would come. Joshua didn't know his mother was an any-day-now case, and she wanted to keep it that way.

"You got a cute son. I bet all the little girls be after him, huh?" Nina said. She loved pissing Valarie off because Valarie was so easy to goad, especially when it came to talking about her son.

"Yeah, but he knows not to be thinking about no girls. His focus is school and ball," Valarie said.

"Yeah, but he sixteen, and he's going through puberty, Valarie. Pretty soon, he's gonna want to get that willy wet, and with you working like you work, you ain't gonna be able to stop that boy from bringing some little girl in your house and turning her out."

Valarie sometimes couldn't stand dealing with this ghetto trick. Everything that came out of her mouth was ratchet. "Well, I trust my son, and he knows not to disrespect me like that. What about your daughter?" Valarie added.

"Oh, Queenie little ass on the pill and the patch, and I got her getting the shots," she said, laughing at her own joke before sobering. "I was a thot in my teenage years. So, I know my daughter going to be one herself. Better safe than sorry."

These parents these days, Valarie thought, *always trying to be their children's friends instead of their parents.* "So, you basically giving her permission to have sex?" Valarie asked.

"Birth control doesn't mean permission. Birth control means I'm helping my daughter with her reproductive rights 'cause I know she ain't ready to be a mother, and I'm not ready to be a glam ma. She likes sex, just like I like sex. So, birth control keeps us from having unwanted pregnancies and running to the abortion clinic every other month like most mothers do 'cause they don't believe in contraception but think abortion is the way. No, quit jiving yourself and understand these kids are going to get it on with or without your permission."

Valarie knew what Nina was saying was true. These kids are going to do what they want, as they please. She has never been on birth control. Valarie was raised in a household that didn't believe in taking or using anything to block God's blessing. But since she had a son, birth control was the least of her concern. And she definitely wasn't giving him condoms. Providing condoms to him meant she was permitting him to have sex and that she wasn't allowing.

Ding Dong chimed the main entrance bell.

"Hey y'all. I'm sorry I'm late," Jenny said. She limped behind the counter to place her books and her purse down. Jenny was a pale-skinned, white woman with short, dirty blonde, shoulder-length hair that looked damped. She wore red lipstick and blush on her cheeks.

"Girl, I don't know what you apologizing for. You always late," Nina said.

"Yeah, but never this late. My therapy session lasted a little longer, and I got out of class late."

Betty entered through the double doors into the front. "Jenny, you made it!" Betty said.

"Yeah, my therapy lasted longer than normal, and my professor had us held up too. Sorry, Ms. Betty." It felt good to have a boss who was understanding like Ms. Betty. Jenny was trying to get her life back in order, and Ms. Betty was trying to help by giving Jenny a job at the café.

"Oh, you good. I was just wondering if everything was okay. That's why I called you." Betty knew about Jenny's past and what all she'd been through. Betty and Jenny have the same trauma counselor. They met at a trauma group meeting. Not only was Betty suffering from losing her husband, sister, and parents, whom she lost while serving her country, she also suffered from Post-Traumatic Stress Disorder or PTSD. Betty had done and seen so much in the Army that she had to go and seek help.

"Yes ma'am, everything is fine," Jenny said.

"Good. If you ladies need me, I'm in the back baking." Betty walked through the double doors leaving Nina, Valarie, Stephanie, and Jenny in the front.

Jenny took a seat at the main table, kicking her feet up in the chair next to her. Jenny and her girlfriend had been moving their belongings from her old apartment into their new place all morning before class and yesterday afternoon. She just needed a moment to relax her feet, which had been bothering her all day. She had dropped a box of heavy kitchen appliances on her foot yesterday, and the pain was still intense. Walking across the campus to her classes didn't make it any better. She was in agony.

"Um. You just got here. Who told you, you could have a seat? You don't see the rest of us sitting," Valarie said with an attitude.

"Valarie, I don't feel up for your crap today." Jenny wanted to explain to Valarie why she was sitting but didn't feel the need to. *I don't work for her, so why should I have to explain to her, why I'm sitting.*

"And neither do I for yours," Valarie replied.

Jenny felt an urge to explain, just to get Valarie off her back. "Look, I just need to rest my feet for a minute. I dropped a box of appliances on it."

Valarie cut her off. "If you were in therapy and class all morning, didn't you sit all day there."

Jenny just couldn't win with her. She angrily stood up from the chair and shouted at Valarie. "There! You happy! I'm standing!" Jenny just didn't get Valarie. She was always trying to find something to call her out on. *What did I do to her this time?*

"Hey?! What's all this fussing, I hear?" Betty emerged through the double doors; upset from the noise she could hear in the back of her store.

"Ms. Betty, we been working all morning, and Jenny comes in and sits. When she just got here. That ain't fair," Valarie said.

Jenny limped over to Betty, trying to explain her case. "Ms. Betty. I'm sorry. It's just that I hurt my foot yesterday, and I wanted to rest it. I got so much going on with moving, school, and counseling that it's exhausting. I'm exhausted."

Valarie hated how Jenny tried to confuse one thing with another. "Exhausted? Honey bye! I work two jobs plus this one. I'm exhausted. You just coming up with excuses," Valarie said.

"Why would I make excuses?" Jenny said.

"'Cause you're white, and that's what white people do when they don't feel like doing something. They come up with excuses. Like that bull crap you just said."

Betty couldn't take it anymore. Valarie had drawn the line with this one. "Valarie! I've done told you about your mouth," Betty said.

"But Ms. Betty. Why me, Nina, and Stephanie have to stand, and she gets to sit? 'Cause she feels it's her white privilege to rest while we work. I done hurt myself plenty of times at my other jobs, and I never get to rest. She's using her white privilege," Valarie argued.

"My white privilege?! I don't know who you think I am, but I'm not what you're trying to make me out to be," Jenny replied.

"Oh, you are definitely what I'm making you out to be. All of you are the same," Valarie said.

"Enough!" Betty shouted angrily. "Valarie, another word, and you're out the door! You will not bring racism into my café! This is not the vision I had for my café. You two are going to have to learn how to work together, or you can't work here at all. Valarie, I hate to do you like this, but this is your second strike. One more, and you're out! Keep your personal feelings to yourself. This is not how I envisioned my dream café, and right now, you two are killing my damn dream!"

Nina leaned over the counter with her coffee. "Like Martin Luther King, she had a dream," Nina said, jokingly.

"Shut up Nina! I'm serious right now," Betty said.

"I'm sorry," Nina replied as she sipped her coffee.

"Now, I'm a need you two to learn how to get along or find another job! Am I clear?" Betty looked at Jenny.

"Yes, ma'am," Jenny replied.

"Valarie, am I clear?"

"Yes, Ms. Betty."

Betty pointed her finger at Valarie. "You skating on thin ice, girl. Now keep your noise to a minimum. I'm baking. Jenny, come help me bag these treats. Nina, get your ass off my clock." Betty and Jenny walked to the back.

"Girl, you don't have to tell me twice!" Nina said. She walked over to the register to clock herself out. "See you ladies tomorrow!" she began walking to the main entrance door. "And Valarie, it's your turn to open." Nina put her shades on, smirked, and exited the café.

"Yeah, almost forgot," Valarie murmured mockingly. After Nina left, Valarie vented her emotions to Stephanie. She trusted Stephanie more than the others. Stephanie was like the big sister Valarie wished she had.

"You know I'm so sick of Jenny and Nina! I wish it were just you and me."

Stephanie walked around from the counter to Valarie. "Yeah, but Ms. Betty needed the help, and you know how that goes," Stephanie said.

"Yeah, but them two, I don't like. Nina keeps all these weird customers coming in, and Jenny always making up some damn excuse to keep from working, and I'm sick of it!"

Stephanie could see her frustration. Valarie was just brewing like hot coffee in the pot. She knew there was more Valarie needed to get out.

"Yeah, but is it worth losing your job?" Stephanie asked. "These girls don't sign your check. Ms. Betty do. Forget them. Just worry about you."

"You know I try, but honestly, I think working all these different jobs is starting to get the best of me. Like, I feel mistreated at all of them."

Stephanie had sensed it was more. "I figure it was a reason you went so hard on her. Let's talk about it. What's been bothering you?" Stephanie asked in a coaxing tone.

Valarie paused a moment before telling Stephanie what was bothering her, but she needed to get it out, and Stephanie was the ear that would listen. "All my life, I've been treated wrong by people. White people, light people, hell even dark people like me and you. At my other jobs… I do the hard work all the time while the light-skinned and white girls get the easy work. I feel it's only because the supervisor finds them more desirable than me, I guess, or maybe it's just in my head. I tell one of my bosses that my hands are bothering me, and could he put me on an easier job, and you know what he tells me?"

"What?" Stephanie asked.

"Oh Valarie, you're strong. You'll be alright. I go shopping, and the store clerks are quick to compliment or help my light-skinned sisters or a white woman before me. The light-skinned and white woman tries on a dress, and they're told it compliments their skin tone. I try on the dress, and I'm told I'm too dark for the dress. Then they always trying to sell me these skin brightening creams, like I care to be light. The entertainment industry has fucked up the imagery of the black woman. This is why so many dark-skinned girls are insecure about themselves and don't feel beautiful because of what movies, and music videos, and music artists see as beautiful. They don't see us, only our bodies if we got one. Then they wonder why I'm so angry! The strong black woman. She so angry; but she doesn't feel anything 'cause she so strong; she can bear everything, but I'm only a woman. I want someone to lean on when I cry. I want someone to talk to when I can't understand why! We're not superhumans, Stephanie! Just black human women. Someone needs to tell people who don't get us to try being us. The most disrespected person in America. The black woman. Then let me ask them. Do you see why I'm angry? Can you understand why I'm mad?"

Valarie's pain made all the sense to Stephanie. The identity crisis every black woman experiences at least once in their lifetime. Stephanie had to put something positive in Valarie's head. Regardless of how Valarie felt about herself, she was beautiful to Stephanie. She just needed to hear it more. She didn't want her feeling low about her complexion when her complexion was the greatest jewel on earth.

Stephanie took hold of Valarie's hand. "Valarie, I understand, but can I tell you something. You are not alone. It's a thousand sisters out there with the same complexion as us going through the same trauma as us. I have been pitted against my light-skinned sister, too. But I still love her 'cause believe it or not, while you want to be her, she wants to be you. She admires your complexion more than her own, and I can't speak for all of them, but some of them do. And you hate your complexion because the entertainment industry tell us lighter is better. Our jobs says lighter is better; society says lighter is better. So, we believe lighter is better. But that's not true. There is no better shade 'cause all shades are beautiful. We got to stick together as women and stop letting them divide us by the shades of our skin, and that goes for not only black women but white women as well," She wiped away the tear that swarmed down Valarie's cheek. "Sista, we can't let the world's view of us tear us apart. We all we got. At the end of the day, we got us, and I got you," Stephanie said. She hugged Valarie tight like a mother would hug her child. Stephanie wasn't that much older than Valarie; however, she did view Valarie like she was her little sister. She could tell Valarie was carrying a lot of baggage. Baggage that she couldn't fully claim, but she had carried a few times herself.

When Stephanie was a child, little boys in her neighborhood would tease her about her complexion and call her names like tar baby. It would hurt Stephanie's feelings, to the point where she thought, what the boys were saying was true. She thought she wasn't pretty. When she went home to tell her Aunt Loventrice, who was her uncles wife, that had stepped in to help her father raise her and her sister, due to Stephanie's mother dying while trying to deliver her during childbirth. She would make Stephanie stand in a mirror, and look at herself, until she saw something beautiful about herself. When Stephanie would stand in the mirror, she realized, how thick and lustrous her hair was, how big and glossy brown her eyes were. She would smile at herself and notice how perfect and white her teeth were, and how fat and dented her cheeks were. After looking at herself in the mirror so much she couldn't see a flaw in her beauty, and insults about her beauty never got her down anymore. Her aunt taught her to have a positive outlook regardless of the situation and trust God's plan. And that she did, even in her marriage, despite the abuse, she was facing, she kept a positive outlook on life and trust God. She stayed mentally drained from pretending to be happy when she was really unhappy. But that was just who Stephanie was, and who she's always been, the light at the end of the tunnel, no matter how dark and gloomy her path was, her spirit and faith in God remained bright. Stephanie could relate to Valarie issue in a sense. She knew in her heart that Valarie is a hurt woman – a woman whose hurt has resulted to anger, and that anger consumes the way she thinks, acts, and treats others. Stephanie only hope, that one day, Valarie would release the anger and be free, but only time could tell that mystery.

CHAPTER 2
~Cream, Milk, Sugar, and Honey~

Today is going to be a great day. Valarie was optimistic as she cleaned the tables of the previous customers. Gerald Coleman wasn't stopping by, and Nina wasn't there spitting her ghetto gospel. The absence of the two made the day feel more relax. She loved being in the café by herself, playing soulful music from the 90s. Her customers that came in were nice, pleasant, and friendly. She placed the dishes and mugs in the dish bucket and started wiping down the table.

"We got another old school jam for ya," the Disc Jockey on the radio said. "Mary J. Blige, *My Everything.*"

"Hey, this my song," Valarie said. She walked over to the counter, grabbed the remote, and turned the volume up on the speakers scattered throughout the café. Valarie loved the instrumental at the beginning of the song. She loved how Mary would come in with the vocals, and the melody would take hold of her voice, like the wind, creating a whirlwind of leaves. The sky would be the airwaves in which Mary's vocals would travel, taking the soft breeze of Mary's voice around the world like the speakers do in people's homes, cars and businesses. Her voice was like the Holy Ghost. It could get deep down into your soul, like a fire warming in the pit of a person's belly, making them feel content and at peace. Valarie wanted the peace and love Mary sang about. She wanted a man to be her everything, even though she had an illness, that most wouldn't except. She still hoped she could get to experience real love before her soul departed this life. But what she didn't know was love was right across the street, making deliveries.

* * *

"Sign here," James said. He was making a delivery at Colemans, right across the street from Betty's Café. Harp, a tall caramel male with gray smokey eyes and long godly dreads, took the clipboard.

"Wow! I didn't know it would be this many papers," Harp said, scanning through the paperwork he needed to sign for the delivery.

"I only deliver the loads. I can't speak on the paperwork," James said. Even he didn't know what all papers the company sent with him on his deliveries.

"Mind if I take a minute to look them over before I sign?"

"Not at all, man; take your time." James looked across the street at the café and saw Valarie wiping down the tables and moving her lips. *She seems happy today.* "Hey, man, while you look over that, I'm going to step across the street and get me some coffee," James said. Harp nodded. James walked across the street, approaching the café. He got closer to the window to see her vibing to the music coming from within the café. *She does know how to have a good time, and she likes Mary J. Blige. She shouldn't give me a hard time today.*

James entered the café.

Ding Dong.

Valarie had the music up so loud; she didn't even hear him come in. She was singing the chorus of the song and putting her heart and soul into the lyrics. James wanted to see how long it would take for her to realize he was behind her. She sounded good singing. Almost as good as Mary herself. She had a lot of pain in her voice, but that pain made her singing come off joyous and happy. He didn't want to interrupt; he enjoyed seeing her smile instead of being so mean like yesterday. As she finished up the song, he began to clap. Valarie turned around, startled.

"Good morning, sunshine," James said, walking closer to her.

What the hell does he want, and how long had he been standing there, listening? Embarrassed over whether or not James had seen her whole café performance of *Everything*, she grabbed the dish bucket and maneuvered around him to the following table. James followed closely behind her.

She looks so beautiful today. She had a glow about her that she didn't have yesterday, and that glow made James wanted to get to know her all the more – even though she was starting to act like her rude self again.

"I didn't know you could sing. You sound outstanding," James said.

"Thank you, and Ms. Betty's not here," Valarie said as she walked to the following table, cleaning and wiping it down.

"I didn't come to see Ms. Betty. I came to see you." She faced him, holding the dish tray and rag. She couldn't believe he came to see her. It had been so long since a man made an effort to see her at all, but she couldn't let her guard down.

"Well, I don't want to see you, so you can leave." She walked behind the counter to put away the dish tray. He followed her and stood at the front of the counter.

"Why you so mean to me?" he asked. Valarie leaned over the counter to face him. James looked decent today. His clothes weren't dirty, his nails were clean, his beard was well-groomed, and he had a smile that would make a woman melt like chocolate, plus he smelled good. Valarie wanted to be mean, but she couldn't. He was just so handsome, and that prompted her to continue with entertaining the conversation.

"I'm not just mean to you. I'm mean to everybody," she said.

"Why?" James asked.

"'Cause I'm angry," she answered.

"Ain't every black woman? But I understand. It ain't easy being a black woman or a black man. You got kids?" James asked.

"I have a son."

"Really? How old is he?"

"Why? You like little boys?" she asked sarcastically.

"Man, don't even play with me like that. I'm just trying to get to know you. I find you cute."

And that he did. Up close, Valarie was more than cute but a gorgeous chocolate woman with honey brown eyes, big fat cheeks, and when she smiled, a dimple formed in the center. James was attracted to her physically, but he wanted to see where she was mentally.

"My son is sixteen. So, what about you? How many baby mamas you got?" she asked, waiting for him to tell her a number that would disappoint her.

"As a matter of fact, I got zero," James announced with a cockiness in his voice.

She could have died and gone to heaven. No children! When every man she used to meet, back when she was dating, had at least one child. Valarie ran her gaze over him, trying to determine if he told the truth. If he was, then James was interesting. Something inside of her encouraged her to know more about him.

"Really? What's wrong with your manhood. All men got at least one child."

"Well, I'm not all men. I wear a condom. I don't touch nothing raw."

Valarie sighed. "I wish more men were like you."

James seemed careful with whom he slept with, and she liked that. Most men always want to enter raw or expect a woman to be on the pill. They never try to protect themselves.

"So, when you're not here, what do you like to do?" James asked.

"Hard to say. I work two other jobs when I leave here."

"Two other jobs?"

"Hey, I got to live. The government don't help those who help themselves."

So, she's hard-working, James thought. Most women, nowadays, looked for a man to take care of them, but not Valarie. She was a grinder who literally got no sleep. James never met a woman with three jobs. This made Valarie even more attractive. He had to know more.

"All that work and no play," he said with an edge of seduction in his voice. He wanted to mask feeling any pity for Valarie. He knew just by the gift of this conversation that she didn't need his pity. "You don't deserve that. There's too much of the world to see to be confined to a job all the time like a slave."

"Then how about you come and sponsor me," Valarie said with her flirtatious tone. "Can you pay my bills?"

"I will. What you need?" James asked with no hesitation. She didn't know if he were serious or joking. But he wasted no time answering the question. Not only that, but he stared deeply into her eyes as if he were reading her soul.

"I was being sarcastic," Valarie said.

"And I was being for real. Let me take you out."

She wanted to be rude and tell him no, but she just couldn't fix her lips to do so.

"I don't have time. My son is the only man I have time for," Valarie said.

"Well, make your son get a job and help you out. Get the weight off of you."

Stephanie had said just as much yesterday. And to hear it come from James' mouth felt like a sign or a message God was trying to get through to her.

"I keep hearing that," she said to herself out loud.

"Hearing what?" James asked.

"Nothing, I don't want him working. I want him to focus on school and basketball. That's my baby's dream."

"Ain't it every black boy's dream. I had a brother who could have went pro, but the street life got him."

"My son isn't like that. He don't be in the streets."

"Baby, you working three jobs. You don't know what little man out here doing."

Now he sounds like Nina. And if he's going to be sounding like a hood rat, then I definitely don't want any dealings with him. His words were like ice water, jolting her out of a dream, his words were slowly turning her off.

"I know he ain't in these streets!" Valarie said with an attitude.

James sensed the sudden change in Valarie as she got all worked up over the conversation about her son. She loved her son and was willing to work herself to death for him. James admired that. She was the kind of woman he had always been searching for. The woman that he didn't have in his mother growing up.

"Look, I know you strong," James said, aligning his eyes with hers, "but you can't do it all. Let me take you out. Give yourself a break. Enjoy yourself. Whatever these jobs pay you, I'll give you, just for your time."

"Your joking, right?" she asked, trying to see if he was serious.

"I'm for real," he answered.

Damn! If it didn't make me a tramp, I would sleep with him on this counter right now and dare whoever walked in that door to watch. James had a certain charm about him, and she could tell what he spoke was law. He wasn't going back on his word like most men would do. James turned her on. He brought out a sensual side to her that had been bursting to arise, but she had to keep hidden.

"I ain't never had a man come at me like that," she said.

"What I tell you? I ain't like other men," James said, licking his lips.

If eyes could fuck, this was the best eye fuck she ever had. She wanted this man more than she'd ever wanted any man.

James grabbed a napkin and wrote his number down. "I just put the ball in your court. You decide when you ready to dribble," James said. He pushed the napkin toward her. "I'll wait on you – whenever you're ready. Bye Valarie." James sauntered toward the door, and she wanted to chase behind him. But, instead, she picked up the napkin and stared at the number, then cast her eyes heavenward.

"Okay. What are you doing, God? You know I can't be falling for no man, but he is cute." She glanced back down at the napkin.

Ding Dong chimed the main entrance bell. Valarie quickly placed the napkin into her apron.

"Good morning, Valarie," Stephanie said.

"Good morning, girl. How are you today?" Valarie asked.

"I'm good. Just gotta get back used to getting up in the morning. I know I hit the snooze button like three times. Then, after that, I didn't want to get out the bed."

Valarie noticed the bruise on Stephanie's wrist that she tried to cover with her sleeves.

"What happened to your wrist?" Valarie asked. Stephanie tried to hide the mark by unrolling her sleeves some more. "Did your husband do that?"

"Look, don't tell Ms. Betty," Stephanie said. "Sometimes me and Melvin have these disagreements that turn into physical altercations, but we be okay afterward."

Valarie couldn't believe Stephanie was permitting herself to be abused. Somedays, Valarie wished she could swap bodies with Stephanie so that she could kick Melvin's ass. She knew Stephanie wasn't the fighting type. She was timid, didn't talk very much, and a down-to-the-bone Christian woman who believed in turning the other cheek.

"Valarie. I'm okay. I promise," Stephanie said.

"Stephanie, him hitting on you ain't right. Ms. Betty can sense it," Valarie said.

"I know she can, and that's why we're not telling her. Okay?"

"Well, I guess it won't be a secret if you turn up dead. I need to go to the back. Ms. Betty made a list of what she wants us to do. You run the front, and I bake and brew her famous Honey Coffee." Putting an end to a conversation she knew fell on deaf ears, Valarie went to the cabinet to grab the items she needed to brew the coffee. Stephanie leaned up against the counter, watching Valarie gather— the milk, cream, sugar, and honey— to make Betty's famous Honey Coffee.

"If you need me, just call me," Valarie said, heading toward the double doors holding the items.

Stephanie knew Valarie was disappointed in her. In her heart, Stephanie knew she was too sweet of a girl to be taking the crap she was receiving from Melvin, and with no baggage, but leaving him would be easier said than done. Valarie exited the room, leaving Stephanie alone in the front. Stephanie turned around from facing the double doors and leaned despondently on the counter. She rolled up her sleeve, looking at the bruise Melvin imprinted on her wrist yesterday. She was in so much pain, but she didn't want to show it in front of Valarie.

When Stephanie got home yesterday, Melvin was upset with her for not being at work when he got there. The incident started with her in the bathroom, tying up her braids so that they wouldn't get wet in the tub. She poured lavender Epsom salt into her bathwater; so, she could soak, relax and remove the stress of the day from her body. Stephanie and Melvin had a beautiful 3,242-square-foot home hidden in the mountains of Mountain Brook, Alabama. Never in a thousand years did she imagine living like this. All she had known before was Gate City, the housing project that she grew up in, where drugs, gangs, and murders have taken over the neighborhood. Now she lived in a quiet, gated community with wooden-gabled ceilings, stone countertops, French doors, and an en suite bathroom, with his-and-hers sinks, and a large soaking tub, along with a huge spa shower. The bathroom was her favorite part of the house. It was the only place she could allow her mind to escape and dream. She dropped her robe and dipped her left foot into the water to test the temperature. It was perfect. She stepped into the tub and sat, enjoying the warm water covering her body, along with the aroma of the Epson salt penetrating her nostrils. She grabbed her earbuds from the side counter of the tub and placed them into her ears. Stephanie enjoyed listening to the relaxing sounds of the sea as she soaked in her spa bath. She closed her eyes and imagined being on the beach. Her daughter, Kinsley, was there. Alive and well. No worries about her illness or death, just enjoying the moment, watching her build sandcastles by the beach. She could also see Melvin there, holding her hand and enjoying the music that the waves created. They were all happy in this dream. They felt like a real family again until Melvin squeezed her hand. She looked over at him in her imaginary dream, and his grip grew tighter.

"Wake up! Wake up," Melvin ordered.

Stephanie was still in a dream state, but she could feel the tightness of his grip around her hand began to crush her bone. She opened her eyes and saw Melvin kneeling over her as she floated in the bathwater. She knew the gripping of her hand was starting to feel too real. He pulled the earbuds out of her ears and placed them on top of the side counter near the tub.

"You embarrassed me today. I stopped by the breakfast spot where you supposedly had gotten your breakfast. And the owner said he's never saw you come in. So now, I'm giving you a chance to tell me the truth before I choke the shit out of you. Where were you this morning?"

Melvin has never checked on anything Stephanie has ever told him, and she wasn't sure what his reason was for doing so now. She couldn't tell him that she went and spoke with a divorce lawyer because she wanted out of their marriage. That would make him want to beat on her even more and longer. Every day, Melvin had a new reason for putting his hands on her. She had finally reached her breaking point. She was ready to divorce his toxic ass, regardless of what her faith says and the vows they made to each other. She wanted to be reborn, and she couldn't do that until the old her was dead.

"I don't know why he would say that," Stephanie said. "I stopped by there."

"So, you're gonna keep lying." He gripped her hand tighter, tempting to crush the bones in her hand. "I know you went and spoke with a divorce lawyer today."

Tears welled in her eyes, and she wasn't sure if it was from the pain or the knowledge he had known of her whereabouts. She knew a blow was coming.

He let go of her hand and grabbed her neck, strangling her. "Listen to me, and you better listen to me good. There's nothing you can do that I won't find out about. I got people watching you." He pushed her down into the water.

Stephanie kicked her legs and swung her arms. Hoping all the wild movement would cause him to loosen his grip around her neck. She scratched him on the neck with her nails, thinking that would cause him to release her, but it didn't. Melvin jumped into the tub with her and shoved his body on top of her. He held her down with his body weight, preventing her from further kicking or moving. She couldn't do anything but lay there. She could hear him yelling but couldn't make out what he was saying as the water-filled her ears.

Take me, Lord, she mourned to herself in her head. *Please, God, take me. I can't do this anymore.* Stephanie felt herself losing consciousness. *This is it. He's finally gonna kill me.*

As the water began to fill her lungs, making it hard for her to breathe. He pulled her up out of the water, with his hands still clutched around her throat. He released his hands and watched her gasp for air like a fish. He stepped out of the tub and continued to watch her gasping for air.

"Next time, be where you say you're going to be." Melvin left the bathroom with the water dripping from his suit onto the floor. Stephanie laid there in the tub, still gasping for air and crying.

Every day she went home, she feared for her life. She never knew when this man would kill her since he had come so close to doing it – so many times before. She knew her days were numbered, but she didn't know how to walk away from a man who was once beautiful but had turned into a beast. *How do you walk away from fifteen years? Who wants to start over after fifteen years? How do I escape this man?* Melvin had her convince; there was no escaping him. This man was friends with everyone, and everyone loved who he was in the limelight. No one knew the monster he was behind the friendly guy persona he fronted. Stephanie stood at the counter in the café, still lost in the thought of how to escape Melvin.

Ding Dong chimed the main entrance doorbell.

First Lady Katrina walked through the door, looking like a sunflower, carrying the Holy Bible. Her husband, Craig Morris, followed right behind her. Craig was a tall bright-skinned man, with a low haircut, big broad shoulders, and dressed in a lime green shirt with khaki shorts and a black hat – the church logo embroidered on it. Craig was an attractive man. All the ladies in the church secretly crushed on him. Some would even flirt with him in front of the First Lady, hoping to piss her off, but it never did. First Lady was a catch herself. Eyes would jump out of the men's heads when they saw Katrina coming through with her short, highlighted hair, supermodel makeup, and her slender, wide-hip frame. She had no behind but was highly favored at the top of the mountain. Her style of dress was classy, and she wore nothing but high heels and pearls.

"Praise the Lord, Saints," Katrina shouted as she made her way to the center table.

"Praise the Lord. How can I help you both?" Stephanie asked.

"Let me get Betty's Honey Coffee that I hear everyone talking about, and for my wife—" Craig turned to face Katrina. "Baby, what you want?"

"Just a plain black coffee," Katrina said, taking a seat at the center table while Stephanie entered their order.

"Okay, that will be seven twenty-five," Stephanie said.

"Seven twenty-five?" Craig asked, giving Stephanie a crazy look. He reached into his pocket and handed her the money. "Sister Betty serving a burger and fries with this price?"

"No Sir, just coffee. I'll bring it to you when it's ready," Stephanie said, then turned to prepare their coffee.

Craig sat at the table with Katrina, choosing the seat across from her.

"Katrina, did you hear that? Seven dollars and twenty-five cents for some coffee!"

"Coffee not cheap, Craig. You see what everyone else is charging."

"Man, I might need to get me a coffee shop," Craig said with a light chuckle. He stopped and noticed the spark on Katrina's face. She looked so lovely in her sunflower dress. Craig knew how lucky he was to have a woman as gorgeous as Katrina. She wasn't the average first lady. Katrina did a lot for the community. She was more than a voice at the church; she was a voice for the Magic City, especially women. That was one thing Craig feared most about her. Her voice. He reached across the table and took her hand in his.

"I got to be the luckiest man in the world to have you for my wife. You're so beautiful. So, what is it you wanted to talk to me about?"

"Well, some of the members want to know when I'm going to take the pulpit and preach. They've been watching me forever speak at women empowerment programs and nonprofit charities that they now want to know when I'm going to empower men and women in our church. And with your honor, I want to preach my first sermon this Sunday." Katrina lets go of Craig's hand. She opens up her Bible to reveal the notes she had written. "I've already written up some words." She passed her draft to him and watched as he scanned the notes.

"Crowning Season?" he asked, raising his eyes at her from the notes.

"Yes. I want to preach, Craig. I have been waiting for this moment since I was a child. I feel the time is now. God has summoned me to preach."

He glanced back down at the notes again before returning them to her. "You sure it was God?"

Katrina gaped at him, confused. She wasn't quite sure what he meant. "Who else could it have been, Craig?" She placed her notes back in her Bible.

"The same person who told Eve to eat from the tree," Craig said.

Stephanie approached their table with their drinks. "Here are your drinks." She placed them on the table.

"Thank you," Katrina said, picking up her coffee and taking a sip of the piping hot brew while Craig did likewise.

"You're welcome," Stephanie said. "Can I get you guys anything else?"

"No, thank you," Craig said.

"First lady?" Stephanie asked.

"No, thank you. I'm fine," Katrina replied in a disappointed tone.

"Well, just let me know if you need anything," Stephanie said, walking back to the counter. She grabbed a broom and began sweeping around the counter.

"So, you believe my calling is of the devil," Katrina began once Stephanie was occupied.

Valarie entered the front and immediately made her way to the counter to place the treats she had just bagged. While arranging the treats, she listened to Katrina and Craig talk.

Craig sips his coffee before answering Katrina. He couldn't understand why they were having this talk. The other pastors in the city weren't fond of women preachers, and neither was he.

"Katrina, Timothy 2:11-12 says, A woman should learn in quietness and full submission. I don't permit a woman to teach or have the authority over a man; she must be silent. We done had this talk numerous times before, Katrina, and you know how I feel about women preaching the gospel in the church." He sipped his coffee again.

Katrina thought about dropping the subject since her husband's mind was already made up, as it had always been before, but she couldn't give up the fight. She was passionate about this, and she had to get her voice heard at this moment by him.

"Yeah… but… Craig, listen to me. I go to outreach programs. I do public speaking for different charities and organizations outside the church, and even though I'm motivating and inspiring people, I'm still preaching. And now you're telling me I can do all this preaching and spreading the word outside the church, but I can't do it in our church. I don't get it! Who do you think brought you those 2,000-plus members and turned yo daddy shack church into a mega-church? That was done through my word outside the church. The people followed me to our church, hoping to hear me. God speaks through me to the people. You too busy trying to impress the other pastors to even get involved with the people, Craig."

"Hold on now. Wait a minute. I'm involved with the people, Katrina."

"When?" she asked.

"Every Sunday, Monday, Wednesday, and Thursday. That's my involvement," he responded.

"Ain't enough. I'm involved seven days a week. I don't believe God himself has a problem with me teaching His word and spreading His love. I think it's just you, not wanting to let your wife outshine you."

Am I right? Katrina took a deep breath and waited for her husband's response.

Craig continued looking at her but wouldn't say anything. She felt her husband was jealous of her sometimes. The last time she spoke at the pulpit in their church was when she gave her testimony on her life, with her mother and talked about the murder of her boyfriend, Jason. So many people joined the church after that, hoping to one day hear her again. Craig was a good preacher, too. When it came to notes, he got a lot of ideas from his wife, and he never gave her any kind of acknowledgment for her assistance, and she never felt bad about doing it because to her, they were one. His word was her word, but she couldn't understand why he couldn't see they were one.

"I'm not worried about that, Katrina. You will never take the pulpit in my church or anyone's church. As long as you are my wife because unlike most of these pastors. We follow God's word. Now, if you would excuse me. Me and Pastor William got a golf tournament this evening, and I don't want to be late." Craig rose from the table and walked over to Katrina and kissed her on the cheek. "I love you," he said, waiting for her to say it back. Instead, she turned her head the other way. She wanted to cry, but just couldn't let the tears fall. Craig straightened and left the café.

How could he kill my dreams like that? This was the reason why she went and talked at so many charities and fundraiser events. Because outside the walls of the church, she could preach. She could touch the lives of men, women and children in the streets. She would welcome those on the streets to the church to hear the words of God, but they always heard Craig, when they wanted to hear her. Her words touched more people than Craig's words, and he knew it. After Craig left Katrina, she sat at the table, with a sad look upon her face.

Valarie was rude to Katrina the first time they met, but this time she wanted to be a voice to her. Her being light-skinned didn't even matter anymore after what she had witnessed. This was her sister through Christ, and she needed to hear the truth. Valarie walked over to the table where Katrina sat and began her argument.

"Hey, why don't you leave that clown and get you a man who shares the same vision as you?" she asked.

"I don't believe in divorce. We Christian people stick it out. We don't run every time there's a disagreement. We pray and the Lord will guide us the rest of the way," Katrina said, despite the melancholy in her voice.

"See, this why I don't claim to be a Christian. I believe in God, but I don't take on the title of Christian. Y'all would rather go through shit that don't make no sense, due to your religious belief, than take your belief out of the equation and do some shit that makes sense. What does it take for a Christian couple to get a divorce when they're not on the same page? I mean, it's too many people in marriages they don't want to be in, but they are, due to religion. I don't believe God would want you to be with someone who doesn't value your vision and tell you not to preach. I don't believe He would want a woman to be with a man who doesn't want to see his woman outshine him; even though her shine is their shine, but he can't see it because he still hasn't grasped the concept that they are one. I mean, come on! If I'm wrong tell me I'm wrong. Does God really want a woman to be with a man that abuses her?" Valarie turned her gaze to Stephanie, taking her attention away from Katrina. She knew part of the reason Stephanie stayed in her marriage was due to religion. "And I'm not just talking physically, but mentally. What about a cheater, a liar, a misuser? What about when the person starts messing with your child? Do you just stick it out in the marriage then?" Valarie asked.

Stephanie didn't want to hear any more of this conversation. She knew what she had going on, but she didn't need Valarie reminding her with this. She had to leave.

"Hey, Valarie. I need to go to the restroom. Watch the front. I'll be back." Stephanie was hoping when she got back this conversation would be over. She didn't need a reminder of what she was going through with Melvin. Betty's Café was her safe haven.

"Valarie," Katrina said calmly. "I hear you loud and clear, and to answer your question, no. God wouldn't want you to keep yourself there. But you have to talk to Him and ask Him to help you break through that wall that's blocking you from getting to the other side of receiving your blessing, His glory, and your joy. I know sometimes we don't like to go through it, but sometimes it's okay to ask God to send me a storm, so that I can get to the other side of the wall, and I'm not talking about a thunderstorm, with the flash of lightning and heavy rain. No. I'm talking about the earthquake that's going to shift the ground and shatter everything. The hurricane that's going to flood the land and wash it all away. The tornado, with winds so strong, it's going to break down that wall. A storm, so strong that you have no choice but to walk through once it has passed. Because it was just… so… devastating… that you can't look back, you have to keep moving forward. You can't hold on; you have to let go. You can't save it all, some of it has to perish. That's the storm that moves you through that wall," Katrina said, preaching like the woman of God she was, before she knew it.

"And for you. I hope that whatever storm moves you, doesn't hurt you in the process," Valarie said. She walked back toward the counter to finish putting out her treats. Katrina stood up from the table, holding her Bible. She admired the voice that Valarie had buried deep inside of her. It was raw, unapologetic and real. Her voice needed to be heard.

"Why don't you preach?" Katrina asked.

"In a church? Naw, I don't think the church would accept me, and besides, preaching ain't my battlefield," Valarie said.

"Sometimes, we have a gift within ourselves that we don't know till a person tell us. You may not believe your battlefield is in the church, but there is a fighting spirit in your voice that could save the lives of so many people who are like you. If you ever want to do public speaking, let me know." Katrina pulled out a card from her Bible. "Here's my card." She holds the card out toward Valarie, who hesitated, then took the card. "You don't always have to spread the word in the church. Sinners are all outside the church. I'll be expecting your call. Have a good day, Valarie."

Katrina gave Valarie a light smile before leaving the café. Valarie stood there, holding the card. She looked up to the ceiling, getting ready to speak to God.

"God, do you want me to preach? Well, speak to women, and help women? I never thought about that, but I do know that there is power in my tongue. Daddy used to always tell me that, and I still don't know how to watch what I say." She slipped the card into her apron pocket along with James' number from earlier. She collected Katrina and Craig's mugs and placed them into the dish bucket. She removed the damp cloth from the edge of the bucket and began wiping down the table, still thinking about what Katrina said. After wiping the table, she picked up the container and hauled it to the back of the café. Still wondering, how the Lord was trying to use her. He'd been sending messages her way since yesterday. *He's preparing me for something.* She knew it and could feel it in the depths of her soul.

Ding Dong, chimed the main entrance door.

Betty and Ruth, dressed in all black, walked into the café and sat at the center table.

"Betty, this is it," Ruth declared. "This is the last funeral I'm attending. I can't keep doing it. Almost every other week, it's somebody's child we know. These damn kids leaving this earth like flies, and they dying younger and younger every day."

"It's sad," Betty said, "The old is outliving the young, Ruth. This new generation ain't like the previous. They don't ask questions. They just shoot. Back in the day, we kept a pistol, but you'd get your behind beat before we took your life."

"True. Hell, you might even get stabbed," Ruth added.

"Might get stabbed, you right. But you knew you were going to live to talk about it the next day," Betty said.

Ding Dong, chimed the main entrance door.

Nina entered the cafe to see Ms. Betty and Ruth sitting at the table, dressed all cute in their black dresses. She walked over to their table.

"Hey, Ms. Betty, Ms. Ruth. Y'all looking cute. What's the occasion?" Nina asked.

"We just came back from a funeral. Our classmate's grandson died last week in a shootout. He would have been twenty-one today," Betty said.

Valarie returned to the front of the café and saw Betty, Ruth, and Nina talking. She went straight to the cash register, acting like she was doing some work while she eavesdropped on their conversation.

"Dang. That's messed up," Nina said, "but it's how they living, Ms. Betty. These dudes stay at war with each other."

"War?" Betty questioned. "They don't know nothing about war. I served in Operation Desert Storm and was blessed to come back alive when most didn't."

"Ms. Betty, I didn't know you was a G.I. Jane," Nina said. She pulled out a chair and sat beside Betty.

"Yeah, I use to be a military gal," Betty admitted.

"How old were you when you joined?" Nina asked.

"I joined the military when I was in my early twenties."

"I bet you were bad with a gun," Valarie asked, joining the conversation and making it known she was being nosey.

"Girl, bad ain't the word. I'm the shit with a gun. You've seen my gun in the back," Betty said.

"I bet it ain't a country you ain't been to," Nina said.

"I been all over. I'm even fluent in some languages," Betty said proudly.

"What all you speak?" Nina asked.

"Let's see… French, German, Spanish, Japanese, Portuguese, Russian. Hell, I can't name them all," Betty said with a chuckle.

"How was it being a woman in the military?" Valarie asked.

"Well, it was an experience. We got treated just like the men did. There was no taking it easy on us just because we were women. A soldier was a soldier, not male or female, just a soldier. The enemy, sure as hell wasn't going to have mercy on me because I was a woman."

"Were you scared, Ms. Betty?" Nina asked.

"Hell yeah, I was scared! Scared of losing my life, but you get used to it. You learn to adapt in an unfamiliar place. You put a lost soul in the desert and surround it with death. You learn that fear can only get you killed, but courage can get you home. So, I learned how to survive, and kill with no remorse, when I was allowed. Back then we were only supposed to help the male soldiers, we weren't allowed to participate in combat, but some of us did. Hell, I was one." Betty said.

"I don't think I could ever be as brave as you and fight for this country. It takes a brave soul, and I'm not that brave," Valarie confessed, awed by the bravery of Ms. Betty.

"But you are, as a matter of fact, I've seen more women in the Army, go harder than men. Not saying men aren't good soldiers, 'cause I know some bad brothers, but women are even better. We're already natural born protectors. So, can you just imagine when we on the battlefield with our platoon, just naturally protecting? The Army was an experience of a lifetime, and I've met and worked with some extraordinary men and women from different ethnicities, and we all had a few things in common. We just wanted to make a difference and be somebody in this world."

"So, did you retire?" Nina asked.

"No, I just didn't re-enlist," Betty said.

"Why didn't you re-enlist?" Valarie asked.

"The reason I didn't re-enlist was because, I began feeling like the military was taking me away from some very sentimental moments in my life. My mother's funeral was one of those sentiments. I couldn't attend it because I was away serving my country, instead of being here, helping my sister take care of our mother. So, yeah, I didn't want to go back after that. I gave Uncle Sam my twenties. He wasn't going to get my thirties, too."

"You hooked up with Stan afterward," Ruth added.

"Yeah, and that was the moment I finally started back breathing. The man I hated so much, turned out to be the man I grew to love. God put me and Stan together. He was my Drill Sargent, and I was his Cadet. Then years later we became husband and wife. I don't think a love story could have been so beautifully written by God, like mine and Stan's love story! It's unmatched."

"Have you ever killed a child?" Valarie blurted out.

This was the question Betty was hoping she wouldn't be asked. Betty saw so many people get killed and killed so many people herself, that she didn't want to answer this particular question. The killing was the reason for the PTSD she experienced.

"If I told you the truth, could you handle it?" Betty asked.

Valarie has always known Ms. Betty to be kind, sweet, and loving. But to know that Ms. Betty had been in the military and could have possibly killed a child would devastate Valarie. She wasn't going to reply to Ms. Betty, but she had to know.

"Well, have you?" Valarie asked again.

"In war everyone's the enemy, even a child. You do what you must to survive. Do I feel bad about it? Yes. Can I take it back? No, but I've asked for forgiveness, and I just hope I'm forgiven. I came home alive, but I brought back some wounds with me – wounds that will never quite heal right. And I'm dealing with it. Hell, I can't stop dealing with it," she said with a deep sigh. "Excuse me ladies, I need to step to the back for a minute and get some fresh air."

Betty rose from the table and hurried to the back. She could feel the pressure building up in her chest from the panic attack she was getting ready to have. Betty knew that killing a child was wrong, but what could she have done back then? She was given an order. She had to do what she was ordered to do. Even though, her first kill was a child, **a** child who should have never been out in that desert in the first place. Valarie and the other women wouldn't understand. Betty locked herself in her office. The window was open, so she went and stuck her head out, letting the wind smack her in the face. Betty inhaled and exhaled the air flowing through the city. She could hear Birmingham, sounding like the Magic City it was. Despite all the pain the city had endured in the past, with the civil rights movement and the bombing at the 16th Street Baptist church. It was still a magical place to be, and Betty's home. She pulled her head back through the window and dropped to the floor in tears.

"God, I'm sorry," she cried. "Lord, I'm so sorry." She sat there and all she wanted was Stan, her husband, who was the only one who could help her calm down when the panic attacks started. Now, she had to calm herself down, imagining Stan's voice and touch, soothing her.

In the front of the café, Nina was getting on Valarie's case, about upsetting Ms. Betty.

"Why did you ask her that?" Nina demanded.

"Well, I didn't mean to upset her. I just wanted to know," Valarie said. Nina gets up from the table and walked toward the counter. She faced Valarie.

"Know this. That lady done put her life on the line for this country, and along the way, has lost not only moments, but herself. You shouldn't have asked her that when you already knew the answer. What have you done for this country, other than blame everyone for your damn problems?" She gave Valarie a bitter look while, wanting to say more but restrained herself. "I'm a go check on her." Nina went to the back. Her blood boiled at the thought of Valarie's loose tongue. She was upset with Valarie for asking Ms. Betty something that was so personal.

Valarie didn't mean to upset Ms. Betty, but she figured since they were already asking her questions about the war, that she could asked whatever it was she wanted to know, too. She just didn't know how much it would disturb Ms. Betty.

"There I go always upsetting people," Valarie said. "It wasn't my intention to upset, Ms. Betty. We were talking. I didn't think it was an inappropriate question."

"That's the problem," Ruth said. "You don't think, Valarie. You react off your emotion. Think about it, before you talk about it."

"Really, your telling me to think about what I say, when you say whatever out your mouth.

"Now see, that's where I'm gonna stop you. I don't just say whatever. I speak the truth, and you can't spell truth without Ruth. I would have never asked that. It was a dumb question, and you already knew the answer. What the hell you think they do in the Army, Valarie."

"You know what, I'm going to take me a break," Valarie said.

Ruth threw up her hands, shooing Valarie away as if she were a fly. Valarie walked through the double doors to the back and passed by Stephanie, who was walking up front.

Valarie was in a good mood earlier. What happened? When she entered the front of the café, she spotted Ms. Ruth and decided to ask her.

"Hey, Ms. Ruth. What's wrong with Valarie?"

"Child, what ain't wrong with her? You know she a ticking time bomb, waiting to explode."

"I see you all dressed up," Stephanie said. "Where you been?"

"A funeral. One of my and Betty's classmates' grandchild passed. So, we went to show our support."

"Oh, sorry to hear that. I know the feeling of losing a child." Stephanie thought about her daughter, Kinsley, who had pass, some years back due to progeria, a rare, progressive disorder that caused children to age rapidly.

"Do you ever wonder why?" Stephanie asked. "Like why God blesses us with children and then take them away from us? For years I felt like I was being punished for something I couldn't understand. To give me a child and take it from me; I still don't get it. You lost a child too, right?" Stephanie said.

"Yeah, my Jason. He was a true rose that grew from concrete," Ruth said with a gentle smile and a faraway look.

"Do you ever wonder why he was taken from you?"

"No, I never asked myself, nor did I ever question Him," Ruth said, pointing up to the ceiling. "To me, God taking my son was His way of removing a secret that I didn't have to hide anymore, and I'm glad I will never have to tell."

Ding Dong, chimed the doorbell. A man in a linen white suit, walked into the café carrying a bouquet of flowers. He wore a hat on his head with a feather in it. His eyes were dark brown, and his frame was muscular and chocolate.

"Good evening," the mystery man said. "I'm looking for Betty. Is she here?"

"She in the back," Ruth said, "but I don't mind pretending to be her." Ruth gets up from the table, trying to see who this man was, dressed like a million bucks with flowers and asking for Betty.

"Ruth, chill," Betty said, appearing into the room like a ghost. "Stephanie, go help Nina in the back."

"Yes, ma'am," Stephanie said, preceding to the back. Betty walked up beside Ruth.

"Betty," Ruth said. "Aren't you going to introduce me to this tall, hot, sexy chocolate?" Ruth gazed at the masterpiece of a man posed in front of her. Betty hadn't plan on introducing Lawrence to Ruth yet, and she couldn't understand why he was at her café. He knew the rules.

Lawrence was a car salesman who sold Betty her Chrysler 300 C. He would always flirt with Betty, even though he knew she was married. Betty never gave in. Until one day, a couple months after Stan had pass, she bumped into Lawrence again at the car dealership, while getting an oil change. Like before, he flirted with her, except this time, he was aware of her husband's passing, but he didn't want to treat her differently. So, he continued with the compliments and friendly gestures until she gave in. Lawrence wanted to be official with her, and do things that couples do, but Betty only viewed Lawrence as her nighttime lover. She would sneak around with him like a young woman. Her and Lawrence would make love, watch movies, cook each other dinner, play cards, and make love again. She enjoyed his company. She just didn't want anything official, and she didn't want to let Lawrence get close to her. She didn't think he could handle her *PTSD*. Betty decided to keep him as a late-night special. Now, because he broke the deal about him not showing his face around the café, she had to introduce him to Ruth.

"Lawrence, this is my best friend, Ruth. Ruth, my friend, Lawrence," Betty said. Lawrence shook Ruth's hand.

"Hi, it's a pleasure to finally meet you. Betty always talks about you," Lawrence said.

"Really, 'cause she ain't never mentioned you," Ruth said, still checking him out.

"I guess I'm just her little secret." He smiled, revealing his pretty white teeth behind his white chocolate beard.

"And I don't know why she keep it, 'cause damn…. you is fine," Ruth said.

"Okay, Ruth, give us a minute," Betty said.

"Do you got some friends?" Ruth asked.

"Ruth," Betty yelled.

"Come on, Betty. Hook a sister up!"

"Go to the back," Betty insisted.

"Okay, I'm a go on to the back." Ruth walked away, switching like Gloria in the movie *Waiting To Exhale* as she made it to the double doors. She looked back to see Betty watching her, and not Lawrence.

He had his head down, laughing at Ruth. "Betty, he supposed to be looking not you," Ruth said.

"Girl, if you don't get to that back!" Ruth went through the double doors but stood exactly behind them as they closed softly in front of her, while she eavesdropped on Betty and Lawrence's conversation.

"Lawrence, what are you doing here?" Betty asked. "We agreed. You wouldn't come around my café."

"I know, but I miss you. I brought you flowers," Lawrence said, holding the bouquet out for her to grab.

"Thank you," Betty said. She took the flowers from him and pressed the blooms against her nose. "Roses and lily's, my favorite," she said. The roses were a fuchsia pink, and the lilies were a blush pink. They both smelled sweet, just like Lawrence. The bouquet was tied together with a white lace ribbon. She undid the ribbon and placed the flowers into the empty vase on the counter. "I'll put some water in there later, but seriously. Why are you here?" she inquired again, fixing her eyes on how nice Lawrence looked in his linen suit.

"I just wanted to see you, Betty. You left so abruptly the other night as if I had done something wrong, and I was wondering, did I do something wrong? You haven't returned my calls, and I still haven't quite figured out the texting thing. So, I thought I'll stop by and make sure we were alright."

"Lawrence," she said, casting a glance back at the double doors where she spotted Ruth's feet at the bottom of the doors. "Ruth, get to the back!"

Ruth stepped away in a huff. Betty didn't want anyone to hear her and Lawrence's conversation. She began to speak softly.

"You did nothing wrong. You were great as always," she said. Speaking in code about his performance in the bedroom. Although he wasn't better than Stan, he was close to it, and that was all she needed.

"Good, because you had me worried. Look, I know it's more of a physical thing for you, but for me it's a little more than that. I don't wanna just lay you down and make love to you every night, Betty. I wanna show you love too. A booty call was cool when I was a boy thinking I was a man, but as a man, I can't go back to thinking like a boy. I want more than just your body, Betty. I want your heart, soul, and mind," Lawrence confessed, pulling Betty close to him.

"Wow. I got you quoting Peggy Scott-Adams," Betty said, removing his hands from her waist.

"I can't help it!" Lawrence grabbed hold of her again. "You play that song every time we make love." Lawrence tried to kiss Betty, but she pushed him away. She took a step back from him. Making the distance known between them.

"I know, but Lawrence, as bad as I want to go there with you. I can't right now. I need space and time," Betty said.

"Space… time…" Lawrence chuckled. His nice guy demeanor turned serious. "Who is he Betty?"

"It's no one, Lawrence. I like you."

"Then why the space? Why the time?"

"I don't know how to put this," Betty said. She wanted to choose her words wisely and not hurt Lawrence. Betty liked him. He wasn't her husband, but he did fill the void left by her husband's passing.

"Just say it," Lawrence said, fearing Betty was gonna tell him she didn't want to see him again.

"I just feel wrong loving you, when I haven't truly let go of my husband Stan." *Lord, don't let this man walk away from me.*

"I see," Lawrence said. Betty saw the hurt in Lawrence's face. She had to say more.

"I mean, I haven't loved another man since him, and I feel by allowing myself to care for you, that I'm betraying the legacy me and him once shared. Truth is, I don't want to replace him, but I don't want to lose you either. I want more than a booty call too, but I just don't think I'm quite ready yet."

Lawrence understood how Betty felt. He once felt the same way, when he lost his wife to a brain aneurysm, some years back. His wife died in her early thirties, leaving him to raise four beautiful kids on his own. He wasn't the best dad, but he tried, and did the best he could as a single parent. Lawrence never remarried or brought any woman into their home. Betty was the first woman in thirty years to come into the palace where his beautiful wife once roamed.

"I understand," Lawrence said. "Losing him is still fresh. It feels like you're cheating on him. I get it. I felt the same way when I lost my wife. She was the best thing that ever happened to me. She was the first woman I ever loved, but I can't say she will be the last. I don't want to pressure you, Betty, because I understand; however, I would like to remain your friend, if that's okay with you."

"That's fine with me for now," Betty said. She was happy he didn't give up on her. His wife had been dead for over thirty years, whereas Betty's husband had been dead for seven months.

"I'll always be there if you need me. Don't ever hesitate to call me," Lawrence said.

"I won't," Betty said. "Thank you, Lawrence, for being so understanding." He walked up and placed a kiss on her forehead.

"See you, Betty. Bye, Ruth." Lawrence walked out the café as Ruth hurried over to stand at the counter. She poured water into the vase that contained Betty's roses. Ruth sat the pitcher down and walked over to where Betty stood. She continued to watch Lawrence until he was out of her line of sight.

"Betty, when was you going to tell me about him?" Ruth asked.

"I guess when I was ready. Besides, he just my friend, Ruth."

"Betty, look. You and Stan had a good life together, true enough, but he ain't coming back."

"I know, and that's the hard part – trying to move on, and yet, still holding on. I been trying to accept the fact that he ain't coming back, but… letting that reality set in hurts."

"Yeah but… you don't want to be alone going through it either."

"Who said I was alone. I got you."

"Like I said, you don't want to be alone," Ruth said jokingly. "Betty, I will always be your best friend, but friend… give the man a chance or someone else will. Have you slept with him yet?" Ruth asked.

"Oh, girl! You know I don't kiss and tell," Betty said.

"You ain't got to tell it all! Just give me a little juice!"

"No!" Betty said, refusing to discuss her sex life with Ruth.

Ding Dong, chimed the main entrance doorbell. First Lady Katrina entered the café, walking through the foyer in a hurry. She wasn't shouting praises to the Lord like she normally did, but she was anxious to get off her chest what she had been holding in on her way there.

"Hey, Ms. Ruth!" Katrina said.

"Hi, Katrina!" Ruth said.

"Aunt Betty, can I have a word with you?" Katrina asked, looking for Ruth to leave the room.

"Sure. Ruth you'll give us a moment?"

"Damn Betty! I just came from the back! Why I always got to go to the back? I don't work here!"

"Well, go home," Betty said. Ruth twisted her mouth and smacked her lips. She wanted to be nosey and hear what Katrina had to say, but Betty insisted she go to the back.

"Fine! I'll go to the back," Ruth said. "Might as well throw on an apron while I'm back there."

Ruth went through the double doors. This time Betty checked to make sure Ruth wasn't standing behind the double doors, listening to her and Katrina. She walked toward the counter and leaned over it. *I don't see any feet*, she thought to herself. She rose from the counter and went to take a seat at the center table and sat across from Katrina.

"Katrina, what's the matter?" Betty asked.

"Pastor Rice called me today. He asked if I could come and preach this Sunday at his church for the Women's Day program."

"Oh, Katrina, that's awesome! Are you going to do it?"

"No. Craig told me if I do it, I might as well pack all of my things and get out of his house."

"What?! That's your house too."

"Tell me something I don't know, Aunt Betty. He don't want me to preach. And I been dreaming of this moment since you placed a Bible in my hand. And to have my husband tell me no, and threaten to put me out if I do? That hurts. Auntie he's not the same man I fell in love with fourteen years ago. The man I fell in love with understood what this meant to me, but this man here… he just wants me to revolve around his world, and know my place, when my calling is the pulpit. The world is evolving, and women pastors are popping up everywhere, and he just wants me to stay stagnant. Well, I can't stay in that place any longer with him. I want a new song because my lyrics ain't flowing with his tune. I think I want a divorce."

"A divorce? Are you sure that's what you want, Katrina?" Betty asked.

"No, but I can't continue to stay in a situation where one of the hands on the clock is stuck, while the other is steady moving by the minute. I can't be that no more. My clock is ticking, and both hands are moving. I'm not the same woman he married fourteen years ago, and he's not the same man."

"As helpful as I want to be and tell you to stick it out. I just can't seem to fix my mouth to tell you that. You have to do what your heart is telling you to do. If it says divorce, then divorce it is. If it says stay with your husband, then with him it is."

"But it's not where I want to be anymore. When I met Craig, I was looking for Jason. My heart still wants Jason. It's going on sixteen years, and I still haven't let go of him. I'm forever indebted to him. He saved me. The day you gave me this Bible was the day he took me to church. He loved God, and he loved me. He was more than a street thug; he was an activist, a man of God, and a voice to the community. His good outweighed his bad. He was more of a protector than a fighter. He was a true warrior turned prince, but was slain before he could reach the throne, and I just wish Malaysia could have met him. He died, the same day she was born. He didn't even get to see her, not even touch her – shot dead, right there in front of the emergency room entrance. He was going to give up the street life. He was going to give it all to God, but it was too late."

"That's why people got to quit putting off getting their selves right with God," Betty said sadly, remembering the day Jason died. "You never know when your time will be up. Me and you need to do something together. I want you to come with me somewhere." Betty got up from the table and walked toward the double doors.

"Where are we going?" Katrina asked.

"You'll see when we get there. Let me get my things, I'll be back." Betty walked to the back.

Ding Dong, chimed the front entrance bell.

Malaysia entered the café, wearing a black oversized hoodie with jogger pants.

"Malaysia," Katrina said, getting up from the table to approach her daughter. "What are you doing here?"

"I was coming to see grandma. Is she here?" Malaysia asked.

"Yeah, she's in the back," Katrina answered. She'd never seen her daughter dressed this way. She could feel in her soul something was wrong.

"What are you doing here?" Malaysia asked, trying to take the attention off herself.

"I came to see Aunt Betty." Katrina noticed how Malaysia tried to take the focus off herself and put it on her. Betty walked back into the front.

"Okay, we can go now," Betty said, until she spotted great niece. "Malaysia!" Betty was shocked to see Malaysia dressed like she had just rolled out the bed.

"Hi Auntie. Where's my grandma?"

"She's in the back."

"Is everything okay?" her mother asked, trying to figure out what was really wrong with her daughter.

"Yeah, I just need to ask her something," Malaysia said. Waiting for her grandmother to enter the room so she could tell her the bad news.

Malaysia tells her grandmother all of her problems. Problems she wasn't quite ready to share yet with her mother. She didn't know if she would ever be able to share what was really going on with her mother.

"Is it anything that I can answer?" Katrina asked.

"No! Only grandma can answer this. It's about dad," Malaysia said, lying to her mother.

Katrina wished when Malaysia had a problem, she would run to her, instead of Ruth. She used to tell her mother all her problems, then one day she stopped. Katrina figured it was because Malaysia was getting older and was embarrassed to tell her certain things, but Katrina wanted to know everything about her daughter. She figured Malaysia wanted to ask Ruth about her father. Although Katrina knew more about Jason than Ruth. For years, Katrina contemplated on the *What If*. What if Jason would have lived? Would she still be the woman she was today, or something else? She could only wonder. Before Jason died, he had planned to turn his life around, get saved, marry Katrina and start a family, but fate decided differently.

A rival gang leader wanted Jason dead for insulting his ego in front of his crew. The leader had his boys murder Jason. Some weeks later the rival gang leader was killed in his home, in front of his five-year-old daughter and girlfriend. After the murder, Jason's crew carried the man's body to Jason's gravesite, making it known to others that even in death, Jason could still catch a body or someone could be murder for whatever beef they had with Jason, his family and his crew. Jason's crew retaliated on the behalf of their deceased leader. Truth was that the streets loved Jason. He was a remarkable man. A big-time drug dealer, but a really sweet guy, who knew that selling drugs would catch up to him one day.

Ruth entered the room through the double doors. She could hear Betty and Katrina saying Malaysia's name, from the back.

"I'm right here," Ruth said, walking toward the counter. "Katrina and Betty, y'all can go. We good."

Katrina stood there looking for Malaysia to just ask her whatever it was she wanted to know about her father, but her daughter remained rooted in place.

Ruth knew the real reason, why Malaysia was there, and what was troubling her, but she wasn't going to talk about it with Katrina and Betty standing right there. They had to leave.

"Well, if you need me call me. I love you," Katrina said as she walked toward Malaysia, hugging her and kissing her forehead.

"I love you too," Malaysia said.

Betty and Katrina exited the building through the main entrance. As they left, heading down the sidewalk to Betty's car, the main entrance door remained open and slowly began to close. Jenny caught the door with her foot before it could close. She had so many heavy books in her hands, she dropped them while trying to catch the door. Ruth and Malaysia thought Betty and Katrina had left once they heard the door shut but didn't know Jenny was on the other side of the wall, gathering her things that she had dropped.

"What's wrong?" Ruth asked. Malaysia reached in her hoodie and handed her grandmother a pregnancy test.

"That belongs to me," Malaysia said.

"Do he know about this?" Ruth asked.

"No."

Ruth stared at the test, looking as if she was waiting for the results to change. "Baby, let me tell you something," Ruth said in a shaky tone. "Some weeds have deeper roots than we expect, and some secrets can haunt you forever. I think it's time your mother knew. You getting pregnant, is the last straw. We can't keep hiding what he is doing to you from her." Tears filled Malaysia eyes as she shook her head at her grandmother.

"No, I can't tell her. We just going to keep praying about it. That's what you told me to do."

"I know what I told you to do, and I was wrong to tell you that. I can't keep letting this happen to you." Ruth stepped away from Malaysia, so she couldn't see her tears. "Every time it happens, you run to me, and you take me back to a place that I don't want to remember, because it hurts your grandma till this day." Malaysia walked up behind her grandmother and place her hand on her shoulder.

"But... Grandma... you pulled through? I'm going to pull through." Ruth turned around to face Malaysia.

"Malaysia, what do you have to lose from this situation? Huh? You already done lost your youth, baby. Why keep putting yourself through this?"

"Because…I don't want to lose my mother," Malaysia cried.

"Malaysia." Ruth tried to place a comforting hand on Malaysia, but she backed away.

"How I know she won't do me like your mother did you when she found out?" Malaysia questioned Ruth.

Jenny couldn't believe her ears. *Malaysia is pregnant by someone, who is touching her, and Ms. Ruth knew who it was.* Jenny stood there longer, wondering if she should make the door chime. That way, they could think she had just walked in, or she could just walk in, making it known that she was behind the wall, listening the whole time. She wasn't sure yet.

"Malaysia," Ruth said, "your mother will never do that to you, baby. She loves you."

"Well, I don't want to know if she will or won't, 'cause we're not telling!" Malaysia grabbed the pregnancy test from Ruth's hand and placed it back into the pocket of her hoodie. "No need to bring the darkness into the light," Malaysia added, feeling confident in her decision.

"But what you don't know is…what's done in the dark always come to the light. It's time we tell," Ruth said.

"Why? Why tell the truth now when it's so much at stake? My reputation at school will be jeopardized. I could lose my friends. This could impact the church!"

"You shouldn't even be worried about the church," Ruth said.

"Why not?" Malaysia asked. "If it weren't for them, my family wouldn't be where they are and who they are today. If we lose the church, we lose it all… then what would we be?"

"Exposed," Jenny said, stepping away from the wall, clutching tightly to her things. She couldn't take listening to this poor little girl any longer. She had to use her voice to let Malaysia and Ruth see that this was wrong. "And the truth shall set you free." Jenny went and placed her books on the main center table.

"I don't want exposure. Some wounds heal better covered then exposed," Malaysia said.

"True," Jenny said, walking away from the table toward Malaysia and Ruth, "but if you cover it, it can't breathe. Don't you want to breathe? Leave the band aid off and breathe."

Where did she come from, Ruth thought? She couldn't believe the audacity of Jenny. *I didn't hear the door chime. How much did she hear?*

"Malaysia, go to the car. Now," Ruth ordered. Malaysia left the café and went to the car, leaving Ruth and Jenny alone. "You have no right listening in on our conversation. This doesn't pertain to you."

"What kind of woman are you, Ms. Ruth? To teach your granddaughter to cope with being raped by remaining silent! You're sick!" Jenny shouted.

"Lower your damn voice!" Ruth said, looking around to make sure no one had come from the back. "You don't know what the hell you're talking about, and you're out of your lane! I been helping her!"

"You call what you're doing helping her?"

"I'm helping her! You were raped as a woman! You don't know nothing about being raped as a child! As a woman you can defend yourself. As a child you are voiceless. This conversation goes no further than this point. It ends here!"

"I can't believe you said that to me, but it makes sense. A child is helping a child because you were raped as a child."

"White girl, leave this shit alone. The conversation ends here. Speak of this no more."

Nina entered the room, carrying a container of cups. She walked toward the counter to place them and noticed Ruth and Jenny, standing toe to toe.

"Jenny, what you up here doing?" Nina asked, placing the cups in their designated spots.

"Uh… nothing I just got here." Jenny grabbed her things off the table and walked around Ruth. She headed toward the back of the counter, beside Nina, where she began placing her things behind the counter.

"Ms. Ruth, I didn't know you were still here," Nina said, still placing cups on the counter.

"I was just leaving," Ruth said; her eyes fixed on Jenny. Ruth wanted to take Jenny outside and beat her ass, but she trusted in her heart that she wouldn't say anything. "See you ladies tomorrow." Ruth headed toward the café's entrance door.

"Bye, Ms. Ruth," Nina said, waving.

Ruth left the café and went and sat in the car with Malaysia. Her granddaughter stared at her. The hope that shone in Malaysia's eyes broke her heart. The only solution to this problem that Ruth could come up with was getting her mother, Katrina, involved. Ruth opened up her arm rest and pulled out a cigarette and lighter. She placed the cigarette between her lips and lit it. She leaned back in the driver seat and enjoyed the taste of the tobacco on her tongue. Ruth was worried about Jenny telling. Ruth wanted to tell, but she didn't want to upset her grandbaby. She didn't want to put Malaysia in the spotlight of shame. Ruth understood the effects of being raped. She knew what it was like trying to convince someone to believe you, and how much it destroyed a family and the people in the community. Malaysia would face a lot if word got out about what was happening to her. Ruth had an idea.

"You're getting an abortion. I'll take you myself and pay for it. And if anything from today comes back up, we'll deny it. We'll say you were telling me about a friend, and Jenny only heard, what she wanted to hear. That's what we'll do."

"Okay, I trust you grandma," Malaysia said.

Ruth wanted to do more than what she was doing but she just didn't know how. She never knew how. She just knew to be quiet, endure, and suffer the abuse. Those three words had been her motto when it came to sexual abuse. She could never catch her tongue.

* * *

In the café, Nina and Jenny were working the front. Stephanie and Valarie worked the back. Stephanie burst through the double doors with Valarie behind her.

"Thank God! We finally finished bagging the treats," Stephanie rejoiced. She flopped over the counter and began panting like a dog out of breath.

"Ms. Betty baked too many treats," Valarie said, leaning on the counter next to Stephanie, watching her continue to pant.

"Do y'all ever think about where you were before you came here?" Nina asked.

Stephanie stopped panting and raised up off the counter.

"I do sometimes," she said. "I worked as a bank teller up until, Kinsley, my daughter, got sick. Then I began staying at home to care for her until she passed."

"What happened to your daughter? If you don't mind me asking," Nina said.

"Oh no. You okay. She died from progeria," Stephanie said.

"What's that?" Valarie chimed in.

"Progeria is a genetic disorder that causes children to age rapidly," Stephanie informed them.

"Is it like the Benjamin Button disease?" Nina asked.

"Opposite. Instead of aging backwards, you age forward," Stephanie said.

Jenny never knew that Stephanie had lost a child. She could hear the sadness in her voice, as she tried to disguise it with acceptance. Stephanie hadn't accept the reality of losing her daughter. Jenny couldn't face the fact that she allowed the humiliation of being raped at a frat party make her give away her son to the foster care system.

"I'm sorry about your loss, Stephanie," Jenny said, feeling a rush of emotion take over her.

"Oh, don't be sorry," Stephanie said, "death happens, but all endings bring new beginnings. God needed her more than I did. How about you, Nina? What did you do before you came here?"

"Well, I was a stripper and a student at Miles College, where I obtained my bachelor's degree in Psychology," Nina said with a proud smirk. Nina was a westside girl with something to prove. She didn't let where she was from define who she could be. She always knew she was destined for greatness. She just needed the extra cash to get out of Alabama. She loved her city, and how it had shaped her into the woman she was today, but sometimes people can outgrow a place, and she had outgrown Alabama.

"So, you're an educated stripper," Valarie asked, having to throw some type of shade on Nina's accomplishment of obtaining a degree while stripping.

"If that's how you want to label me," Nina said, already sick of Valarie's misery loves company parties.

"So, why'd you quit?" Valarie asked, trying to get into the history of Nina's past.

"My daughter was the reason; plus, stripping was getting old. Stripping was like selling drugs. Some days the money came fast, then others, the cash trickled in. Even though I had my degree, I was addicted to the lifestyle of being a stripper. Just being on that stage and controlling the mind of a man with my body and getting paid for it – I loved it." Nina smiled reminiscing on her past. "Stripping was fun, especially when you had hot southern artists like, Boosie, Webbie, Gucci, 8 Ball & MJG and many more coming through blessing the Magic City with their presence. It was the place to be, before the club and after.

"Did you sleep with any of the guys who watched you dance?" Valarie asked.

"No," Nina said, insulted by Valarie's question.

"I don't believe that," Valarie said. She knew most strippers slept with their clients, she had friends who were strippers and they slept with their clients on more than one occasion, and she found it hard to believe that Nina was one of those who didn't.

"Why I got to lie?" Nina responded.

"Because I've heard stories of how you nasty girls get down."

"Nasty girls?" Nina twisted her face at Valarie, while batting her lashes. She was about to let words slip out that would crush Valarie's soul, but she quickly collected herself and allowed Valarie's bitter comments to roll off her back, knowing there were other ways to get back at Valarie. "I can brush that off, but not all of us get down like that. But I'm only speaking for myself. I can't speak for other strippers. Some girls really have to use what they got to get what they want. I never had to go that far, but I don't knock no stripper for making a living. I've seen motherfuckers do much worse to put food on the table. I've seen dope fiends sell their kids to put food on the table, but I don't judge. Until you lived it, don't judge it."

Nina never understood the hate women who used their body to make a living received. Stripping to her was no different than a model strutting on stage in front of millions of people half naked, but when you include nudity, it's a problem. Add twerking and it's still a problem. Women never get the rights to their body without someone having a say so in it. *It's a sad truth, but your body ain't your body*, Nina thought.

"Did you ever have to get high to get on stage," Jenny asked.

"Some nights I did. Alcohol became my first best friend," Nina replied.

"I was on drugs real bad before I came here. You name it I did it," Jenny confessed. She wanted to speak on her past, after listening to Stephanie and Nina tell theirs. They all had more in common than she thought.

"What led you to drugs?" Nina asked, loving the leap Jenny was taking after Valarie's toxicity towards her story. She was curious to know why Jenny was doing so many different drugs, when nothing about her physically or mentally showed drug abuse, but Nina knew that in certain moments and situations, people knew how to mask different faces.

"Rape and giving my son up for adoption. I was shattered and couldn't figure out how to piece myself back together. I was lost, and the drugs took me places that I couldn't go sober."

"How long have you been clean?" Stephanie asked.

"Six years now," Jenny said.

"So, what led up to the rape?" Valarie asked.

"There you go with them damn questions," Nina snapped. "Girl, you don't have to talk about that."

But Jenny did, no one else knew her full story about being raped, they only knew about the addiction. It was time she talked about it, so she could be set free from her past.

"Honestly, I don't mind telling my story," Jenny said. She inhaled and exhaled, steeling her nerves as she prepared to share one of the darkest times in her life. "It happened when I was in college. I went to a frat party with my roommate, Holly, who decided while at the party to keep introducing me to all the guys as her lesbian roommate, Jenny. Now at first, I thought nothing of it; until she did it again. So, I pulled her to the side, and I was like, 'Hey, Holly, you're going too far with the lesbian introduction. If I want people to know I'm queer I will tell them I'm queer. You don't have to do it for me.' Then she said, 'But ain't that who you are? Are you ashamed of who you are?' I told her, 'No, I'm not ashamed of me, but I feel you're putting a label on me, and I don't like it.' Holly goes on to tell me to have a drink and relax. 'I won't do it anymore, I'm sorry,' she had said. The drink she gave me was spiked. I woke up in an alleyway with my clothes ripped off and my private area covered in blood. I was raped and I can't tell you who did it. I just know it was more than one, and they were the guys she introduced me to at the party. They took my virginity that night, and a few weeks later, I was pregnant. I was ashamed, confused, and humiliated, and even though I had an idea of who did it I said nothing. I didn't speak of it to anyone, not even Holly. I was scared to even confront her about it. I just continued like nothing happened. I dropped out of college, and I became a stripper." Jenny glanced at Nina to see her reaction, which was puzzled. "And I gave my baby up for adoption, because I didn't believe in abortion. Pride got in the way of me asking my daddy for help. So, I turned to drugs and alcohol. I did anything that could take the pain away. And now that I'm clean and sober, I just want my child back." Jenny's face turned red. Tears formed in her eyes and rolled down her cheeks. "What happened to me was not his fault, and I'm finally understanding it wasn't my fault. I forgive them. Everyone who had an involvement in my rape. I forgive."

Stephanie walked over and pulled Jenny into her arms to comfort her. "It's okay, Jenny," Stephanie said. "What you lost will come back to you. I promise. It will come back."

Valarie and Nina stood in silence, watching Stephanie comfort an emotionally wrecked Jenny. Both Nina and Stephanie, felt sorry for Jenny, but not Valarie. She was shocked that someone would even want to rape Jenny, considering that Jenny looked like trailer park trash to her.

"I didn't know you were a mother," Valarie said. "Honestly, I'm shocked."

Jenny raise her head from Stephanie shoulder and set her sight on Valarie.

She just won't let me have my moment, Jenny thought to herself. *I'm hurting and she's shocked that I'm someone's mother.* "It's a lot of things you don't know about me," Jenny said.

This bitch is a bully, Nina thought to herself. *Jenny was healing herself, by admitting and accepting what happen to her, and all this bitch can say is I'm shocked.* Nina was tired of Valarie picking with Jenny. It was time for Valarie to tell her story. Nina was anxious to know why this bitch, was such a bitch.

"So, Valarie. What's your story?" Nina prompted. Everyone had told their past, except Valarie. She held on tightly to hers. *What's her secret,* Nina thought?

"What do you mean?" Valarie asked. "I don't have a story."

"All of us have a story," Nina said. "And I know you have one too." Nina tried to get Valarie to expose herself, but it just wasn't happening.

"My story is two jobs, plus this one, and my son. That's my story," Valarie said.

"Why do you hold back from people?" Nina asked.

"I'm not holding back. I just don't have a story, not one to talk about," Valarie said.

Her life was none of their damn business. The only person who she would tell her story to was Stephanie. She wasn't about to discuss her past and present, with Nina or Jenny, and she didn't care to know theirs.

Ding Dong, chimed the main entrance doorbell. Joshua came running into the café like someone was after him.

"Mama," Joshua said, out of breath. "The police is after me!"

"What?! What happen?!" Valarie asked, panicking.

"I was walking from practice, and the officer pulled up on me, talking about I was involved in a robbery."

"A robbery?"

"Yeah ma. I told him I was heading home from practice and coming to see you. I didn't know nothing about no robbery. He told me to come with him to the station, and I ran."

"You what?! Why did you do that?! You could have been shot!"

"Mama, I could have been shot if I got in that car."

Ding Dong, chimed the main entrance doorbell. A thin, tall white man, with hair like hay on a scarecrow, walked into the café, dressed in a police uniform, with Randy on his badge, and his gun out, pointed at Joshua.

"Freeze, boy! Put your hands up!" Officer Randy said. Joshua stood there frighten. The officer appeared as the Grand Reaper, coming to collect his soul. Joshua slowly rose his hands and stood still like a statue.

"Oh my God!" Valarie said, watching this man point his gun at her son – her biggest fear, in living color. So many black males had been killed due to unscrupulous cops. Back in 2018, a black male was killed in the mall by a white police officer and Valarie couldn't allow what happen to that innocent man to happen to her son. Valarie slowly tried to move in front of her son, hoping that if the officer fired any shots, the bullets would hit her, and not her son.

"Hey! Don't move!" Officer Randy shouted, pointing his gun at Valarie.

"Mom," Joshua said, upset his mom was trying to move in front of him.

"Officer, what is this about? This is my son," Valarie said, trying to make sense of the situation.

"We had someone call in about a robbery at the gas station down the block from here."

"What was the description of the person?" Valarie asked.

"I'm waiting on the dispatcher to radio me that," Officer Randy said.

"Then why do you have this black boy at gun point, if you don't even know the description of the person you are looking for?" Nina asked. She was tired of the racial profiling that these officer stay doing of black men and getting away with it.

"When I tried to question him, he ran. That made him suspicious to me," Officer Randy replied.

"Of course, he would run! Look at how y'all are killing our babies. Black boy can't even walk the street without being racially profiled," Valarie added.

"I'm just doing my job, ma'am," Officer Randy said, swaying his gun from Joshua to Valarie.

"Do your job and put down your gun! Ain't no threat here," Nina said. She hated the police. She couldn't see the good in none of them, not even the black ones. To her the police was nothing but an overseer, making sure blacks knew their place, and remained in it.

"I can't do that. When he ran, he became a threat," Officer Randy said.

"But ain't all black boys and men a threat to you? They fear for their lives when they see you, because they know one wrong move, could lead to a dead end for them," Nina said.

"Ma'am, this is not personal. I need you to be quiet and for you to step away from the boy," Officer Randy said.

"No, I'm not letting you massacre my child," Valarie said. "If I'm stepping anywhere, I'm stepping in front of him!" She raised her hands and stepped in front of Joshua.

"Ma," Joshua yelled, "what are you doing? Stop!"

"No, baby. I'm protecting you. You're the only one that can show that I had an existence in this world. I can't lose you," Valarie said.

"Ma'am, step out of the way…" Officer Randy ordered, pointing the gun at Valarie. He wanted to shoot her but was afraid of the reaction from the other women. He was scared. He hated that he even stopped Joshua at this point.

When he saw Joshua walking, Joshua was close to the scene where the store had been robbed. Randy just wanted to ask him a few questions. He wanted Joshua to ride down to the station with him, but instead of giving him a yes or no answer, Joshua took off running. *If he's innocent then why he run*, Randy thought. He wasn't racially profiling Joshua; he was just doing his job. Joshua was close to the crime scene and looked more suspect than the group of white boys, who were also walking the same path as him, but Randy didn't bother to stop and question them. Because they didn't look suspicious to him.

"No. You want to point that gun at somebody, point it at me. I'm not letting you get a pat on the back for this one. Ain't no celebration at the station in honor of you killing my son. You going to have to crown me before you crown this one!" Valarie declared.

This is what we need, Nina thought. *Instead of waiting for the next leader to come and lay his or her life on the line for black people. Black people got to start dying for their people. Martin Luther King and Malcolm X did. Why shouldn't we, as black people? People always want to be part of the movement, but don't wanna die for it. You got to be willing to die for these children… you got to be willing to die for your people.*

Nina raised her hand and positioned herself beside Valarie. She realized that no matter how much she disliked Valarie, it was something going on, way bigger than their beef, and that was the lives of black men, women, boys, and girls.

"Hey! What are you doing?" Randy asked.

Nina fearlessly stood beside Valarie and grabbed her hand. Valarie looked at Nina in shock. She couldn't believe Nina was standing beside her, ready to put her life on the line for her son, whom she didn't even know.

"Get back," Randy said, waving the gun, "I said get back!"

"Do what you got to do, Jack. Black lives matter here," Nina said. Stephanie and Jenny, raised their hands, and stood beside Valarie, hiding Joshua from the sight of Officer Randy.

"Stay back! I don't want to use this gun! Don't make me use this gun!" Officer Randy shouted. *I should just shoot all of them,* he thought, trying to figure out which one to shoot first to get to the boy.

"Well, you might as well get your trigger finger ready, and make that bullet stretch long and wide, 'cause we tired of y'all killing our babies," Valarie. said.

"Change can't wait," Jenny said.

"Crown us," Stephanie said.

Ding Dong, chimed the main entrance doorbell. Another police officer entered the café. His badge read Jake. He was a short, stout, dark-skin male, with a beer belly and a wobbly walk. Nina and Jake knew each other. They both grew up in the same hood on the westside. Jake was a D-boy, way before he became Lieutenant. Jake and Nina brother, Bird, use to run the streets together. He went directly to Officer Randy and pushed his gun down.

"Hey, what's going on in here? Put your gun down they caught the boys who rob the store! It's not him! It was four Caucasian boys," he announced. All of the women dropped their hands, relieved that the true criminals were caught.

"Thank you, Jesus," Stephanie said. She folded her hands to give God the praise. Valarie turned around to hug her son. He was still holding his hands up, until he felt his mother's tight embrace. He lowered his hands to hug her back.

"Have mercy, Father," Valarie said. She thought she had lost her son. Valarie's biggest fear happened on the day she thought was a good day. Outside looked beautiful, but the acts of the officer made a beautiful day look bad outside.

"Ladies, I'm sorry about this. Randy's still learning," Lieutenant Jake said.

"That don't mean nothing!" Nina said, stepping up to Jake. "He racially profiled her son!"

"No, ma'am I did not! I thought he was the suspect because he ran!" Randy said, feeling attacked by Nina comment.

"You thought 'cause he was black," Nina corrected.

"The devil will never admit his wrong," Valarie added.

"Randy, get out of here. I got this," Lieutenant Jake said. He saw the direction the conversation was going, and he wasn't about to let these women insult his officer, on his first day in the field. Randy exited the café, leaving Jake alone to defend his badge. "Ladies, I understand your frustration. Trust me, I watch the news, and this was a misunderstanding on my watch. It won't happen again."

"But it did, and it can tomorrow," Nina said. "You can't be around to keep your eye on all of them, and you most definitely can't change a system that's not meant to be changed. The people are getting tired of trying to fight evil with good, and him pointing that gun at her son wasn't a misunderstanding. That was very understood! We're tired of the brutality, Jake!" Jake threw his hands up in defeat to Nina's preaching.

"So, what you want, Nina?" Jake asked. "You want war?"

"The war was here long before you and me! The question is when will it end, Jake? When will black mothers and fathers be able to stop worrying about what will happen to their children when they step out the door? When?"

"I can't answer that, but you have to understand not all cops' intentions are bad."

"And not all are good. You remember what happen to your friend, my brother, Bird. What was the cop's intention that day?"

"Like I said once before, Nina, sorry for the misunderstanding. Ladies, Nina, have a nice evening." He nodded to each of the individuals, as he exited the café.

Valarie released her arms from around her son to look him in the face. "Are you okay?" she asked, glad to see all parts of his body were bullet free.

"Yeah," he said, "thankful to still be standing." Valarie looked over at Nina, and saw she was still traumatized from what happened. Valarie had to thank her.

"Thank you, Nina," Valarie said. She could never be mean to Nina again. Nina showed her that she was willing to lay her life on the line, along with hers. And for that, Nina earned her respect, so did Jenny.

"You're welcome," Nina said. She could tell things between her, and Valarie were going to change.

"You know that cop?" Jenny asked.

"Yeah, we grew up together. I need a break," Nina announced, walking toward the back of the café. She had to get away and go write in her journal about what just happened. Seeing that cop with that gun bought back memories of her brother, Bird, who was killed by a white cop, for speaking his mind. The cop had his gun pointed on someone else, but as soon as Bird started speaking on how police needed to stop harassing black men with no probable cause, he became the target. No justice was ever served for Bird's death. The news channels made matters worse. They started finding old charges from her brother's past to make him look bad and enhance the image of the officer who killed him. Months later, Jake had left and joined the military. Then years later, he came back a police officer. People from the hood, who knew Jake, was stunned by his decision to become an officer, especially Nina. She couldn't understand how he would want to wear the same uniform as the man who killed her brother and his best friend. It never made sense. She had to escape that room; she needed to release her thoughts and feelings.

* * *

Later that evening, Betty and Katrina drove down the dark, rough country road that seemed to be out in the middle of nowhere. There wasn't a house until another forty miles. Katrina hadn't traveled this sad, dusty road since her mother's funeral. She wished she would've known, before she had gotten into the car that, this is where Betty was taking her.

"Why are we going to the graveyard," Katrina asked.

"I met a man, Katrina," Betty said, "His name is Lawrence."

"You love, Lawrence," Katrina asked.

"I care for Lawrence a lot. I can't quite say its love, but I do care for him."

"Is this why were headed to the graveyard."

"Part of it. The other reason is for you. When was the last time you seen Jason or bought Malaysia out here to her father's grave."

"It's been a while, Aunt Betty. I don't like coming out here."

"You should, and you should bring Malaysia as well."

"Malaysia doesn't care to know about her father, and if she does, she goes and asks Ms. Ruth about him. She doesn't ask me."

"Well, maybe you should just start telling her things. You know just as much about him as Ruth, maybe even more." Katrina did. She knew more about Jason and Ruth's past than Betty did. Ms. Ruth had a secret that only Jason knew, but with Jason being dead, Ruth figured no one would ever know her secret. But Katrina knew, and she knew Betty didn't.

"We're here," Betty said. She pushed the ignition switched off. They both sat there, staring out at all the tombstones.

"When was the last time you been here," Katrina asked.

"I haven't been here since the funeral. It's been hard to come out here. I still can't fix my eyes to come and look at a tombstone with his picture on it."

"Jason's tomb is right down there," Katrina pointed.

"Go visit him and talk to him. You gotta let him go, Katrina. That way you can stop holding on to the 'what if.'"

"Aunt Betty, I understand the fact that he's not coming back. It's been almost sixteen years. I've accepted it, but I can still miss him, and love my husband. It's nothing wrong with that. It's part of grieving, especially when they were so close to your heart. I will never spiritually let him go, but I have physically."

"Well, looks like this drive was for me. I'll be back." Betty got out the car and walked to Stan's grave. He still had the big flower arrangement sitting on his tombstone from the Army. As she stood there, looking at the tomb, her eyes began to fill with tears.

"Hey there, baby." She could feel the tightness form in her throat. "I miss you, Stan. Lord knows, I miss you so much. It's so lonely here without you. I don't know how I'm gonna make it. I know you're in a better place and that you're still here with me, but I can't move on. I just don't know how," wiping her tears from her cheeks.

"I met a man, and he's so nice and sweet to me. He put me in the mind of you but he ain't you. Honey, I could never find another like you. You were special and it felt good to share my world with you. When we got together, you made living and loving easy because for years, living and loving was so hard for me to do. Who would have ever thought that I would wind up marrying a guy, who I already knew, but couldn't stand? The Lord really does match people up in some crazy ways." She laughed. "I love you, Stan, and I just want to let you know that I enjoyed every moment of this life with you. The good, the bad, the ups, the downs. Thank you, Stan, and thank you, God, for blessing me in this lifetime with such a great man. Can't wait to see you again."

Betty leaned over and kissed the tombstone. She felt good speaking that to his resting place. She never got to express her love or say her final goodbyes before Stan had passed. She was trying so hard to keep him happy through his treatment and bless him with good news, that she never just took the time to really tell him how much of a difference he made in her life. He was the first man to love her spiritually and not with his fist. As Betty stood there reminiscing on their life together, she saw Katrina get out the car and walk over to Jason grave. Betty smiled whispering to the Lord. "She needs healing, too, Lord. She needs healing too."

Katrina walked up to where Jason is buried. She didn't know what to say and she didn't want to cry. "Hello King. I know it's been a while, but I hope you understand." She twisted her mouth. "I miss you." She placed her hands to her eyes. "I miss you." She continued to say those words repeatedly, as she fell to her knees, crying a harsh cry. Being at his tomb made Katrina heart feel like it was breaking into a million pieces, her breathing began to get heavy, her throat began to swell, knelling on his grave was like laying on top of him. She could remember the moments they were together making Malaysia. Feeling her heart pump due to her anxiety was like feeling his heartbeat when she would lay next to him. Looking at his picture on the tombstone made her stomach weak, she wanted to puke. The last sight she had of him was in his casket, which is why she never came to his resting place, being at the gravesite made her sick, but after seeing her aunt build up the courage to go to her uncle Stan grave. She had to build up her strength to go to Jason. But going to Jason grave made her weak, it took the life out of her, she needed to stand, but couldn't find the strength to. Betty walked up to see Katrina on her knees in tears. Betty placed her hand on her shoulder. Betty suffered from anxiety, and she knew that's what Katrina was experiencing, as she watch her cry and breathe at the same time.

"Rise up child… Rise up." Betty grabbed Katrina by the arm to help her stand up. "Go on," Betty said, "talk to him. Calm down and talk to him." Betty stepped away so Katrina could have her moment with Jason.

Katrina wiped her face and stared at Jason tombstone. Looking at his picture brought back so many memories that she had of him. The time he saved her life from someone trying to rape her in an alleyway.

Their first date, which was going to church and Sunday dinner at Betty's, who was the first to find out they were dating. Katrina had so many more memories she could reminisce on, but she had to focus on her words. The words she had been wanting to tell Jason for years.

"I wish you were here. I wish you were here a lot. Craig means the world to me, but you meant so much more." She wiped the tears from her eyes. "I love my husband, but the what ifs, and the what could've been haunts my marriage. I just wish you could be here; Malaysia deserves you. I deserve you. I know if you were here, you would let me preach. You would want me to preach. You was the one who saw how God would use me before I ever did, and regardless of all the bad you did in the streets, you did so much good as well. People don't know that the night you died, you had gotten baptized. People don't know you were giving up the life, so you could get closer to God. People don't know and that's okay. As long as the Lord knows. I never got to tell you, but I love you and I promise I will do better by bringing Malaysia to see you. Just understand, I wasn't expecting you to go home so soon. You left before the book of our life could get good and I understand why. I love you, Jason. Just know that wherever you are." Katrina turned around to see Betty standing off in the distance. She walks up to Betty. "That man," she said, pointing at Jason's tomb, "will always be my first love. I love Jason, but I love my husband more. I just need him to step it up." Katrina walked away, heading toward Betty's car. Betty watched her as she disappeared into the vehicle. Betty had made her peace, she just hoped that Katrina had done the same.

* * *

Late that night, Nina sat at the table in the dark back room of the smokey club. Her bandmate Harp, was sitting across from her, reading over the poem she had written for them to perform at the poetry club downtown, called Voice Your Pain. Nina continued to watch Harp look over the paper. She couldn't tell if he liked it or hated it because his facial expression was emotionless. She had to ask him.

"Harp, what you think?" she asked.

"I like it," Harp said. "It got a Billie Holiday and Nina Simone vibe to it."

"That's the idea," Nina said. "for it to sound blue."

"Very blue indeed. You want a drink?" Harp asked.

"Yeah, pour me one." Harp rose from his seat to pour him and Nina a shot of Hennessy.

After what happened earlier with Valarie's son, Nina had to make her poem reach the people more. Harp placed their shots on the table and resumed his seat next to Nina. The club owner entered the room.

"Hey, you guys are up next," the club owner said, as he closed the door behind him.

"Let's drink up," Nina said. Nina and Harp tossed back their shots. They both squinched their face and twisted their nose as the cognac burned a trail of fire down their throats

"You look beautiful tonight," Harp said, admiring Nina in her gold sequence dress.

"Thank you, Harp. You clean up well yourself." He looked nice in his gold and white suit, which complemented her dress. They left the room and walked down the hallway, where other poets were chatting and enjoying themselves behind the curtain. Nina stopped at the stage entrance. She could see the audience was full, no empty seats. As a stripper you don't necessarily have to make eye contact with the audience when you perform, you can just blink out and express yourself, without wondering what people were thinking, but performing as a singer/poet was different. You had to look at these people or look at something in the crowd with them. For the first time, she was nervous about being on stage and people looking at her.

"We got this," Harp said, building her confidence. Harp was such a great musician. He was a tall, caramel man, with sparkly white teeth and dark gray eyes. Nina tried not to let temptation lead her into the arms of Harp, but sometimes she couldn't help it. This man was exquisite, talented, and smart. She knew about Harp's other women, but she didn't care. Harp was just fun to her. She previously had so many failed relationships that she didn't want anything serious. She enjoyed having fun and sex with him. And sex with Harp was the best ever. Nina entered the stage. She stepped to the microphone and Harp went to the keyboard. Nina began to speak.

"This poem we are about to perform, is for all of us. You remember when you could ask a person, how is it out there…outside, and they would say, it's nice out or it ain't too bad. But outside consists of more than just the weather. It also consists of people and what they're doing out in it. Slow drag it, Harp." Harp began to play his keyboard. Nina started to sing.

"They say it ain't too bad outside. They say it ain't too bad outside. Open the door and step on out. We about to walk through fire. They say it ain't too bad outside."

Harp maneuvered from the keyboard and began to play the saxophone, while the keyboard played a prerecorded sample that he prepared. Nina scatted over the instrumental that Harp played. The base from the saxophone is hitting deep into the souls of the audience. Some started to sway from side to side, while others looked as if they wanted to shed a tear. Once the music decrescendo to a nice calm, the music settled back into a slow drag blues. Nina continued to sing.

"They say it ain't too bad outside. They say it ain't too bad outside. Close your lips and open your eyes. We're about to see the fire. They say it ain't too bad outside."

Harp was a genius with how he made the sax sound angry and yet melancholy. A cloud had formed over the room. Patrons were hypnotized in the audience. As the music pulled them in with haunting notes. Even a waitress had to stand to the side with her tray due to the sax's hypnotizing sound. Harp played that sax like he was speaking through it. Everyone's attention was on Harp. Nina's scatting was shoved to the background as Harp's masterful performance stole the show.

"They say it ain't too bad outside. They say it ain't too bad outside. If you're black, you better beware. Strange fruits no longer dangle in the air. They're the red carpets in the streets out there."

As Nina points to the audience with her finger, she pours her heart out onto the lyrics as she feels the atmosphere in the room. Despite her fear, the pleasure of being on the stage, and delivering a message that can change people consumes her. She tosses her head back and belts out a note that twists at the heart of the audience. Nina took a step back from the microphone and pointed to Harp who went crazy again with the sax. He stole souls out of their seats when he played that sax. Nina was turned on by it. As he played, he watched her. She imagined every note he hit was her, sending a wave of ecstasy throughout her body, causing her to bite back a moan. The more he gripped that sax and expertly ran his fingers along the mother of pearl keys, Nina felt those same hands gripping her body, playing her like an instrument She was secretly crazy about this man. He watched her perform as if she was the great Billie Holiday, and he was Lester Young, himself. She love performing with Harp. Once the performance was over, the duo had left the audience speechless. Seats were empty and hands collided together in a roaring applause. They made such a good team and they would celebrate with great sex later.

CHAPTER 3
~Stirring~

The next day Betty decided to open up the café. Valarie had reported to her that she needed some time off due to the traumatizing event with her son. Nina and Stephanie wouldn't pick up their phone and Jenny had class, so that left Betty to get the day going. *Something is stirring in the air,* Betty thought. Raindrops rapidly tapped on the cafe rooftop. She was the only one there. Cleaning and wiping down the tables, while the Lord did his work outside. *A storm is coming,* she thought. As she listened to the wind howl outside the window, God was really stirring something up. The rain got heavier, and the wind howled louder. Betty stopped cleaning and walked to the window. The sky was dark as if night were approaching when it was still early in the morning. People were running inside buildings and jumping into cars, trying to escape what the Lord was stirring. *It's going to be a rainy day,* she thought to herself. *No sunshine, just tears from heaven.*

Ding Dong, chimed the main entrance bell. Betty heard the bell but didn't pay it any mind. She was still watching the Lord work. Craig entered the café and noticed Ms. Betty's attention was fixed on whatever was happening outside the window.

"Ms. Betty," Craig yelled, aiming for her attention. She turned around to face him and was surprised to see him standing there. It had been months since they had spoken or seen each other. "How are you today?" he asked, standing in the main entrance doorway. His heather gray suit was soaked from the storm.

"I'm good," she responded. "How are you, Craig?"

"I'm great. Are you here alone?" he asked.

"Yeah. Why?" she asked, wondering why he wanted to know. He stepped closer to Betty, making sure only she could hear him and no one else, in case she wasn't there alone.

"Well, you see, I need a favor, Ms. Betty. I need you to talk to your niece for me."

Betty figured him stopping by had something to do with Katrina. Craig never came to visit her. Even after her husband passed, he never showed empathy nor sympathy – never said a word.

"About what?" she asked, hoping nothing crazy happened between him and her niece.

"She wants to preach, Ms. Betty, and Katrina knows I'm against women preaching the gospel. It goes against God's word of the woman's place in the church, and I just need for you to talk to her and make her see that what she wants to do is not what God intended. Now, I know you're a woman of God and a firm believer of the word and I'm sure you can talk some sense into her."

This nigga must be crazy, Betty thought. *How dare he come in here, wanting me to stop my niece from fulfilling her calling.* Betty was ready to disappoint Craig with her answer.

"But Craig, I can't say what God's intentions are for her. She's been wanting to preach since she was a child. It was your father's church where she realized her calling. The same church where she gave a word that brought in the people who were in search of God and found Him through her word before you ever touched the pulpit."

"You talking about the day she gave her testimony?" Craig asked.

"That testimony turned your daddy's church into a mega church. You should thank your wife for that." Betty could tell by the frown on his face that he was dissatisfied with what she said. He knew the impact his wife had on people, but he just wasn't ready for her to co-pastor with him in the church. He liked having her as his first lady, not his competition within the church.

"I'm very appreciative of my wife. I just don't want her falling into Satan's trap."

"I doubt she will ever do that, but let me ask you something. Why don't you want Katrina to chase her dream? How is her preaching affecting you?" Betty asked. She didn't want to believe that Craig could be jealous of his wife, but jealousy and insecurity would be the only reason to why he didn't want her to preach.

"She's not taking over my church," Craig blurted out.

The truth finally comes out, Betty thought. "It's not your church. It's y'all's church. Her glory be your glory. Let your wife preach, Craig. Support her." There were so many things that Craig supported his wife in, but preaching wasn't one of them. He just couldn't do it. He feared what others would think of him, since his church and a few others never allowed women to preach.

"I support her knowing her place and staying in it," Craig said.

"Preaching is her place," Betty said, defending Katrina's dream. Betty knew what this meant to Katrina, and if she could use her voice to show Craig he was wrong, then she would continue to speak in her niece's defense.

"You sound like her. I guess there's no need for me to get you to talk to her, since you seem to be on her side."

"I've always been on her side. The question is why aren't you?" Betty was right. He needed to stand with his wife instead of against her, but how could he stand for something he was against? Katrina may have been the reason for the rise of his church, but he would be damned if she would be the reason for its fall.

"You know women have always been the fall of man," Craig said. "The Bible is a written testimony of it. Starting with Eve. The first woman God ever created disobeyed him and unleashed the deadliest curse known to man. Potiphar's wife, the first real desperate housewife, accused Joseph, a Hebrew slave, of rape; all because he refused to sleep with her. So, she had him thrown into prison. Delilah, the money hungry girlfriend of strong man Samson, revealed the secret of his strength to the Philistine for money and had him imprisoned. See, Ms. Betty, I know men like Joseph incarcerated or dead like Emmett Till due to a lie that a woman told. That woman, who had Emmett Till killed, waited till she was close to her death bed to tell the truth. So, you see, I know men like Samson, who wear their heart on their sleeves, for some woman to come along and have him set up by his enemy. Now, I ask you, is woman not the fall of man?" Craig just knew Betty would agree with him on this. He felt his point was made. When men fall, women are always involved. However, Betty didn't agree.

"No. Man is the fall of man, and you're not about to come at me with downplay about women in the Bible because while some were wicked, others were wonderfully made – brave, compassionate, faithful and patient. Your wife has been all those things and more. I put the Bible in her hand when she was a child and she fell in love with the word. Then she met someone who loved it just as much as her."

"You must be talking about Jason?" Craig asked, twisting his face in disgust.

"No, I'm talking about you. What does Jason have to do with this?" Betty asked.

"A lot," Craig said. "She still sneaks and look at his pictures. She got a picture of him now that she carries around in her bible. Hell, I married a woman who still mourn over her ex-boyfriend, who died fifteen years ago. Why do I have to live in his shadow of what could have been. I hate that mother—"

"Whoa," Betty said, stopping Craig from swearing on the name of her late Godson. "Now, we ain't going to talk on the dead! Yes, Katrina loved Jason, but she is in love with you."

Craig grinned and shook his head in disbelief. Craig didn't feel Katrina loved him. He felt like he was just a shoulder for her to cry on during her years of grieving and a backup to get over Jason. *Fourteen years of nothing to show.* He wanted a child, but Katrina refused to give him one. The only child she wanted was Jason's child, Malaysia.

"She in love with me, you say?" Craig asked, his voice cracking. "Then answer me this. Why my wife still have dreams where she call out his name in her sleep? You know I could have left the first time she ever did it, but I found another way to channel my anger, while she's laid up in our bed, dreaming of Jason."

"Channel your anger," Betty said. "What do you mean by that?" She didn't understand what he meant by channel his anger. *What is Craig doing when he feels his wife isn't giving him the affection and attention he's been seeking? Or is the question, who is he doing?* Betty thought to herself as she watched Craig. She could read his thoughts through his movements. She noticed a wicked grin teased his mouth. His whole aura had turned wicked.

"You don't want to know," he said. "Matter of fact, I got to get going, Ms. Betty. It was nice chatting with you."

He had said too much. He knew what he said had raised a question mark in Betty's head. Before he could reach the door, Betty shouted his name.

"Craig!" He froze in his tracks. He was more afraid to turn around and face her, than to walk out the door. Hesitant and nervous at the same time of what she wanted, he forced himself to face Betty. As he turned, Betty eyes aimed at him like a pistol pointed in his face, ready to shoot with questions. "What skeletons you got in your closet, son?" she asked. She could feel the evil that was hidden and stirring inside of him. The presence of the evil was surreal. Craig had been hiding his true self behind a false representation as a man of God.

"You mean what monster still rests under my bed?" he said, giving Betty a death stare.

"You know, I used to hear stories about your father," Betty said. "Folks from y'all church back then said he would beat on you and your momma and did some unimaginable things to y'all." Betty wondered, *was Craig still suffering from the abuse his father had caused when he was a child?*

"Did they mention he had a drinking problem?" Craig asked. "Did they tell you how he used to bloody me and my momma's nose, and lock us up in a room with no food, no water? We couldn't even take a bath or put on decent clothes. So, he could be out all night, cheating in the next room with one of those low-down women from the church, while me and momma were still locked in the next room. Did they tell you that?"

This man is hurting, Betty thought. *He needs help.* "No," Betty responded to Craig's questions. "But I always knew. You mask your pain so well for a man of God who still hasn't healed himself."

"What you saying, Ms. Betty? I'm a wolf in sheep clothing?" Craig asked.

"More like a sheep who can't break loose from the wolf," Betty replied.

What Betty spoke was true. Craig's childhood was rough. Anyone would think that since he was the son of a pastor, he had a good Christian upbringing, but he didn't. Bible scriptures and praises to God weren't the only thing happening in his family home. His father would beat, starve and rape him and his mother. Some days he would get so drunk at the local bar, he would go home and lock them away in a room. That way he could bring random women into their home and have sex with them. Craig and his mother could hear it all, the banging of the headboard on the wall, the moaning and groaning of the women and his father, and the tears his mother would cry, while listening to his father have sex with women that she knew were from their church.

Some days, his father would forget that he locked them away, and they would go days without a meal, a bath, and fresh, clean clothes. Craig hadn't healed from the trauma his father had caused. Instead, it enraged him and made him participate in pleasures that would tarnish his name as a pastor.

As Betty continued to talk, all Craig could think about was his childhood and his mother, whom he hadn't seen in years. His father caused so much pain and despair, that Craig's mother lost her mind. He had to admit her into a mental institution after the passing of his father. His mother being locked away in a nut house was hard for him to deal with, until he met Katrina. She took away the pain and brought joy back into his life. Her uplifting words and love for God made him want to do better as a person and a pastor. Katrina helped him heal, but she also helped him un-heal. Craig wanted a child with Katrina. He wanted to raise his child better than how is father raised him, but

Katrina didn't want any more children. Craig loved Malaysia as his child, but Malaysia wasn't his. He wanted his own image of himself to love and father, but Katrina denied him the right, and he had to accept that fact and live with it.

Ding Dong, chimed the main entrance bell. Melvin stormed into the café, bringing the rain and wind with him as he rumbled through the café foyer.

"Hey, lady," he said, roaring at Betty until he saw Craig standing there with her. "Oh, sorry to interrupt."

Craig was happy to see Melvin. He was the perfect escape route to get away from Betty, who had thrust him into the memories of his atrocious past.

"Oh no, brother, you're good," Craig said. "I was just leaving. See you around, Ms. Betty." There was so much more Betty wanted to ask Craig. She wanted to help him, but Melvin's big black ass had to come and mess that all up.

"Who that?" Melvin asked, smiling at Betty. "Your boy toy?"

"Mind your business," Betty said, "and your wife not here. So, what do you want?" Betty went back to the table she was cleaning before Craig came in and the impending storm tore her attention away from the task. She grabbed the dish bucket and carried it over to the counter, hoping Melvin would see she wasn't interested in talking and leave. However, it didn't work, it only made him follow her to the counter.

"Well, she didn't come home yesterday, and I was wondering if you'd seen her?" No matter how concerned Melvin tried to look or pretend to be, Betty could smell the bullshit all over him. He wasn't concerned. He was just pissed because he had no control over Stephanie's whereabouts.

"Well, maybe she came to her senses and got the hell away from you," Betty said, hoping that her smart remark would run him off.

"There you go getting out of your place again," he said.

"Out of my place?" Betty responded. "I done had it with this!" She walked up to Melvin and poked her fingernail into his chest. "You in my place! From the ceiling to the floor is my place. You come in my domain, looking for your wife but telling me my place. Have you not looked around to see where you stand and who you stand before? You have no authority here, Satan, and shit is out of your control here. You young ass men and boys talk of a woman's place, but where's your place? Huh? I know mine... and if you keep beating on that woman, God is going to put you in your eternal place!"

"I've already received my eternal place," Melvin shouted at Betty, wanting to put his hands on her.

"Receiving and accepting is two different things. Yeah you received it, but did you open it."

"Open it," he said, mocking Betty. "What you know about losing a child?"

"Losing a child?" Betty said, now mocking him. "What you know about killing one?" Melvin anger turned to shock. No matter how much pain he inflicted upon Stephanie, he never touched their child. He loved their daughter, Kinsley. But to hear Betty say she had killed a child made Melvin a little nervous. *What kind of monster is she*, he thought?

"I aborted my child, just so I could escape a motherfucker like you, and give new birth to my life, and have killed even more in combat. So, yes, I've danced with my devil and lived with the consequences of my decisions along the way. When I got out the military, I learned to be better than the person I was before I joined and greater than the person I was while I was in. You can do the same, but you got to stop using that child's death as an excuse and go back to what shaped the creature you became. What made you hit the woman you loved? Why

117

the beating of this woman? You forgot who was watching you. He's been watching you, Melvin."

Ding Dong, chimed the main entrance bell. Nina, Ruth, and Jenny entered the café together, discussing how bad the weather was outside. They were just chattering away until they saw Betty and Melvin standing toe to toe. Ruth pulled out her knife, trying to figure out how she was going to stab this big ass man.

"Betty, what's going on?" Ruth asked, holding her blade, ready to poke Melvin.

"Nothing. Me and Melvin was just having a talk." Betty walked around him and approached Ruth, signaling her to put away the blade.

"Yeah, and if any of y'all see my wife, tell her I'm looking for her. I got to get back to work." Melvin exited the café, leaving the women alone to discuss Stephanie whereabouts.

"He didn't touch you, did he?" Ruth asked, checking Betty for marks.

"Naw. He knows better," Betty said. She took a seat at the main table.

"Where is Stephanie?" Ruth asked, joining Betty at the main table.

"From my understanding, she stayed with Valarie yesterday." Nina said, approaching the table where Betty and Ruth sat, while Jenny went behind the counter to clock in at the register.

"Yeah, that's where she's at. She didn't wanna go home to his ass, he bruised her wrist and Valarie opened up her home to her." Betty said. "They told me about what happened yesterday. Matter of fact, I watched the tape. That was real brave of you, Nina. You standing up to that officer like that put me in the mind of Miss Simone herself."

"I was named after her," Nina said. *"To Be Young, Gifted and Black* was played in my house every day when I was a child. That was my mama's way of reminding me, how important I was, in this white man world as a black little girl. That happens to be one of my favorite songs by her."

"Mine too," Betty added, "and it's still relevant till this day. Along with her other song, *Strange Fruit.*"

"Oh, Ms. Betty. Girl, yes. Which was originally performed by Billie Holiday, but I love how Nina Simone delivers it," Nina said.

"Me too," Ruth said. "That was a deep song."

"And still nothing has changed," Nina remarked, thinking about how black people are still fighting for the same shit they were marching for years ago. "Black bodies went from strange fruit hanging and swinging from a tree to a red carpet in the streets. The streets are now filled with the blood of black men and women. What have we really overcome? These white folks still don't give a damn about us." Nina spoke, forgetting Jenny was white and in the room.

Jenny had an idea of what Nina spoke of, but Jenny had questions too. Questions like, why black folks always point their fingers at the white man for their problems? Why do they keep holding on to a past they never had? Jenny wasn't going to allow herself to be the voiceless white girl in the room. She had to defend her race.

"Well, can I say something on the behalf of white people?" Jenny asked. Everyone looked at Jenny as if she had called a public service announcement.

What is she about to say on the behalf of white people, Betty thought?

She better not say no stupid shit, thought Ruth, *or I'm going to cut her ass.*

I'm cocked, ready, and loaded, Nina thought. *Ready to verbally assassinate Jenny if she spoke something, she didn't like on white people behalf.*

Jenny began. "When are black people going to stop blaming white people for what was done to their ancestors? It didn't happen to you. So why not get over it?" Before Betty could speak, and Ruth could cuss, Nina let loose.

"Well, since your ancestors where thieves, you wouldn't understand what was stolen from my ancestors. Homes invaded, lives ruined, families broken. The black family ain't been the same since we came to your America, which is really our America since my ancestors built this bitch with no profit in the end, only oppression, depression, subjection, and still waiting for the resurrection which has yet to come. When your ancestors enslaved my ancestors, they enslaved every generation after them. I never been through slavery; but that doesn't mean that I don't feel the trauma of slavery. Mothers and fathers watched their sons get whipped, and now we watch them get shot, and the world sees it, but still does nothing. We riot when we get angry at the shit that's going on with our people, just like the slaves revolted, but when the smoke clears, we go back to what we were rioting for and revolting for. No progress." Before Nina could get out another word Jenny interrupted her.

"But you have made progress. Look at how far black people have come. You are more ahead now than you ever been. Education, music, film, writing, owning your own businesses. I don't think there could be a more perfect time to be black than now, but y'all got to stop looking at white people and the past to solidify what you can't have and what you haven't overcome. Yes, police brutality is wrong, killing an innocent black life is upsetting, but what can you do about it other than point the finger at my race? You can't blame every white person for their ancestors' mistakes."

Nina shook her head in disbelief of Jenny. *White girl still don't get it.*

"I wish it were that easy, 'cause for black people, y'all so easy to hate. The suffering you caused, the pain you give, the hate you make us inflict on ourselves and others like us. The reason for black-on-black crime. The need to belong in your world, when we know, y'all will never accept us for us. Even when we polish ourselves to look like you, the feeling of not being good enough, when you know we are more than good, but we are better than you, that's why you steal, copy, and take everything that we do and put your name on it. The separation of families is still dormant till this day. Black men need to take their place. If you going to plant a seed, then stick around to water it and watch it grow, then black folks don't know their true religion because you done stripped, took, and raped everything that was us, and now my people don't know themselves due to you. The sins of your fathers—"

This has gone far enough, Betty thought, stepping in to deescalate the tension between the ladies.

"Okay, Nina, baby. "Let's take it down a notch," Betty said, standing between the two of them, making sure no one laid their hands on each other. "Now, let's back it up and calm down. Nina, I want you to go to the back and take a break. Jenny, I want you to do the same. This why I don't like talking politics in here, too many opinions, that lead to conflict with no real resolution. So, let's breathe, relax, and calm down. Can y'all do that?" Betty asked.

"Yeah," Nina said.

"Jenny, can you?" Betty asked.

"Yes, Ms. Betty," Jenny said. Betty hoped once they got in the back that they wouldn't be fussing or fighting. She would hate to pull out her gun and shoot both of them if they destroyed her dream café.

"Okay, let's do it. Take a break," Betty said. Jenny exited through the double doors, followed by Nina, keeping a six feet distance between them. Betty went and sat back down at the main table with Ruth.

"Now that's what you call educated and black," Betty said. Even though she had a soft spot for Jenny, she loved how Nina stood up and was a voice on black people's behalf.

"Like they say, 'You can take a girl out the hood, but you can't take the hood out the girl,'" Ruth added.

Ding Dong, chimed the main entrance bell. Stephanie entered the cafe. She had on big black shades, looking like Lil' Kim from back in the 90's. The shades were overlapping her face so bad that you could hardly see her face. She walked past the table without speaking or looking at Betty and Ruth. She went behind the counter to place her things and clock in at the register. Ruth had to call her out.

"Well, if it ain't Lil' Kim, the Queen B," Ruth said, picking.

"Biggie came by looking for you," Betty said, joining in on the joke with Ruth.

"I know," Stephanie said sadly. "I've already talked to him." Betty and Ruth joking cease. Betty could hear it in Stephanie's voice that something was wrong.

"That don't look like all you did," Betty said, bumping Ruth, signaling her to go to the back so she could have a word with Stephanie and see what she was hiding underneath those shades.

"Well, I'll go back here and check on Nina and Jenny," Ruth said, getting up from the table. "Make sure they ain't started the next Civil War." Ruth went through the double doors, leaving Betty to speak to Stephanie. Betty got up from the table and went behind the counter with Stephanie, who had her back turned toward Betty.

"So, when you going to take them shades off," Betty asked. "So, I can see what he done did to you now."

"Ms. Betty now ain't the time," she responded. Betty could hear the exhaustion in her voice. She sounded like her and Melvin had been fighting and he knocked the wind out of her.

"Now ain't never the time, but I done read you wrong you say. Hell, I done lived your wrong. Your secret ain't no secret, Stephanie."

Stephanie still wouldn't turn around and face Betty, so Betty acted. She walked around to stand in front of Stephanie and snatched her shades off her face. "Give me them shades," Betty demanded. What Betty saw, made her grab her mouth and cry. Stephanie's right side of her face was swollen, it looked as if honeybees had attacked her and made her swell. Her eyes were matted shut and she couldn't see.

"Ms. Betty, give them to me," she cried, snatching her shades from Betty's hand, and covering her face with them. It hurt Betty's heart to see such a sweet, beautiful woman going through hell like this.

"Child, let me help you!" Betty said. Her eyes filled with tears. "You can live with me, until you get on your feet."

"I don't need your help, Ms. Betty," Stephanie said. "I can help myself!"

"If you can help yourself then leave him because if you don't, that man is going to kill you, girl."

"If he wanted to kill me, I would be dead by now, Ms. Betty" It was amazing how Stephanie could convince herself to believe that lie, even though, she knew it was true.

"Well, you damn sho can't say he ain't trying. Look at your eye! You can't even see out of it!"

"Ms. Betty, why can't you just leave it alone? Why you all in my business?" Stephanie stormed away from behind the counter to stand beside the center table.

"'Cause your business came into my café," Betty said, storming after her. "I didn't go out looking for yo drama, yo drama came to me. That's why you was sent to me."

"Here you go with that God sent me here to you," Stephanie said sarcastically.

"Damn right!" Betty said. "And I'm not stopping till you hear me. I've walked your path. I had a man that used to beat the dog shit out of me, and I took it, 'cause he told me if he didn't hit me, then that meant, he didn't love me. Hell, I watched my father beat my mama and she still stayed with him till her dying day. That was my childhood. I grew up thinking that love was abuse and abuse was love, even though in my heart, I knew that wasn't love, but when you grow up seeing it, and you live through it, you become conditioned. It took me getting pregnant to realize I couldn't take the love abuse any longer. I was tired of being treated like shit, slapped on, beat on, spat on. I was tired of feeling like less of a woman to a man that didn't know how to control his own damn devil. So, he released his demons on me, and I had had enough. I was two months pregnant when I saw my way out. I was walking downtown, and I saw these women in a camouflage uniform, and these sistas were looking bad, and I don't mean bad as in appearance, I mean Shaft bad. Ain't no man kicking they bad asses. They were confident and with the stance of a tree. I wanted to be like them sistas. I wanted to kick ass like them sistas. So, you know what I did? I said do you know what I did?!"

"What did you do, Ms. Betty?" Stephanie reluctantly asked.

"I went and had an abortion, and I enlisted into the U.S. Army."

"You killed your baby? How could you do that?" Stephanie said, disappointed in Betty's decision at the time.

"If I would have kept the baby, I would never had gone to the Army. I couldn't deploy pregnant! And I wasn't going to wait to get my taste of being free from his ass. I didn't want that baby, no more than I wanted the father. But I paid the price for what I did. Lord knows I paid for what I did because I had to walk through the pits of hell before I could even get to the gates of heaven. Girl, you don't know my story."

"And we obviously don't share the same tale. I could never had killed my baby just for a new start."

"But the Lord did it for you, and you still can't figure out how to break your chains."

Stephanie knew Betty was right. What was really keeping her in their marriage? There was nothing to hold onto but memories.

"He wasn't always like this, Ms. Betty. I've been with him since high school. He wasn't like that until Kinsley's death."

"So, you believe her death brought the rage?"

"It did," Stephanie said, convincing her mind to accept the lie she was telling.

"You can't really be that blind to your own situation. That rage was always there, Stephanie, before her death." As Betty continued to talk, Stephanie started having flashbacks of the first incident when Melvin put his hands on her, but she was still trying to convince her mind to believe a lie. Stephanie grew emotional again.

"No, it wasn't," Stephanie said, still forcing herself to believe in the lie. Betty walked over to her and grab her by the arms to face her.

"Yes, it was," Betty shouted. "Think about it! You just didn't see it! You been blaming it on her death when the rage was there all along!" The first flashback of abuse, continue to swarm her mind like ants in a bed. Every flashback she thought was the first wasn't.

"No, it wasn't" Stephanie said trying to fight, what her consciousness was revealing.

"Yes, it was!" Betty shouted at her again. "The death just gave the fire a little oxygen so it could blaze."

Stephanie began to weep. The last flashback was when, her and Melvin was in high school. The true start of the abuse. "And now you see it," Betty said, realizing Stephanie was done lying to herself. "You remember it."

"I don't want to talk about this no more," Stephanie said.

The first time Melvin had hit her played in her head like a movie in a Blue Ray. Stephanie jerked away from Betty and went to the window where she could see the storm still stirring, and the wind still blowing and the rain steady pouring. Betty walked up beside her and stared out the window with her.

"Stephanie. Oh, honey. You done ran away from the truth for far too long. Let's talk about it. Come sit down." Betty took her by the hand and walked her to the center table, where they sat. Stephanie kept her eyes to the table. "Heal yourself," Betty said. "Holding it in, ain't going to free you. How old were you when he first hit you? You said y'all been together since high school. He had to have shown some kind of sign then."

Stephanie raised her eyes to meet Betty's. "I was seventeen," she said.

"The same age I was when I met my abuser. Go on," Betty said.

"He slapped me for looking at a guy that I thought I knew, but he said he was sorry, and he wouldn't do it again."

"And he did? How long did it take till the next incident?" Betty asked.

"Three years later, he pushed me down the stairs in our home, and I twisted my ankle. He was mad about something that happened at work, and I didn't move fast enough when he called my name, and I…don't want to remember that day."

"Why? What happened that day that you don't want to remember?"

"He tried to kill me." Stephanie placed her hand over her mouth to hold back the sob that threatened to break forth. She removed her hand, so she could continue talking. "But I made it out of the house. After I fell and twisted my ankle, our neighbor saw me crawling out the door and ran over to help me. I told him I had tripped over a shoe and fell down the stairs. I never told I was pushed." Stephanie looked away.

"It's okay. Let it out," Betty said, rubbing her back, trying to calm her, as she spoke.

"Then when Kinsley was born, he seemed happy, loving, and changed but that was at the hospital. As soon as we brought her home, he brought the devil. I was in the bathtub bathing, and she was crying, and she wouldn't stop crying. He got mad 'cause I wouldn't get out the tub to get her. So, he came in the bathroom and put his hands around my neck and pushed me under the water."

"My God," Betty said. She could just imagine Melvin drowning Stephanie.

"He tried to drown me, but the doorbell rang, and it was some of his colleagues from work who had come over to see the baby. So, he didn't get to kill me that day."

"It's okay, keep letting it out. That's his second time trying to kill you," Betty said. She was keeping count of how many times this man has attempted on Stephanie's life.

"Then when we discovered Kinsley was sick. He blamed me, due to my family's history of genetic disorders. He started hitting me in front of her. He told her mommy gets beatings, 'cause she a bad mommy, but I knew, she had known otherwise. Then when he realized how much the physical abuse was affecting her. He turned it into mental abuse and ordered me to stay home and take care of her or he would kill me for real this time."

"And the day he revealed his true self?" Betty said.

"The day we buried her. We got home and I tried to comfort him. He walked away from me, then minutes later he came back, and I became the punching bag. Every day since then and it hasn't stopped. No breaks, just a constant fight every day." She began crying again but was losing her breath in between tears. Betty continued rubbing her back.

"Breathe, baby, breathe. That's how they do it baby. Some don't always come full force like my abuser. Some spread it out over time. The way you were done, my father did my mother the same exact way, and he told her the same shit Braxton told me. I do it, 'cause I love you. But don't no man love you like God. Do you hear me? You got to figure out how to go inside the enemy's camp and take back what he took from you, so you can break through. And if I could do it, so can you. God gives his toughest battles to his toughest soldiers. Now it's time for you to come home, soldier." Betty cracked a soft smile at her. "Don't you think so?"

"Yeah," Stephanie said, still weeping.

"Yeah, I do too. Come here." Betty hugged Stephanie as if she were hugging her old self. She saw so much of her younger self in Stephanie. *God don't make no mistakes*, she thought, as she continued hugging Stephanie. "It's okay, sweetheart. You're going to break through. I promise." Stephanie released the hug and looked in Ms. Betty pretty, dark, soft eyes.

"Thank you for the talk," Stephanie said.

"You're welcome, darling. I'm here for you if you need me. Okay?"

"Okay," Stephanie said.

"Now go to the back and clean yourself up. We got java to serve."

"Yes, ma'am," Stephanie said. She exited the front through the double doors. Betty had to figure out a way to help Stephanie, even if that meant offering her home as a sanctuary until Stephanie got back on her feet. Ruth walked back to the front to see Betty lost in thought. She took a seat beside Betty.

"Is she okay, Betty?" Ruth asked.

"Yeah, she's okay. She just started the first step to healing. She still got a way to go."

"What about you," Ruth asked. "Are you okay?"

"Yeah. Talking to her was like talking to my younger self. I just wanted to give her the talk that I wish someone would have given me. My family didn't wanna save me from Braxton. I had to save myself. And I don't regret doing what I had to do to live the life I wanted to live. I used to regret what I'd done, but I'm over it now. How them two back there?" Betty asked, wondering how Nina and Jenny was getting along after their debate earlier.

"Oh, they good."

"Good," Betty said with a smile.

Ding Dong, chimed the main entrance bell.

"Praise the Lord, saints! Praise the Lord," Katrina said, bringing in some joy from all the pain that was filling up the café.

"Praise the Lord! How you doing today?" Betty asked, excited to see her niece.

"I'm doing better than I was yesterday. How about you?" she asked.

"I can say the same," Betty said.

"Ms. Ruth, how are you?" Katrina asked.

"I'm here," Ruth said. Nina, Stephanie, and Jenny entered the front. They could hear First Lady all the way in the back. They had to come out and say hello.

"Ladies?" Katrina said, watching them post up behind the counter. "How are you all doing today."

"I'm good," Nina said.

"Great," Jenny said.

"Happy to be alive," Stephanie said.

Katrina could tell the ladies were having a bad day. The energy in the room seem depressing and sad. It wasn't the energy she was use to in the café. "That's awesome!" Katrina said, trying to figure out what had been stirring up in the café.

"You want some coffee?" Betty asked.

"Yes ma'am." Katrina walked over to the center table to sit. "I'll take one."

Betty got up from the table to fix herself, Ruth, and Katrina a cup of coffee. The café was quiet, while Betty prepared the coffee. Even though, Nina and Jenny were back cool, they still remained distant from each other, while Stephanie watched the storm worsen outside.

When will this storm go away, she thought. *How can I get out of this marriage?* She had been walking around with the divorce papers and a poem she wrote to end her marriage since yesterday, plotting out ways to get Melvin to sign. She couldn't face him again alone. While Stephanie was wrapped up in thoughts of how to persuade Melvin to sign the divorce papers, Ruth had received an alert on her phone that was blaring throughout the café.

Ruth picked up her phone to silence the alert that had captured the attention of all the women. Ruth began to read the alert, about the law that Alabama was passing on abortion.

"Y'all listen to this," Ruth said. "Alabama is passing a law making it illegal for a woman to have an abortion, even if it was incest or rape. The abortion is illegal."

"I can't believe it," Betty said. "They stay putting laws on us."

"Now hear this," Ruth continued. "The new law is punishable up to ninety-nine years for any doctor caught performing or attempting an abortion." Jenny walked from behind the counter and closer to Ruth.

"That's ridiculous! That's more time than the rapist will ever get," Jenny said folding her arms, upset by the news.

Stephanie was happy to hear the news. She couldn't understand why they weren't. To her, this meant saving the lives of babies, who were killed every day, because of their unprepared parents, which to her, wasn't fair.

"Okay, maybe someone can help me understand," Stephanie said, walking away from behind the counter and closer to the center table. "But why do women in America feel so oppressed? Like, there are women overseas who are truly oppressed and here we are, upset about killing a child, when we are really beating the odds here. We don't have laws that dictate what we can and can't do. So why are we complaining?"

"So, you're saying this abortion law is not what you just said. A dictatorship," Nina asked. She leaned over on the counter, ready for the debate with Stephanie on abortion. "Cause it seems to me that a bunch of white men, who don't know shit about being a woman, and ain't never experienced being raped or molested, and then wind up pregnant, wants to take away my choice of how I control my reproductive system. So yeah, I have a problem with that! Why not you?"

"'Cause," Stephanie said, folding her arms. "I don't believe in killing babies!"

"Is that you talking with common sense or religion?" Nina asked. Stephanie was appalled by Nina's questioning of her intelligence along with religion. "I'm just asking," Nina said, knowing how most Christians feel about abortions, while disregarding the underline truth of why women do it.

"I agree with you, Nina," Betty said, walking back over to the center table with the coffee mugs placed on a serving tray. "It's bull crap." She placed the mugs in front of Katrina and Ruth, then took a seat in between them and sipped her coffee. After letting the coffee heat up her tongue Betty was ready to further express how she felt on the matter. "What gives them the right to interfere with our freewill? As women, we should be the only ones with the right to make a choice about our bodies, along with our doctors, family, and friends, if we choose. Like this country is steadily giving off the perception that we are moving forward, when in reality, we are steadily moving backwards. Nothing has changed."

Ruth raised up her mug, agreeing with Betty on the matter. "Your right, Betty," Ruth said. "Nothing has changed. It goes back to slavery. Women didn't have rights to their reproductive system then. Forced and sometimes paired with men to produce a child for labor, or to be sold for profit. Most women were bred like dogs, just to produce children for financial gain on a breeding farm, where they could be sleeping with their son, father, brother, or cousin and vice versa with men. Could you imagine being on a breeding plantation? Just making kids so they can be sold off? But you know in this day and time that's considered foster care now. How they manipulate these women into keeping their babies and giving them a better future, then once the child is born, it becomes property of the state. I can't imagine having a child out there and not knowing where he or she is. Some should just have an abortion."

Jenny silently agreed with Ruth. She had a child out there and didn't know where he was. *Would I have been able to live with myself if I would have had an abortion*, Jenny wondered.

"Ms. Ruth," Stephanie said, "an unborn child shouldn't be punished for the sins of its parents. Jeremiah 1:5 says, 'Before I formed you in the womb, I knew you; Before you were born, I sanctified you; I ordained you a prophet to the nation.' Abortion is the number one murder in the African American community. One hundred to a million babies a year are killed due to abortion. Atlanta has a billboard stating that. Black children are an endangered species."

"Girl, listen to yourself," Nina said, sicken by people who always believed in statistics, with their false theories and number games that they try to run on the people. "Where these folks getting that information they feeding you? We were endangered the time our ancestors got off the boat, and still an endangerment, but it's not just due to abortions. Police play a part; we play a part. I mean anybody can come up with numbers and theories and put it on paper, don't make it true."

"First Lady, how do you feel about abortions?" Stephanie asked, wanting to hear the opinion of a woman of God, whom she just knew would side with her against the other women. Katrina sipped her coffee, when Stephanie picked her out, like a rare flower in a garden.

"To be quite honest with you," Katrina said. "I don't view an abortion as a good thing, but I don't view it as a bad thing either."

"Really?" Stephanie said in shock.

"Yes, really," Katrina said. She knew what Stephanie was expecting to hear, considering her position in the church, but her position couldn't overrule what her heart truly felt about abortions. "I mean the church, we don't discuss abortions due to the sensitivity of the issue, but there are more Christian women than any other religion having abortions and giving their child up for adoption every day. I feel, as a woman of God, that the church shouldn't be so quick to judge these women when they turn up in a situation where the pregnancy is unwanted, or the mother is financially unable, or just not ready due to whatever the social reasons are. We shouldn't judge. That's not our place, but instead, we should support these women in whatever decision they make. My goal is to get the mother to keep the baby. No abortion or adoption. Unless rape is the case, then I'm for abortion or whatever the mother wants to do."

"What about adoption?" Jenny asked. She had all these mixed feelings while listening to the ladies talk.

"If that's what the mother chooses, then I will support it, even though I would rather she kept the baby, than to surrender it to the state," Katrina said. She could hear the voice in her heart telling her that *Jenny had given up a child.*

"So, do you consider yourself pro-life or pro-choice?" Stephanie asked.

"Neither" Katrina answered. "I choose pro-voice."

"Pro-voice?" Stephanie asked. "What does it mean to be pro-voice? 'Cause I'm pro-life."

"You only pro-life because of your religious beliefs," Nina said.

"All human life is precious, Nina." Stephanie returned.

"I know that," Nina said.

"Well then, if you know that, why are you agreeing on abortion," Stephanie asked.

"'Cause, I believe in choices."

"Okay," Stephanie said, getting frustrated with Nina. "Explain. If a woman wants education and a career, with no children, then why have sex?" Before she knew it, Nina burst out laughing at the foolishness of Stephanie's reasoning.

"Did you really just say why have sex?" Nina asked, still laughing at Stephanie.

"Yeah! Why hop in bed with every Tom, Dick, and Harry, when you know you're not ready to be a mother?" Nina stopped laughing when she saw the seriousness in Stephanie face. So, she put on her serious face.

"'Cause women love sex," Nina responded, "just as much as men do. Hell, sex is beneficial. It helps relieve stress, it clears up acne, and it's considered a cardio work out. God wouldn't have placed it here if He didn't want us to enjoy it. Why make us have all these sexual desires at an early age if you don't want us fucking. I mean be real with yourself; don't jive yourself!"

"Oh, I didn't," Stephanie said. "I waited till I was married to have sex and even then, I still used every preventive measure available to not get pregnant, until we were ready for a child. I used condoms."

"They break," Nina objectively said. "Plus, I had a few dudes try to trap me with, 'I got the condom on,' but it don't be on. Men low down too," Nina added.

"And the pill," Stephanie added, but Nina interrupted her again.

"But ain't the pill still stopping life," Nina argued. "You pro-life people kill me. No abortion, but what you think the pill is doing? Not only is it stopping the process of life. It's hurting the mother to where in the future she may not be able to have kids without health issues. See, if you never been on that side of the track, then you wouldn't understand what this means to the women who have." Stephanie caught it. The whole time her and Nina had been debating on the matters of abortions, she happened to ignore the fact that this issue meant so much to Nina, because she had experienced it firsthand.

"Well, obviously you must know," Stephanie said. "Help someone like me understand it, 'cause I don't." Nina could see she had finally caught Stephanie's attention, and now she could voice why abortions mattered to her.

"Most women who have abortions, don't do it 'cause they don't want the baby. That's not the case all the time. It's other factors that play a role in the decision. I got friends who did it, including myself. I never been married before, but I want a baby by a man who wants one with me. My second abortion, I was forced by my boyfriend at the time to have it. He didn't want no baby with me, but I wanted a baby with him. At the time, I already had a child, and it was hard raising her alone. Then here comes another one, and I got to raise it by myself, 'cause this dude don't want to be tied down. But I'm like, dude, you bust in me. I didn't bust in you, and yet I got to walk around feeling bad about my decision. While this dude is relieved, that I did it, he feels no shame, but I do. He don't blame himself, but I do. Can you imagine, wanting to keep something that someone else doesn't want, and they make you feel some kind of way about wanting to keep it – that you one day decide you need to get rid of it, 'cause even though it may be what you want, it's not what they want, or maybe just not with you. A life that you both created, but only one of you want."

Stephanie could see the tears Nina wanted to release, but she held back. If words could be erased, Stephanie would erase everything that she had said to Nina. She didn't have the full knowledge of why women had abortions. She just knew it wasn't right. But she understood Nina. It was something she wanted as well, but Melvin didn't want, and that was peace. She could see that Nina too wanted peace, with whatever she had done, to her unborn seeds.

"You say your second one was forced," Jenny asked, wanting to know more about Nina's abortions. "What about the first one?"

"Out of my control," Nina responded. "I had no choice. I was fifteen years old, still in school, no mother, living in a house full of men, who weren't going to raise my child for me. So, my daddy forced me to have an abortion. I wanted to keep them too."

"Them?" Jenny questioned.

"Twins," Nina said. "I guess God didn't want me to have them anyway. When my eggs shot, one of them made it to the womb, and the other got stuck in my fallopian tube. I could have died from internal bleeding. After all, the abortion had to be performed, so I could live. Even the baby in the womb couldn't survive this procedure. It had to go too. The guy, whom I was dating at the time was pissed at me for not standing up to my father and allowing the abortion at the time. He didn't care that my life was on the line. All he cared about was the fact that I had killed our babies. He so desperately, at the time, wanted to be a father, and as young as I was, I wanted to be a mother, even though, I wasn't financially stable to have a child, and neither was he. We wanted those babies, but we had no say in the matter. I was living under my father's roof, that was my father and God's decision, not ours."

"Do you ever regret having an abortion?" Jenny asked.

"Yeah, sometimes I do, but that's my trial and error to live with. No one else can live it for me. The first abortion wasn't my decision, it was my father, but the second one was mines. I still have regrets about what I've done, but it doesn't change how I feel about abortions. I was once like you Stephanie. I was against it, because our religion is against it, but then my father showed me that... I could do it as many times as I pleased, as long as I repent. That's what our religion teaches us, and that's a sinners crutch – repentance. But regardless of my regrets, I'm still pro-choice. I'm for abortions… end of story."

"Nina, baby," Betty said. "Your story is sad, but I can relate. You ain't the only one in the room who done had an abortion. I have too, but those tears you're fighting, and that regret you been feeling, let it go. Don't let nobody make you feel bad about what you had to do. We all must sacrifice something to live the life we want to live. Even if that means a child. And your father was wrong, to make you feel like you had to repent for a sin that he committed, not you. That wasn't your fault."

As the rain hit the roof harder, Nina's tears began to flow. She had been holding those tears for so long, that it felt good to let them go. She had to forgive herself, because for years, she had blamed herself for those babies. Stephanie and Jenny walked over to hug her. Nina needed the love and support, not a judge. She had been judged for her choices all her life, but this time, she finally felt the support and love she needed from the women in the café.

"I read a quote yesterday," Betty said, admiring the healing that was taking place in the midst of the storm going on outside. "It stated, 'Society is unwilling to provide all children with what they need to thrive in society.'" Katrina nodded her head, agreeing with the quote.

"That's true," Katrina said, "and I'm going to tell you something. I heard Dr. Willie Parker say to an interviewer, and I agree with him 100 percent. He stated, you can't answer religious questions with scientific answers, and you can't answer scientific questions with religious answers. Science gives mankind knowledge which is power. Religion gives mankind wisdom which is control. The two are not enemies."

"That's a powerful statement," Nina said, still flushed with tears. "It makes me wonder. People always talk about it, but I wonder is it true. Was religion used to control us?" Everyone looks at Katrina, the woman of God, waiting for her response. Even Ms. Betty was eager to hear what she had to say.

"Wow," Katrina said as every eye in the room fell on her. "You pulled a gun out on me there, but I can honestly say, for our ancestors, it was. I visited a museum in Washington, like two years back, and they had a slave bible, and in the bible, it was missing chapters and verses, that they took out the Bible to keep the slaves from uprising and oppressed. About ninety percent of the Old Testament was removed, and about fifty percent of the New Testament was removed. Exodus was redacted, and there was no book of Moses leading the people to the promise land in the slave bible. The book of Galatians and the book of Jeremiah were removed. Anything that would have made the slaves want to revolt or rise up was removed."

"Wow," Nina said, amazed by Katrina's honesty in what she knew. "And what's the name of the museum?" she asked.

"Museum of the Bible in Washington, D.C." Katrina said.

"Interesting. I got to check that out," Betty said. After learning the truth of how religion was being used to keep slaves from overcoming their plight. Jenny felt bad in what she had said earlier to Nina. She could never understand the suffering of black people, but she felt sorry for them, and all that they had to go through just so they could be considered human. Jenny wasn't like those people who mistreated black people. She loved everyone, and she had to apologize to Nina.

"Nina," Jenny said in a sad voice. "I'm sorry for what I said earlier. I may have been out of line, but not all white people are responsible for all white people. Like not all black people are responsible for all black people. But I do understand that as black people, you got it harder than most, and that is due to my ancestors. We can't change the past, only the future. The change starts with us. Because at the end of the day, the real issue is not black or white, the real issue is…" *BOOM!!!* Thunder rumbled, shaking the café and causing Jenny not to be able to finish her sentence. They all looked around as the lights in the café flickered.

Ding Dong, chimed the main entrance bell. Melvin entered the café. Dressed in a blood red suit, looking like the devil himself coming from the pits of hell. The lights continued to flicker, making Melvin appear as a creepy, big, black figure.

"There you are," Melvin said in a sinister tone, staring at Stephanie. "I thought I told you to stay at the house. And you said you were going to call me if you see her." He looked at Betty like he wanted to kill her, and Betty was ready. She hadn't danced with the devil in years. Betty stood up from the table. She clinched her fist, making it known she was ready for war.

"You think I would actually call and tell the wolf where little Red Riding Hood was hiding? I don't think so," Betty said. The lights continued to flicker like an evil presence was in the room with them.

"Old lady," Melvin said, walking to the table. "I ain't got time for your foolishness. As of today, my wife quits! Stephanie let's go!"

She didn't want a showdown in the café with Melvin and the women. She had to leave and take whatever blow was coming afterwards.

"I said let's go!" His voice bellowed throughout the room, like the thunder rolling through the sky outside. Lightning flashed upon the darkness that followed him. Stephanie began walking toward him and stopped.

"Melvin," she said. "I don't want to go with you! I'm tired." She began to cry. The lights in the café suddenly stop flickering. "My body can't keep taking this." She pulled out the divorce papers. She trembled while holding them. "I want a divorce, Melvin."

Melvin looked at her and laughed. *This bitch is funny.* "See this why I didn't want you getting a job," he stated. "You start hanging around people, and talking to people, and letting them put encouraging words in your head. These damn women are trying to get into your head and you're letting them."

Betty came around the table and went toward Stephanie. "Better us getting in her head than you banging up against it," she said.

"You know what," Melvin said, pointing his finger at Betty. "I'm not arguing with you about my wife. Stephanie, let's go!"

"Bruh, didn't she just tell you she ain't going nowhere?" Nina said, walking up beside Stephanie.

"Hey, bitch, this don't concern you! Stay out of it!" Melvin said.

"Bitch?!" Nina said, scoffing at him. "Nigga, who you calling a bitch?! If I'm a bitch, yo mama, sister, auntie, grandma and niece a bitch!"

"Nina!" Betty shouted. "That's enough." Betty walked away from Stephanie's side and went to the back of her café.

"See how you embarrassing me?" Melvin said to Stephanie. "Got this chicken head talking crazy to me. Now this my last time asking, or I'mma drag you out of here and embarrass you in front of them. Let's go!"

She knew he meant what he said. To avoid him putting his hands on her, she began to walk to him.

"That's a good girl," he said, coaxing her like she was a child.

"Stephanie!" Nina shouted. She stopped and looked back; Nina walked up to her. "Don't go. I been with dudes like him. He ain't worth your life. Don't leave here with him. You can come stay with me."

"Or me," Jenny said, walking up beside Nina. "Nina's right. You don't deserve this. You may be a damaged bird, but you can still fly Your wings are not broken. You don't have to stay caged."

Stephanie's heart melted at the knowledge that these women were willing to help her, when her own family never tried to support her to leave Melvin. They encouraged her to stay, while the women in the café were encouraging her to leave and was willing to help. *They are my family.*

Betty returned from behind the double doors, holding something behind her back.

"Stephanie," Betty called to her. Stephanie turned around to see Betty, standing in front of the double doors. "I love you, but if you walk out that door with him, you can never come back here. I can only help you if you want to help yourself, but if you leave, I can't help you."

"You bitches doing too much chit chatting," Melvin said. "Stephanie, let's go!" His voiced rumbled with the sounds of the thunder again.

These women love me, she thought, watching them all gather around her and beg her not to leave. *I love me,* she said to herself. She had made her mind up; she wasn't leaving with Melvin.

"I can't," she said, looking back at Melvin.

"What?!" he said angrily, with the thunder meeting his roar again.

"I can't!" she repeated.

"I guess I got to drag you out of here!" He stalked quickly in Stephanie's direction. Betty removed her gun from behind her back and met his pace. Before he could touch Stephanie, Betty had the barrel of her .357 magnum pointed at Melvin skull.

"Give me a reason," Betty said, "to shoot your ass!"

Melvin froze, afraid to move. He'd never had a gun pointed at him, and for the first time, in a long time. He feared for his life.

"I been waiting for you, devil! I been waiting on you!" Betty said as the thunder now began to roll off her voice.

"Ms. Betty," Stephanie implored, "please!" Ruth and Katrina walked over to Betty.

"Betty, put the gun down!" Ruth said, watching how Betty maintained eye contact with only him. She could see the others out of her peripheral vision, but her laser focus was zeroed on Melvin. *Mentally insane,* she thought. That was her plan to get away with murder.

"Auntie, please put down the gun," Katrina said, hoping Betty would exit out of this shellshocked focus that she had on Melvin.

"No, Katrina," Betty answered, with her eyes still locked on her target. "I'm sick of this. I had to watch my mama go through it, my sister, me, and then it comes into my café. Why a man hate a woman so much, he got to black her eye? Out of all the shit you could be hitting on, you hit what loves you. You abuse the image of what gave birth to you. Why? Why so much hate toward this woman? I'm sick of it! Always bringing her close to her death. It's about time somebody bring you close to yours!" As Betty fingered the trigger, Stephanie moved in front of the gun.

"No! Ms. Betty, please. I can handle this! I can fix this! You don't have to do this," Stephanie cried. Regardless of everything Melvin had done to her. She could never wish death on him or watch him die. She wasn't that kind of person. She always knew God would come and seek justice against the wicked, but this was not the justice she wanted for Melvin. What Melvin was doing to her was deeper than what they knew. Her husband needed help, not death. Betty lowered her gun and cautiously walked away to the back of the counter, with Ruth and Katrina trailing behind her. Stephanie turned around to face Melvin. He still had his eyes locked on Betty and her gun. "I can't do this no more," Stephanie said. "Melvin you need help, and I can't help you. I just want to be free."

Tears formed in Melvin's eyes. "Free? What's free?" he asked. He had been the enslaved dragon of his past for years. Free didn't make sense to him. Free was nothing more than just an illusion.

 The rain began to lighten, the wind gently howled, and Stephanie was ready to read the poem she had wrote. The storm that had been stirring for years in her marriage was finally coming to an end. Stephanie placed her hand into her apron and pulled out the poem. She unfolded the paper and realized everyone's attention was on her, including Melvin. Her stomach twist, and her hands trembled. Her cheeks were burning as she let out a soft sigh. she began to read.

"Melvin, I wanna breathe again, I can't keep taking you pounding on me. I wanna see again, and for years you been blinding me. You took away my voice and left me voiceless. You blocked out my sound and now I can hear again."

After reading that line of her poem, she felt like a rock trapped between two hard places. She couldn't stop reading like her pounding heart was directing her to, she had to keep going.

"No weapons formed against me shall prosper. I been battling you before we lost her. I don't know why you put your hands on me, but I do understand… why you're so angry. It's not our fault that God had a plan we could not see. Every day I prayed it was me. Our baby girl… she was a blessing, and when she died, her death became our lesson. How could you not know when you lost, I lost too. How could you not see when you hurt, I hurt too. But instead, you turned your back on me, and when I tried to soar, Melvin you came, and strike me."

Stephanie paused as she caught her breath. Reading this poem to him was harder than writing it. Flashback of his abuse clouded her memory, sending a ray of emotion through her, but the sun continued to shine through those clouds. Her happiness and peace, was stinging at her pounding heart, waiting on her to break free from his storm. She gathered herself and continued on with the poem.

"Even though I walk through, our home, the valley of the shadow of death, I never feared you. You could throw, drop, and crack me, but you never broke me. You hate me, 'cause your mother didn't love you. You abuse me because you had been abused. It's not your fault your mother didn't know how to love you. The only reason she raped you, 'cause she saw him in you. Your father… he went and got away, and when he left, she put you in his place."

Stephanie crumbled up the paper and threw it to the ground. She look Melvin in the eyes, which was filled with tears. She haven't seen him cry since Kinsley's funeral. She walked closer to him and took hold of his hands.

"The battle ain't yours. The victory is ours, and we shall see. If God could save Daniel and Jonah, then Melvin, he can save us. The abuse is no longer the escape. You can live by the sword, but I refuse to die by it."

She released her hands off of his and raised her hands to the ceiling.

"Break my chains, set me free, I don't wanna be here. I loved you long enough to stay and take the abuse. But it's time, we go our own ways. Today's a new day, and I got my parade 'cause I'm going to breathe again. No more pounding on me and

blinding me. No more taking away my voice and drowning me. I just need you to set me free. Break these shackles off me and let both of us go free. So we can both just breathe. Melvin I just wanna breathe. Please!"

As Stephanie stood there waiting for an answer Melvin had a flashback of where his rage started. As a child, Melvin had what was once a good life. Both parents were present, and both parents, on the outside, had appeared to have been in love. His father had so many affairs on his mother, until she reached the point of putting him out. She tried to convince his father to take him along, but he didn't. He didn't want Melvin and neither did she, and since she was so miserable, she wanted to make her son's life miserable as well. She would mentally attack Melvin –physically and sexually, making him hate her. He could see no love in his mother. She was a monster, and she created a monster in him. When he met Stephanie, he fell in love with her kindness. She was so kind to him and caring, but she was also an easy target to hurt. He realized then that he should have sought help before they married. She didn't deserve the abuse.

"Give me the papers," Melvin finally said, his shoulders slumped in defeat and regret. She handed them to him.

"I hope you find the peace you're looking for," he said, scrawling his signature across the bottom of the papers, and handing them back to her. He didn't want this divorce. He feared losing his wife. He knew this woman loved him, and he hated the fact, that he couldn't stop his rage from destroying their marriage. He wanted a second chance, but knew it was too late. He started walking toward the main entrance. Stephanie couldn't believe it. He had finally set them free.

"Hey, wait!" Stephanie said. He stopped and turned around to face her, hoping she was coming home with him. She ran up and hugged him. For the first time in a long time, he didn't want to let go. "I forgive you," she said. "I just hope you can forgive her for abusing you."

Melvin nodded and made his way out the door. He realized it was time for him to seek help and for Stephanie to live. As Stephanie watched Melvin make it to his car and leave, she noticed the sun coming out from behind the clouds. It was bright and lit up the café with its rays.

Betty stepped beside her, catching gaze of the smiling sun. "Are you okay?" Betty asked. Stephanie tears of sadness and pain turned to tears of joy as she continued to cry.

"I did it, Ms. Betty," Stephanie said, laughing while crying. "I broke my chains." She continued laughing. Betty took hold of her like a mother to her daughter and hugged her.

"Yes, honey you did, and I'm so proud of you!" Betty said. *The storm is over*, Betty thought. *The storm is finally over,* as the sun continued to shine down on them.

CHAPTER 4
~Espresso-Yourself~

It had been three weeks since Katrina's last visit to Betty's Café. With all the tension and emotions that were stirring up in the café, Katrina decided that she needed a break. She had to put her focus back into doing community work, public speaking, being a mother to Malaysia and a wife to Craig. She had to get back on top of things in her life. However, during the course of those three weeks, Craig finally allowed her to preach. He also God-ordained her as a second Pastor of their church. Katrina taking the pulpit was what the members of the church had been waiting for. When she stepped to the podium and began preaching on her subject, "Crowning Season," the congregation was ecstatic. They laughed, they danced, they cried, and they praised.

Katrina's preaching was the best gospel experience in the Magic City. She was proud of herself and even more thankful for God, who had laid it on Craig's heart to allow her to preach. Katrina sat at her desk in her home office, going over her checklist for Malaysia's birthday party. Katrina, Craig and Malaysia lived in a beautiful two-story home with plenty of space, privacy and an outside living area on cul-de-sac in Redmont. Secluded among trees on one of Birmingham's most exclusive streets. The outside of their home was a tropical paradise. It had a brick patio with wrought iron gates, waterfall and koi pond. However, the inside was the fairytale. Every room was spacious and painted in pastel-colored paint with floral striped wallpaper. The ceilings had a 3D mural of African American angels in white gowns with gold instruments looking down over the home with white fluffy clouds hovering behind them. The living room, den, and other rooms in their home were filled with traditional luxury Rosa antique styled furniture, made from solid mahogany wood and chenille fabric upholstery with a floral pattern cushion. There were paintings in oil, watercolor, pastel, and acrylic scatter throughout the home of their family and other uplifting and spiritual masterpieces.

"I got to get the cake, pick up the flowers, and go to Ms. Pam's house and get Malaysia's car." Katrina sigh. "Lord, I hate birthday parties." As Katrina continued circling everything she needed to do on the check list, her gaze drifted to her mother's picture. She put down the list and grabbed the frame. "How I wish you were here. If you were here, this day wouldn't be so stressful." Katrina set her mother's picture back on the desk. She couldn't allow herself to get distracted with her sorrowful feelings that always emerged when she missed her mother. She had a birthday to prepare for.

"Mom," Malaysia said, barging into Katrina's office like a gust of wind. She held Katrina's phone. "Aunt Betty been calling you. She said she's waiting on you to come and get my cake."

"Right," Katrina said and hurried from her chair to grab her phone from Malaysia. "Hi, Aunt Betty. Yeah, I got caught up with this checklist. Oh no, auntie. Don't trouble yourself. You're a guest. I'll come get the cake. Okay, see you soon. Bye." Katrina hung up the phone.

"Can I come with you," Malaysia asked.

"Not this time. I still got a lot of stuff I need to get for the decorator, and your cake is a surprise."

Malaysia twisted her mouth and began looking sad.

"Hey, look, today is a special day, baby. I don't want you running around and getting sweaty with me. I want you to relax and get beautiful and enjoy this day. Enjoy being sixteen." Katrina kissed Malaysia's forehead. "Tell Craig when he gets here to go to Ms. Pam's house. He knows what's there."

Katrina exited the room, leaving Malaysia alone in the house with the decorator, Elizabeth Hill, who was creating Malaysia a magical birthday party in the backyard.

"Malaysia," Elizabeth called. "I got to go by the florist to get the flowers for your party. Do you need anything?"

"Can you bring me back an espresso. I know mama got a list of activities going on for the party, and I think I'm going to need the shot of caffeine to make it through the day."

"Anything for you, little lady. Be back soon." Elizabeth left.

Alone, Malaysia rushed out of her mother's office and into her bedroom. She needed to write in her journal before Craig got home. She lifted up her mattress and pulled out her journal and began to write.

Saturday, June 8, 2019.

When will she ever see me? She so busy chasing her dreams and giving me this extravagant party, that's not even my style, when truly, she doesn't even know me. Why did God have to choose my mother to be the voice of Him? To go out and speak and heal people? Does he not see the healing that's needed in me? There's a demon that lurks in this house. A false man of God, who touches me. Whenever she's not here, he's inside of me, and it confuses me. This man taught me how to ride a bike. He was the first one to push me on a swing. He tied my shoes, bathed me, brushed my teeth and now, he rapes me. What changed from the time I was three up until I turned thirteen? What possessed him to touch me? He fucks me more than he fucks my mother, and yet he can stand in front of the congregation after a sermon, and call me his daughter, knowing that later that night, when mama's gone and we're alone, he's just gonna come into my room and take it. You're gonna take it because we're both lacking my mother in our lives. You're gonna take it because I am my mother's daughter and your enemy's child. So, I will wait for you, to come into my room and rape me, and I will take it, because this is how I will protect our family, our image, our secret.

Signed, Malaysia
The protector of family secrets

As she finished writing in her journal, she closed it up and placed it underneath her pillow, along with an empty pill bottle and the paper her grandmother signed for her medical abortion, to terminate her pregnancy by Craig. She sat on the bed, waiting for the arrival of the Devil. Her room door opened, and there he was.

"Where's your mother," he asked.

"She went to Aunt Betty to get my cake. But she said, you needed to go by Ms. Pam house now."

"I got time to do that, but, since no one's here. I can get my quick fix." He began to unzip his pants.

"Are you sure that's a good idea," Malaysia said, trying to keep him from raping her. "It's a busy day, and people coming in and out."

"Hey, I know what I'm doing. You just lay there and cry. Like you always do."

Malaysia plopped back on the bed with tears in her eyes. *If you love me God, reveal it. Let him be caught.*

* * *

At the café, Betty was behind the counter looking through her appointment book, noticing she was booked up with orders for the month. June was the season for not only birthdays, but weddings. Big and beautiful wedding cakes was Betty's specialty.

Ding Dong, chimed the bell. Katrina entered the café. She walked up to the counter, opposite of where Betty stood.

"Praise the Lord, saints!" Katrina said.

"Praise the Lord," Betty said. "Here's your cake?"

Katrina lifted the lid off the cake to see Betty's latest creation. "It's a masterpiece, Auntie! Thank you."

"You're welcome," Betty said. "By the way, I did put my foot in it!"

"Yeah, I think I see a footprint!"

The cake had a castle and a little princess in a carriage being carried to the castle. It was beautiful. Katrina couldn't wait to get home and show it to Malaysia. *She's gonna love it*, Katrina thought. "How's Stephanie doing?" Katrina asked.

"She doing better. I gave her some time off to get herself together and I took her by the doctor to see about that eye."

"What did the doctor say?" Katrina asked.

"If he would have hit her any harder, he could have damaged her sight."

"Lord have mercy, Jesus! I'm so happy she walked away."

"Me too. She got to go to court in another week about spousal support."

"She got a lawyer?" Katrina asked.

"The very best in town," Betty said.

"Well, I guess bad news is good news," Katrina said.

"It's my new philosophy," Betty said.

Valarie entered the front of the café, holding a box full of Styrofoam cups. She went to the cup slot on the counter that was empty and began filling the compartment with the cups. Valarie didn't dare glance at Betty or Katrina. She wasn't in the mood for conversation. She had a lot on her mind – her condition, her son, all the jobs she was working. She needed a release. It was time to give it up.

"How you been Valarie?" Katrina asked. Valarie knew she couldn't ignore Katrina. She had to speak back.

"Making it. I can't complain," she responded.

"How about your son?"

"He's good."

"I saw you in church last night. You left before I could come speak."

Valarie didn't even think Katrina had seen her that night. She had sat in the very back of the pews, hidden along with the others who didn't want to be seen.

"Yeah, I just wanted to get the word and go. I see he let you preach."

"Yeah, it surprised me too." There was a lull in conversation. Valarie had nothing else to say, and Katrina rambled on to keep the conversation going. "Have you thought about what we talked about?"

"Kind of," Valarie answered.

"Well, you know the doors of the church are always open, and I'm here for you if you need to talk."

"Thank you. It was good seeing you, and you preached an awesome sermon last night."

"Thank you," Katrina said.

Valarie did need someone to talk to but would Katrina be the one she could unpack her suitcase on. She didn't know if First Lady could handle the weight that she had been carrying or if anyone could.

"Well, if y'all would excuse me," Valarie said. "I got to get back to work. See you around, Sister Katrina." Valarie left the room.

"She's not okay," Katrina said, still watching the double doors that Valarie went through.

"I said the same thing," Betty added. "Hey, you ain't got time to worry yourself with that. You go ahead and set up for Malaysia's party. She'll be fine. She just need some time."

"You still coming to the party?" Katrina asked.

"Yeah… I'm riding with Ruth."

"Alright then," Katrina said, picking the cake box up off the counter. "I'll see you both soon. Bye, Auntie."

"Bye, sweetheart."

Katrina carried the cake box and exited the building to her car. As she sat in her vehicle, she worried about Valarie. She didn't know why God had Valarie on her heart so heavy, but it was an unsettling feeling. But she had to think about what Betty said. This was her daughter's day, not the women who she wanted to save day. Katrina cranked up her car and drove off. *I hope Craig went and got that car*, she thought to herself.

"Valarie!" Betty shouted, hoping her yells would carry from the front of the café to the back. Valarie hurried to the front, thinking something was wrong.

"Yes, Ms. Betty?" Valarie said, out of breath.

"Hey, I need to run to the bank and get some change for the register before they close. You think you can hold it down for me?"

All hell, she called my name like that just so she could go to the bank, Valarie thought. "Yes, ma'am," Valarie said, relieved that nothing was wrong with Ms. Betty. "Is Nina or Jenny coming in today?"

"Jenny is, but Nina is off today. So, it's just us three." Betty gathered her things. "I shall return." Betty exited the café, leaving Valarie more intwined with her thoughts.

All she could think about at this point was James. The past two weekends she had spent with him were incredible. After the incident with her son, she decided to dial up his number. They chatted on the phone for hours, like teenagers in their first trimester of love. Even Joshua couldn't believe his mother was smiling. It overjoyed his heart to see her happy. Their first weekend together, they went to Atlanta, while Joshua stayed over a friend's house. James took Valarie to the amusement park and a popular soul food restaurant, in the heart of Peach Street. She enjoyed the time she spent with him. It was exciting, riding on the thrill rides, bumping each other in the bumper cars, playing games to win teddy bears, and gliding on the skyline. It felt good to have a partner. When night came, they sat on the hotel sofa and watched all the reruns of *Martin, Living Single* and *Fresh Prince of Bel-Air*. James never tried to take advantage of her or touch her in a way that was uncomfortable. He was a man, and he respected her as a woman. When it came time to go to sleep, he would sleep on the sofa and let her have the bed. He didn't want to tempt her or himself. So, he would keep his distance as they slept. But she wanted him in her bed, even though, she knew she couldn't have him sexually.

The next day of their getaway, they went to the Georgia Aquarium. The aquarium was beautiful. She loved walking through the tunnel and viewing the ocean life above her head. The aquarium was a magical place, and being there with him, made it even more magical. They spent the past weekend in the Magic City of Birmingham. James had hired a chef to prepare them an elegant dinner at his place. He also hired a live band to come and perform some soulful tunes. Once the entertainment and chef had cleaned up and left, there was no one there but him and her. He offered to take her to the Botanical Gardens or a movie to end their evening together. Instead, Valarie charged him with a kiss. Before they knew it, he was undressed down to his underwear and so was she. James picked her up and carried her to his bedroom. He gently laid her down on his pillowtop mattress and began kissing her neck. She dug her nails into the center of his back.

"I love you," he whispered into her ear.

She looked at him in shock. She couldn't believe he confessed his love for her first. "I love you too," she said back to him.

"Wait! Let me get a condom," he said. He got up out the bed and went to his dresser. He slid the condom on and turned around to face Valarie, who was fully dressed.

"I'm sorry, James," she said. "This was a mistake. I have to go."

"Wait, you just gonna leave me like this," James said with a boner. As much as she loved him, she couldn't have sex with him. She wasn't ready and she didn't know how to explain why.

As Valarie stood, bent over on the counter, replaying her past weekend, James watched her from outside the café window. *I finally caught her*, he thought. James entered the café and sauntered over to her, catching the eyes of Valarie, who was shocked to see him. She walked over to him.

"James," she said. "What are you doing here?"

"Well, it seems as if this is the only way I can reach you, since you blocked my calls and won't return my messages. What went wrong the other night? We were getting close." He grabbed her hand.

"And that's exactly what I don't want – to be close." She pulled her hand away from him and walked away. "I think it's best you go your way, and I go mine."

"What? Why?" James asked, confused in how Valarie was treating him. "Where is this coming from? The other day you were in love. You said you loved me." Valarie turned in his direction. She hated seeing him like this, but she couldn't love him, like he deserve. So, she had to tell him a lie.

"I lied; I didn't mean none of what I said. I just want to be left alone, okay. I don't want you."

"Valarie that's cold," James said. He walked up to her, so she could see him. "Even though you said that I know you don't mean it. Love is such a rare gem now a days. You shouldn't just leave it on the ground for someone else to pick up, especially when God placed it there for you."

"Not everything we find on the ground is ours to keep. James, I'm sorry. You're a real nice man. Beautiful, inside and out. In another life, you would be everything I want in a man. But in this life, you are wasting your time. I don't deserve you! And you most definitely don't deserve me. Let's save ourselves the heartbreak, and just leave."

"Valarie, I love you!" he pleaded, grabbing her hands again.

"James, no. Just go. Please… get out of here." She jerked her hands from him and went behind the counter. James felt defeated in his attempt to win her back. He made his way out the door, but his heart wouldn't let him leave. He needed to know why she had such a change of heart. He walked back through the café foyer to get the answers he so desperately needed.

"What's wrong with you, lady?" James shouted at Valarie, as he began walking toward her. "Why are you suddenly treating me so cold." As James approached her, he stopped to look at her, waiting for her to give him an answer, but Valarie just stood there with her arms folded and her gaze opposite of his. He took his hand and placed it on Valarie's chin, slightly turning her distracted gaze on him. "Baby… all I wanna do is love you. Valarie, I love you."

Valarie heart began to race in her chest. James plea of love felt like a train pounding down the tracks. It was overwhelming to accept when she fought back receiving it. She turned her face away, effectively removing her chin from his hand and shook her head in disbelief that James was still trying to be with her, after confessing the lie of not loving him. She couldn't take looking into his meek eyes. She loved him back. She turned her gaze away again and walked toward the counter, hoping her silence would end his pleading.

"So, you just gonna turn your head and walk away from me?" James walked up behind Valarie and turned her around to face him again. "Why you doing this to me, Valarie? You really got me bugging out over you. I ain't never been the type to chase behind no pussy or begged on bended knees."

But James did just that. He lowered himself down to one knee and grabbed Valarie hand. "Baby, I want to be with you. If I got to get down on my knees and beg you until you give in, I will." Valarie smiled. She admired the consistency in James pleading. But she just couldn't bargain with his love. She had to close shop.

"James, you see. I don't want no company, and I never asked you to get down on your knees." Valarie pulled her hands from his grip. James stood up with a displeased look on his face. Valarie couldn't just come out and tell him why she couldn't be with him. She wasn't ready to reveal her secret, so she spoke in code.

"James, my love, you couldn't take it. You be gone if you taste it." Valarie saw the sour look come across James' face, She could tell her words confused him, and she wanted to keep letting her code talk throw him off. "I don't believe in wasting time and what you feel for me may feel good to you, but it's a lot you gonna have to sacrifice. So, just save yourself and walk out that door and don't look back. Go find you a woman who can love you back," Valarie said, pointing at the door for James to leave. Her heart went from pounding to burning. It set her heart on fire to tell James that, knowing it wasn't truly what she wanted.

James let out a mirthless laugh. "This why I don't get you women. Don't know a pot of gold when it's in front of you. A man just wanna show you the world, but y'all just wanna see the stars and the moon." James grabbed Valarie hands again, hoping she wouldn't give him another let down. He was falling to pieces inside and her facial expression, body language, and tone, let him know she didn't care. "I ain't got nothing on my hands but time and a true love is so hard to find; but I want your love. Baby I don't know what I'm going to do if I walk out that door, knowing this is it for me and you. Valarie, your my true love."

Before James could get out another word, she placed her index finger to his lips to silence him. No man has ever considered her a true love. Before she spoke, she had a flashback of her past history with men. All the men she ever dated and loved, made her feel less than what she was. Men and women were the reason she hated herself. To have the first man she ever loved, her father, tell her at a young age, that she would never look better than her sister, who was light-skinned, was devastating to her soul. Out of all the men in her life, he should had been the one to applaud her beauty and build her self-confidence, but instead he broke it and never tried to fix it. He just left her broken. So, when every boy and girl teased her about her complexion, and when every man and woman made a remark about her skin color, it just lowered and lowered her self-esteem to the point where she felt what her father had said was true. She would never be beautiful like light-skinned women. The three men she loved set out to be with light and white women, after they left her. She never had anyone in her corner to tell her she was a beautiful black woman, except Stephanie and now James. She finally had a man who saw her, and he was begging to love her.

I can't keep doing this. I must tell him my secret. It's time to break free. "True love 'x' me out, 'cause that ain't me. I have no pages for eternity. Offer me the world and I swear, I wanna take it. The moon and the stars, ain't why I won't take it. I can see why they say love is blind. I done gave you too many warning signs; but you want my love and in order for me to give it, I must reveal this secret to you." Valarie stepped back from James as it felt like honeybees were swarming in her throat stinging her as she began to unveil her truth. "Look up toxic and there is me. I love you, James," she said, seeing the relief in his face as he began to walk near her again, but she stepped back from him, causing a puzzled expression to form across his face. "But damn. Can you love me?"

"Yes, I can," James said. "Come here, baby." He began to walk toward her again, except this time, she raised her hand to stop him.

"My condition," Valarie hesitated. *If he loves me, he will accept this.* "It's contagious…HIV… and today I decided to carry my papers." She held the paper out for James to grab. He took the document and looked over it. "That's the reality of my life and some people don't like to deal with my kind. But you love me. And if you love me, like you say, you can accept this, right? James, can you accept this?"

James was frustrated. He couldn't believe she had HIV and didn't say anything to him about it before.

"James," Valarie said. "Can you look at me? You can't look at me? Can you?" He dropped the papers and walked out the café. "James," she shouted his name. She retrieved her papers and placed them in her apron. Lighting had struck her heart. She thought he would say yes. She thought he would have understood why she couldn't tell him. She couldn't understand how he could just drop the paper and leave. After all the begging and pleading, he was able to walk away.

Her heart stopped beating when she saw him walk out the door. She died in silence on her feet with her eyes open and her body going cold, as she watched the man she loved not return. *He's not coming back.* Tears ran down her cheeks, like a marathon race. She had revealed her biggest secret to a man who now felt like a stranger, with the tea talk on her. She feared who he would tell, and how they would look at her once knowing her truth. She wrapped her arms around her waist as her stomach began to cramp. She could feel the pressure in her stomach radiating all over.

I thought he would accept me, as she continued to hold her stomach and catch her breath. She was beginning to feel ill. She was displeased with herself, and the fact that she had allowed herself to fall in love, and yet love was the reason for her regret and pain. But being in love with James felt good. He opened her up, made her feel sexy, and he showed her that she was beautiful, and she could be loved, but just not with her condition. Valarie was tired of feeling sorry for herself and being nasty toward others 'cause she wasn't happy with herself. She wanted to change her nasty attitude; she wanted to stop being so hypocritical; she wanted to stop being insensitive to other's feelings and problems, and most importantly, she wanted to love herself. She looked up to the ceiling and began talking with God.

"I must admit, Lord. I feel stupid. A part of me wish I would have never told him, and another part is happy I did. See, that's why I don't like to share my story. People can't accept it. They hear those three letters, and they leave. And I'm the one left to hurt. But you know what? I'm tired of letting my condition get in the way of my life. I'm tired of being afraid to love because of my condition. I'm tired of worrying about how someone is going to react or treat me. I'm tired of being a victim to my condition. I'm no different than a person who has seizures, cancer, diabetes, high blood pressure, thyroid disease, lupus, sickle cell and the list goes on. Don't none of those diseases got cures, but they still a condition that you got to live with. But one thing that I am going to accept about me, that I could never accept about myself, is my condition. Because I knew a man could never accept it. And I was wrong, to ask a man, to accept something that even I haven't accepted myself. But today, Lord, I'm taking that step to accept it. My condition is my condition. My healing is in your hands. People can cast me out and shatter my name. But while they trying to defeat me, Father you gonna always be raising my hands. Because I'm a winner. The devil is a liar. As long as I keep my faith in you, Father, I won't ever worry about why. I'm gonna go and tell it on the mountain, Lord! I'm gonna scream it and shout it. I'm giving this all to you, Lord, because I believe in eternal life. I accept my condition. Yes! I accept. I'm tired of living a lie, God. I'm tired."

As she wiped the tears off her cold cheeks. She could feel warmth infuse her spirit. She was free. No more hiding behind the anger to protect the secret. No more being untruthful to herself. The battle within herself was over.

Jenny entered the café and saw Valarie standing in the center of the floor, bent over while holding her stomach. Jenny immediately ran over to her.

"Valarie!" Jenny yelled. "Are you okay?"

"No," Valarie said, still hunched over, holding her stomach.

"What's wrong?" Jenny asked. She was concerned about Valarie. She was always so tough that Jenny wasn't used to seeing her cry.

"I'm sick, Jenny," Valarie said. She caught her breath and stood up tall, wiping the tears from her cheeks. "Like I'm really sick, and my son don't even know. You don't know. No one knows but me and my doctor. I'm HIV positive and I've been ashamed of it for years. I found out the day my son was born, and to be honest, I don't even know who gave it to me. I've only been in a relationship with three people. And those three people are the only people I've ever slept with in my entire life. I was in a monogamous relationship with all of them, and I thought they were with me. And now, I have met someone who has stolen my heart. And I feel like he done ran away with it, forever. And I ain't never getting it back." Jenny couldn't believe her ears. Valarie's truth was finally out, and it wasn't the truth she was expecting. HIV! This was a serious matter. A secret that you just don't share with everyone. This was worse than her addiction.

"As my mother always told me. If it was meant for you, it will come back to you." Valarie hugged Jenny's neck. For the first time, Valarie didn't see Jenny as an enemy, but a friend. A sister. Jenny hugged Valarie back. Their beef was over, and their friendship had just begun.

"Jenny. I got to go," Valarie said. "Just tell Ms. Betty. I'm not feeling well, and I had to leave. Okay?"

"Okay," Jenny said. "I won't say a word about this to anyone. I'll let you tell when you're ready."

"Thank you," Valarie said. She grabbed her things and exited the café. Jenny went to sit her things behind the counter. She was still in shock about Valarie's secret. *All these skeletons and secrets we have,* Jenny thought. She realized that every woman that worked at the café had a skeleton, that had to be excavated. A past that must be forgiven. A secret that must be told, and a soul that must be healed. Every woman that worked in the café was placed there for a reason. To remove their skeleton, tell their secrets and heal their souls. This was the purpose of Betty's Café.

* * *

It's time to put the finishing touches on this party, Katrina thought as she pulled up outside her lavish home. *Craig car is still here? Why hasn't he gone to Mrs. Pam's house to get Malaysia's car?* Katrina got out of her classic Lincoln Navigator and proceeded to the house with her purse dangling from the crook of her arm and Malaysia's cake in hand. She couldn't wait to show Malaysia her cake. She went into the kitchen to place her purse and Malaysia's cake on the counter. She saw Craig's keys were laying on the counter, when they normally would be hanging on the key holder. Katrina got his keys and placed them on the rack.

Craig is a neat freak. He never leaves things all over the place. She was surprised to see that Craig did that, since he considered himself to have OCD. As Katrina turned away from the key rack, Elizabeth's decoration outside on the terrace caught her attention. She opened the glass, gold, trimmed door and stepped out onto the terrace. She was in love with the work Elizabeth Hill had done. Most people in Birmingham would go to Peaches for an extravagant event. But if people wanted something sophisticated, classy and with a touch of elegance, Elizabeth Hill was who they sought. As Katrina walked around admiring the décor, fabric, and center pieces. Elizabeth snuck up behind her.

"What do you think, Katrina?"

She jumped and grabbed her chest. Elizabeth had frightened her. She was in deep thought as she examined the decoration.

"Sorry, I didn't mean to frighten you. I just want to know if you like it." Elizabeth said eyeing her work.

"Elizabeth, this is breath taking. I love it. The fabric, the centerpieces, the floating candles in the pool. Everything is beautiful. Has Malaysia seen it yet?"

"I don't think so, which reminds me. She asked for an espresso. I got to go give it to her. I'll be back."

"Okay," Katrina replied with a gracious smile, watching Elizabeth enter back into her home. Katrina continued to walk around the terrace, admiring Elizabeth's work. Elizabeth made it look like heaven in her backyard with the lights, drapes, balloons, flowers and the big water vase with floating butterflies and candles.

"Elizabeth, really out done herself." Katrina said to herself as she folded her hands and praised God. "Lord, I'm so pleased. Thank you, Father. This is going to be a magical day. Thank you for blessing Elizabeth hands to create such nice pieces and décor. Thank you Father! Thank you, so much for this day that you gave my baby. Amen!" As she unfolded her hands from the praise, a memory of how her mother would decorate for her on her birthday came to her. It made Katrina feel so special and loved, knowing her mother put all that time and effort into making her day special.

"Mama," Katrina said out loud and placed her hand on her heart, "why you been so heavy on my heart today." She raised her coffee-colored eyes to the sky. "I been missing you and thinking about you a lot. And I don't understand why. Why you so heavy on my heart mama?" As Katrina stood in the center of the terrace, floating on thoughts of her mother, Elizabeth was walking briskly out the house. She had an alarmed expression on her face. "Is something wrong Elizabeth." Her marching out the house was so intense, it startled Katrina. Elizabeth let out a hard puff and sealed her eyes with Katrina's.

"You need to come into your house right now." Elizabeth said in a calm but demanding tone. Panic welled up in Katrina.

"What? Why? What's going on?" Elizabeth raised her hand to stop Katrina from saying another word.

"Katrina, you're wasting time. Go in the house, get your gun and walk upstairs. Someone is having sex in your house." Katrina's heart did a triple sprint when she heard the word sex. She danced through the idea that Craig could be in their home with another woman.

"Impossible! Craig wouldn't bring another woman in our home. He wouldn't dare disrespect our home and Malaysia isn't like that. He must be watching porn. I hate to admit, it's a sin that's been taunting our marriage for years, but he does it from time to time." Elizabeth gave Katrina a sad and disappointed look.

"Katrina! Why don't you go upstairs and listen for yourself! It's not porn!" Katrina took off like a starting pistol was shot. She needed to hear; what Elizabeth had heard. She hoped Craig didn't have a woman in their home or in their bed. She opened the glass doors and went straight to her purse to retrieve her Smith & Wesson MP Shield. She pulled the safety and started upstairs.

Her mind and thoughts were everywhere. She wondered who this lady could be, bold enough to come into their home on her daughter's birthday and sleep with her husband. She thought back to when she pulled up. Craig's car was the only one she saw, and there wasn't any parked cars on their secluded street. She felt a sudden flare of trouble. As she made it up the stairs, she could hear the headboard banging on the wall. She listened to see if she could hear a woman, but she only heard Craig. Howling like a foul and disgusting animal. As Katrina made it to her bedroom door, the banging grew louder. She couldn't believe it; Craig was having an affair. Katrina took a deep breath and released it. Her throat began to swell as she reached for the doorknob. She grabbed the knob and quickly turned it. She quickly opened the door to see no one was there. No Craig, no woman. But the headboard continued to bang on the wall into Malaysia's room. Katrina felt razor blades slashing at her flesh as the reality set in that someone was having sex in Malaysia's room. She hurried out of her room and turned down the hall to Malaysia's room. She speed walked as fast as she could in her heels. The closer she got to the door, the clearer she could hear Craig's howling.

"No, not my baby!" Katrina cried as she raced to the door. She flung open the door and was stabbed in the heart. Her eyes screamed in silence, as Craig's moans ceased. Everything began to move in slow motion as she placed her hand on her heart. What she saw couldn't be unseen. Craig was fully naked, pounding his manhood into Malaysia, while she laid there with tears in her eyes, looking toward the ceiling. Craig had his hand clutched around her throat, choking her and ramming his manhood into her, like a proud pedophile warrior. Katrina stood there paralyzed in shock at how much he was enjoying fucking their little girl. He raised up her legs and began to stand up in her vagina. Pouncing up and down, making the bed frame squeak. Malaysia let out a scream. Craig moved his hand from her throat to her mouth, sealing off the sound, so he could continue to fuck her in this painful position of thrusting his large erect penis deep into her gut.

"Shut the fuck up and be quiet! Let me get my nut!" he whispered harshly at Malaysia. Suffocating her screams with his hand. Katrina removed her hand off her heart and placed it around the gun. She raised it up and pointed it at Craig's left ass cheek. *Pow,* sounded the gun as the bullet pierced through the flesh of Craig's ass.

Aww! he whimpered, falling to the floor, rolling and holding his ass.

"Mama!" Malaysia cried. She got up off the bed and ran to her mother's side.

"Get behind me, baby!" Katrina yelled, holding the gun pointed at Craig. Elizabeth came up to the door and witnessed what she had hoped wasn't true. She shook her head in disbelief.

"Katrina, what do you want me to do?" Elizabeth asked.

"Take my daughter in my room and call the police." Elizabeth took Malaysia and left Katrina with Craig, who was still lying flat on his chest, holding his left ass cheek. "I can't believe you, Dirty bastard. How could you?" *Pow!* The gun sounded again. This time, the bullet penetrated Craig's right ass cheek.

"Aww. Katrina! Katrina! Please!" he begged, while holding both his ass cheeks.

"Don't you dare beg when your sad ass touch my baby." Katrina moved Craig's hand from his left ass cheek with the toe of her shoe, then pressed her heel down into the bullet wound. He screamed and squeal at the top of his lungs, as she yanked her heel from his wound. She was enjoying this, seeing him hurt and suffer like he was just doing to Malaysia, satisfied her. But the ass shot's wasn't enough. She had to get him where it would really hurt.

"Turn your punk ass over!" she ordered.

"Katrina, I can't…" he said panting. "You shot me in my ass. I'm in pain. I can't move."

"If you don't turn the fuck over, I'm going to shoot you in your ass crack!" Aiming the gun at the crack of his ass.

"No!" he squirmed. "Give me a moment! Let me try to turn over."

"Hurry up," Katrina yelled.

Craig struggled to roll his body over due to his bleeding ass wounds, but he managed to flip his self over to see Katrina, whose eyes were on fire. She took the tip of her heel and stuck it up to his throat.

"For years, I thought you were such this godly and holy man, going around talking about God and how much you love God. When all this time, you been a snake. You ain't nothing but the fucking devil. False claiming you love the Lord. But me and you both know the Lord ain't make you do what you did today. How come I never saw this in you? Huh?" Katrina took her heel off his neck and pointed her gun at his penis. Craig held up his hands, trembling, trying to protect his dick. "I'm going to make sure you don't ever fuck another little girl again."

Pow! Blood splattered on her Dolce & Gabbana heels. Craig hollered with his eye's popping out of his head. He raised his hand up to his face to see blood from his penis on it. He began breathing heavy, with a scared look on his face of what Katrina was about to do next. She aimed the gun at his head. She wanted to kill him. She wanted him dead. She leaned over and placed the gun to his forehead and whispered, "I hope you rot in hell." She stood over him and leaned close. She wanted to make sure the bullet went straight through his skull. To do this to him was frightening. She never killed anyone before. She knew it would be a sin that she would have to repent for.

"You gonna kill me," Craig wept. "Well, go ahead and kill me. You already done shot my dick off, you bitch."

Katrina closed her eyes and placed her index finger on the trigger as she began to squeeze. A rough heavy hand overlapped hers.

"You got him, first lady. You don't have to take his life. Trust me. It won't help you sleep at night."

Katrina lowered the gun after hearing the familiar masculine voice that she had heard once before. She opened her eyes to see a badge that read Lieutenant Jake. She looked at his face, and immediately felt saved. She didn't have to live with killing Craig. Jake had it covered.

"We got it from here, Katrina. Give me the gun and let the crew help you."

She knew that meant Jason's crew was gonna handle this matter she just had to go along with whatever Jake said. She handed him the gun and hugged him. Katrina and Lieutenant Jake knew each other. He used to work for Jason, selling drugs and was still apart of Jason's crew.

"He needs to die, Jake," Katrina whispered. "He raped my baby. He raped me and Jason's baby."

"I know he did," Jake whispered, "and you can mark my word, he gonna pay. We got it from here." He signaled the paramedic to come into the room and get Craig. The man and woman lifted him up onto the gurney and covered him with a sheet. He laid there on the stretcher, looking pathetic and powerless. He grabbed Katrina's hand with a tight grip.

"Katrina, forgive me! Please! I'll repent! I promise! I'll never touch her again!"

Katrina reared her hand back and slap him in the face with all the strength she had left. He released her hand. She took the twenty-four-carat princess cut ring and band off and place it in his hand. Craig's eyes and mouth widen.

"Your days are number," Katrina whispered. "Get him out of my house," she yelled to the paramedics. They rolled him out of the room. He cried and begged for Katrina. His voice echoed throughout the hall.

Malaysia and an officer entered the room. She went to embrace her mother, while the officer talked to Jake.

"What a sick fuck," Jake said to the officer. "I'm going to do their report and talk to the family. Tell forensic to wait outside when they get here." The officer nodded his head, while holding open a Ziploc bag. Jake placed the gun inside. "Give this to forensic when they get here and tell them to wait on my call before they enter this room." The officer nodded again and left. Jake reached in his shirt pocket and took out a pad and pen. "Malaysia let me talk to you sweetheart."

She walked over to Jake, who had a miniature size notepad. She was worried about what all he was going to ask her in front of her mother.

"How long has this been going on," he asked.

The main question Malaysia didn't want to answer in front of her mother. "Three years," she nervously respond.

"Oh my God!" Katrina covered her mouth with her hands. She didn't know it had been going on that long. She thought this had just happened today. She dropped her hands from her mouth. "Where was I at when this was going on, Malaysia."

"The church, outreach programs, community events. Craig knew when you would be gone long enough for him to do it." Katrina still couldn't stomach this information. Her heart was still sour from what she has seen.

"Did Craig threaten you? Is that why you went this long and not tell," Jake asked, trying to see why she had allowed this to happen for so long.

"Yes, somewhat," she responded, hoping this was his last question.

"One more thing," Jake said. "Do you mind going to the hospital and undergo a forensic exam. This will be helpful if you plan to prosecute him." Malaysia looked at her mother, waiting for her answer.

"If we want him to pay, then you need to do it," Katrina stated to her daughter.

"Yes sir," Malaysia answered. "I will."

"Good! Katrina, do you want to take her or us?"

"No! I'll take her, Jake." Katrina didn't want to let her out of her sight. "Can you give us a moment? I need some time with my daughter before the news hits the street."

"Sure, but Forensic is going to have to come into this room to collect evidence, so if you can, try to leave everything as it is." Jake walked out the room and closed the door behind him.

"Baby girl, come here." Malaysia fell into her mother's arm. "Baby, I wish I would have known this sooner. I would have gotten rid of him a long time ago. I'm so sorry this happen to you."

As Katrina continued to hug Malaysia, she noticed a pill bottle, journal, and paper partially hidden underneath a pillow.

"Malaysia," Katrina said softly, unwrapping her arms from around her daughter. She walked over to the bed and removed the pillow, revealing the pill bottle, journal and paper. "What's that pill bottle for?" Malaysia didn't respond. Katrina picked up the bottle and saw it was empty. The label had Malaysia's name on it. She picked up the paper and read it, then focused her eyes on Malaysia. She looked back down to pick up the journal and flipped it open, slowly glancing through the pages. She turned to the next page and stopped. Her eyes trailed over the words on the page till she dropped the journal, paper, and bottle to cover her mouth again. She focused her eyes back to Malaysia, who this time, was looking very scared. Katrina dropped her hands from her mouth. "Malaysia!" Katrina said emotionally. "Did your grandma know about Craig touching you? Were you pregnant?"

Malaysia didn't say anything. Instead, she looked away, afraid her mother would shoot her grandma, like she did Craig.

Katrina thought back to Malaysia going to the café wanting to talk to Ruth and not her. "That Bitch!" Katrina shouted. She picked up the journal, the paper and medication bottle then grabbed Malaysia's arm before heading out of her daughter's room. She passed Jake, who was entering the room with the forensic team and Elizabeth, who was giving her statement to the officer. Outside, she shoved her way through a host of news reporters that flooded her front yard. She couldn't believe how fast the news had gotten out. She rushed through the yard and assisted Malaysia into the passenger side of her Escalade before jumping into the driver's seat.

Her heart broke at the pitiful look her daughter gave her. Katrina switched on the ignition, put the gear in drive and stomped on the gas. She was on her way to Betty's Café, where she knew Ruth would be.

* * *

Ding Dong, chime the main entrance doorbell.

Ruth entered the café in her rose gold sequin dress. She was looking all fancy for her granddaughter's Sweet Sixteenth birthday party. She looked around the café and noticed Betty wasn't there.

"Where Betty?" Ruth asked.

"I don't know," Jenny said. "She wasn't here when I got here. Valarie wasn't feeling well so she left." Ruth realized Jenny was alone. It was time she addressed her about what she heard, when her and Malaysia were talking.

"You never said anything to anyone about what you heard, did you? About Malaysia?" Jenny knew this conversation was gonna happen eventually. She just wasn't expecting it today.

"No, that karma is for you to deal with. I've forgotten all about it."

Ruth walked closer to the front of the counter. She knew what Jenny said was true. She would have to face her karma one day. But at this moment, she felt she owed Jenny an apology in regard to her being raped. "I'm sorry about what happened to you. I was wrong to have said what I said to you."

"You're fine, Ms. Ruth. Like I said before, I've forgotten about it. I've erased every word that was spoken from my memory." Jenny didn't want to discuss the matter anymore. She knew whatever hell, Ruth was gonna endure, would be the hell designed just for her.

"Did you ever tell your parents about being raped?" Ruth asked.

"No," Jenny said. Still not wanting to have this talk with Ruth, but she didn't want to be rude to her either. "My father, he never had time for me when I was younger, so, I figured he wouldn't have time for me then. But he did pay for me to go to rehab."

"At least he did that. What does your father do for a living?" Ruth asked walking toward the center table.

"Why these questions, Ms. Ruth?" Jenny wondered. *Where is this conversation going?* She had already given her word on not saying anything. *What else did she want?.*

"We're just getting better acquainted, that's all," Ruth said, taking a seat at the center table. "You don't have to talk. I'm not forcing you." But Ruth did wanna talk. She felt her and Jenny had more in common than any of the other ladies. She felt she could express herself to Jenny.

"My dad is an oral surgeon, and my mom, before she died, was a social worker at the foster home. What about your parents?" Jenny asked.

"I never knew my father. And my mother... well, the woman I considered my mother, she cleaned white folks houses for a living. She died when I was thirteen."

"What about your real mother?" Jenny asked.

"She was married to a pastor, my stepfather."

"Do you hate your mother?" Jenny asked.

"Baby, hate ain't the word. I hope she rots in hell!"

"I feel the same way about my stepmother. She a bitch. I felt like she was the reason my father disowned me after my addiction. She couldn't stand me anyway. Then, the year she found out I was bisexual, she nearly flipped. And dad... he was just dad. Always going along with whatever she say. He wasn't always like that."

"Your mother's death had an impact on him."

"I couldn't tell. He had a new woman like two months later. It made me wonder if he was already having an affair while my mother was alive."

"You never ask, you'll never know," Ruth said.

"Well, I guess I'll never know."

"I'm sure your dad still loves you," Ruth added.

"I'm sure he does too. Do you think your mom still loves you?"

"That would be hard for her to do, to love someone who you never loved to begin with. My mother abandoned me when I was a baby... for a man. Then she came back for me, just so he could rape me. She never loved me."

Jenny didn't understand her position in the café. Everyone was setting themselves free to her, and all she had to do was listen. She felt sorry for Ms. Ruth. Like she felt sorry for Valarie. Both women hid their hurt through their attitudes. But once you got to know them, you could see the pain and exhausted woman, each woman carried, hidden behind the strong woman, that they had to use to carry the hurt and tired woman.

"I guess I'm sorrier for you, Ms. Ruth. At least I can say that, once upon a time, my father loved me. You know, he would send me the most expensive gifts he could find before he'd actually spend time with me. He was always buying gifts."

"Well, you know when a man buy gifts, that's his way of saying, 'I'm sorry.'"

"Sorry." Jenny slightly laughed. "Yeah, he's sorry – for all those years he didn't know how to be a father. Money couldn't buy my love, and it never brought me happiness. It only stole my joy. I didn't need the Louis Vuitton bags, or the Christian Louboutin shoes. I needed guidance, attention, and love. If you don't love your child, someone else will. And not all love is good love. I just wish my love could have come from him and that my mom was still alive. Maybe things would have been different."

Ruth used to feel the same way. If her grandmother had still been alive would she had ever been sexually abused? *Only God knows why He takes those we love from us.* "We lose people for a reason," Ruth said, "and while we think they're not there, they be right there all along – guarding us, protecting us, watching over us. Our guardian angels. Your

Mother's death was the same reason as my Big Mama's death. God needed them to fulfill another mission, not on earth, but in heaven. He sent us to them to love in the flesh, but took them away so they could look after us in the spirit. He knew the road we were traveling and knew they could steer the wheel better in spirit than in flesh. That's what I believe."

That was beautifully put, Jenny thought, but she herself, didn't feel that way. "I wish I could allow myself to believe that, but I don't. I just feel like a…" Jenny caught herself. She wasn't expecting her and Ruth's conversation to get so personal. Talking about their rape and parents was becoming a tad bit overwhelming for Jenny.

"You feel like a what?" Ruth asked. "Don't hold back now. Express yourself." Jenny walked from behind the counter and faced Ruth at the center table. She had a song to sing. A song that she had been wanting to sing for years.

"Can I sing you a song I wrote." Ruth gave Jenny a friendly head nod. Jenny cleared her throat and began to sing.

"I'm just a motherless, fatherless child (mm… hmm…).
I'm a seed that has yet to be watered.
I'm the lone wolf that lingers at night (well, well).
Howling to the moon for its mother.
I'm the soldier too afraid to fight (mm… hmm…).
Everyone wants war but where's the peace?
I'm a woman but still I'm a child.
Everyone has rights to me but me.

I'm just a motherless, fatherless child. I never asked to be me.
I'm just a motherless, fatherless child. Why has the world made a bed for me?
I'm just a motherless, fatherless child. Tell the world to keep their hands off me.

I'm the lion in search of its heart. I want the courage to kill what's been attacking me.

I'm the caterpillar that died before it flew. My true beauty, I'll never see.

I'm the tree branch too afraid to break. If I fall then who will carry me?

I'm a woman searching for a child. That little girl I no longer see.

I'm just a helpless, victimized child. Who put this curse on me?

I'm just a worthless, corrupt child. Who's playing this trick on me?

I'm just a motherless, fatherless child. Tell the world to keep their hands off me."

As Jenny finished the song, Ruth began to clap. Ruth held back tears as she continued to carry on with a standing ovation. The song resonated with Ruth. She felt the same way as Jenny. She felt motherless, fatherless, victimized, corrupt, and cursed. All those things Ruth felt, and it unsettled her spirit. After she finish giving Jenny her praise, she sat back down in her chair. "That was beautiful, Jenny. I guess we're two peas in a pod," Ruth said.

"I guess we are," Jenny returned with a small smile.

Ding Dong, chimed the main entrance bell.

Betty entered the café, startled to see Ruth there before the time they had planned on leaving for Malaysia's party.

"Ruth, you're here early," Betty said. She went behind the counter to place her things and deposit the money in the cash register.

"Yeah, I just wanted to get out that house," Ruth said. "You know how it is on this day." Betty almost forgot. Malaysia's birthday was on the same day Jason was murdered.

"Yeah. Today is the day that Jason died," Betty said. She began preparing her and Ruth an espresso. She had just ordered a new espresso machine, and today was gonna be the first day she used it to help her friend espresso-herself.

"Who is Jason?" Jenny asked.

"My oldest son," Ruth answered. "Malaysia's father."

"Wow, he died on Malaysia's birthday?" Jenny asked, saddened by the discovery of Ruth's son's death on Malaysia's birthday.

"While Katrina was giving birth, my son was being gunned down like Scarface. He got caught up in a life that he couldn't turn away from."

"Where is Valarie?" Betty asked, noticing she haven't seen her.

"She said she wasn't feeling well, so she left," Jenny said, hoping Betty couldn't see through her lie.

"Oh, I kind of figure she had a little bug. She wasn't acting like herself."

"Well, I guess I'll go to the back and bag some treats. Do you need me to do anything before I get started?"

"Oh no, go ahead," Betty said.

Jenny walked to the back, relieved to be away from the presence of Ms. Betty, who could sense everything like a hound dog.

Betty walked over to the table with her and Ruth's espresso. She handed Ruth her coffee.

"Here," Betty said, "have an espresso." Betty took a seat across from Ruth. She could tell by the look on Ruth's face that something was bothering her. "How are you feeling?" Betty asked.

"I feel like some shit about to go down," Ruth said, patting her pack of cigarettes in her hand. "I don't know why I'm feeling this way, but my nerves are real bad. I already done went through my first box of cigarettes. I don't know if I'm about to have a nervous breakdown, or if it's something else." Betty could see the tenseness in Ruth's demeanor. She spoke softly, calm and sad, unlike her usual tone. Her eyes looked tired and worried. Either Jason's death was really bothering her, or it was something else.

Ding Dong, chimed the main entrance doorbell.

James entered the café, looking even more tense than Ruth.

"Hey, Ms. Betty. Is Valarie here?" he asked, while looking around the café for her.

"No. Jenny said she wasn't feeling well, so she left."

The nerve of this boy, Ruth thought, *walking straight over to Betty and not speaking to me – his mama.* "You don't see your mother sitting over here?" Ruth asked.

"What up, ma," James said.

Ruth couldn't believe the disrespect. *Who addressed their mother like that*, she thought? "That's how you speak to me?" she asked.

"I don't know what else I'm supposed to say," James said, raising his voice at Ruth. He didn't come to Betty's café to mingle or talk to his mother. He needed to find Valarie. "Hey, Ms. Betty. Can I talk to you about something outside?"

"For what?" Ruth asked. "You my damn son! What you got to say to Betty that you can't say right here in front of me?"

Here we go, James thought. He hadn't talked to or seen his mama since he got out of prison, and he wasn't about to discuss his relationship problems with her.

"The truth is, I don't want to say it in front of you. Ms. Betty, can I please talk to you outside?" Betty could see that what James needed to talk about was important. Although, she didn't want to step in between him and his mother, she had to see what he needed. Betty began to get up out her chair, but Ruth grabbed her arm and stopped her.

"No!" Ruth stood up to face James. Ruth and James had a horrible relationship. She made a lot of mistakes by him, as his mother, but that gave him no right to disrespect her. "You my damn son. Betty, that's my son. I'm your mother!"

"Really? Are you?" James asked. "Ms. Betty been more of a mother to me than you ever been."

Plap! Ruth slapped the spit out of James mouth. He held his cheek. "How dare you say that shit to me?! You don't know a damn thing about being a parent. Especially a mother! Yo father wasn't shit!"

"No, ma. You wasn't shit," James shouted.

Ruth raised her hand to hit James again, but this time, he caught her by the wrist. He tightened his grip around her wrist and stared into her eyes. "You're not going to keep putting your hands on me. I'm not your little boy anymore!" He forcefully threw her hand away from his face. "I came here to talk with you, Ms. Betty, but I think it's something my mama needs to hear. Something I been burning to tell her, but I never did 'cause Jason used to always say, she our mama, and we got to love her regardless of what she do. And may bro rest in peace, but that was some bullshit! Mama, I hated you! From the time I grew up to know you was my mama, up until the time I got locked up, I hated you! When I was younger, I used to wish you would just die, so Ms. Betty could just take us away from you! You abandoned us for a motherfucking nigga!"

Ruth couldn't argue with James on this matter, what he said was true. She did abandon them. When James' father took all her money and left her for another woman, it ruined her. Ruth thought she had finally met a man that accepted and loved her and Jason. But he changed. He started out nice, kind, family-oriented, and hardworking, but somewhere down the line, he stopped being all those wonderful things and became mean and lazy. James was too young to remember the hell his father put her through – staying out all night and not coming home, losing jobs and putting her through financial hell, which started her on the path of selling drugs and maintaining two jobs to support her household. The situation had broken her down. Having to be the man and woman of the home had been exhausting. When James' father left, he left Ruth destitute. He found her secret stash and cleaned out their accounts. Ruth had to start over, in ways that she didn't want to – sleeping with men for money and putting them before her children. This was low of her, but it also filled that void of wanting to be loved by a man, something she had never received properly before his father or after. As James waited to see if Ruth would have a comeback to what he said, he was perplexed when she never responded. She just stood there like she was waiting for him to say more.

"I remember when me and Jason would wanna watch TV, but you would send us to our room with no TV 'cause yo nigga wanted to watch it! Me and my brother would be starving. We couldn't wait till you got home and cooked us a meal, except those cooked meals wasn't for us. They were for him. Mama, you wouldn't even feed us until that nigga ate and was full! And we were your sons! We would have done anything for you, especially Jason! We had to go to school looking like shit, while you kept you and your nigga fly. You would stay gone two to three weeks at a time. Somedays we had no food, some days no lights. What do you expect young boys to do when they're forced to be men? Love begins at home. And when you don't have that love at home, you turn to the streets looking for it. You the reason Jason started selling drugs! You the reason my brother dead! I blame you! You put him on!"

"Wait a minute!" Ruth shouted. "You're not going to put his blood on my hands! I was just showing you boys how to make a little money on the side if you ever had to. I never said to go out and become a kingpin. Now that was never my intentions. That was his!"

"But you put the fire in his hand, and you burned him. It's your fault!"

"No, it's not! No, it's not!" Ruth said, refusing to accept the responsibility of her son's death.

"Yes, it is!" James said. "Own up to your mistakes, mama!"

"Don't you ever call me mama!" Ruth shouted. "You ain't no son of mine! Matter of fact, it should have been you. Jason should still be here. That bullet should have hit you!"

"Ruth!" Betty said, shocked by her friend's choice of words.

"Thank you, Ruth," James said, "for telling me what I always needed to hear out your mouth 'cause I wish it were you instead of him too."

"James, Ruth, y'all don't mean this," Betty said. "Ruth that's your son."

Betty could only hope that Ruth would take back what she said, but she didn't. Her tongue got worse.

"Betty, my son is dead. I don't know this nigga."

James knew this day, this talk, with his mother was coming, but he didn't want it to end, the way it was about to end.

"You know, when we were kids, Jason used to always tell me, 'Mama can't love, 'cause she never been loved.' As a kid I never understood what he meant, when he said that you were robbed of love. Now I can see it. I feel sorry for you!"

Ruth shed a tear. Jason was the only one besides Malaysia that knew her truth. And the truth hurts more now, than it did before.

"Get out," Ruth shouted at James. "Get out now!"

James never meant to hurt her. He just wanted to express how he always felt to her, even if that meant the end of them. James exited the café. Ruth stood there in tears, still hurting from the words her son said. Betty was confused. She knew Ruth wasn't the perfect mother, but she never thought Ruth would let her emotions make her stoop so low with the words she said to her own son.

"Ruth, what done gotten into you?" Betty asked. "How the hell you gonna tell that boy it shoulda been him? He's your son!"

"No, he's your son!" Ruth said, pointing her finger at Betty's chest. "Why you always cleaning up my trail? Who asked you to step in and play my role?"

"Wait a minute," Betty said. "You getting mad at me over some shit that happen thirty something years ago?"

"Hell, yeah, I'm mad! Mad my son thinks of you as more of his mother than me."

"You mad 'cause you couldn't play your role as a mother, and I did it for you?"

"See, that's the thing, I never asked you to play my role!"

"Well… Ruth. You couldn't pour from an empty cup. Someone needed to play your role. The boys needed someone. While you were out partying and chasing men, you left boys to be men. When all they wanted to be were your children. You made them boys grow up faster than they were supposed to."

"Hell, I grew up faster than I was supposed to," Ruth said.

"I don't recall that," Betty said. "I grew up with you. You had a very decent upbringing. Now what made you go left other than right, I don't know. But your folks were decent people."

"You don't know shit about them folks! You only knew what you saw, and what you saw was a lie!"

"Then tell me the truth so it can set you free, Ruth. What you been keeping from me? What parasite been feasting on your heart that you so cold?"

"Some things are better left in the dark. You can't save the world, Betty."

"But who's to say I can't try?"

Ding Dong, chimed the main entrance bell.

Katrina entered the café, holding the pill bottle, Malaysia journal and a white piece of paper. She sounded like a stampede of elephants running through the café, as she stomped inside with Malaysia trailing behind her. "Ms. Ruth," Katrina shouted, making her way toward the centered table.

"Mama, wait!" Malaysia yelled, chasing behind her. She tried to grab Katrina's arm, but she jerked away from her.

"Move Malaysia," Katrina said.

Ruth turned around to see Katrina approaching her with Malaysia tagging along.

Jenny could hear Katrina shouting Ruth's name all the way in the back of the cafe. She walked upfront to see what the problem was, but when she saw Malaysia, she knew exactly what the problem was. *The truth has come to the light.*

"Katrina what's wrong?" Betty asked, stopping Katrina in her tracks. Katrina was heading toward Ruth like she was about to snatch her up, and Betty wasn't about to allow fighting in her café.

"Ms. Ruth knows what's wrong." Katrina stepped around Betty and went to stand in front of Ruth, who stood there looking confused. "How could you?!"

"How could I what?" Ruth shouted.

"Know that my husband was having sex with my child, and not say anything?!"

Ruth's confusion turned to shame. This was not the way she planned on discussing this matter with Katrina. Ruth dropped to her seat at the table and looked away. *I'm not answering that. I can't answer it.*

"I went home with my baby's cake and caught my husband having sex with my daughter. I pulled out my gun and shot him in both ass cheeks! And then I made sure he would never, use his manhood again. Once the paramedics came and got him, me and Malaysia was in her room alone, comforting each other until I spotted all this." Katrina showed what was in her hands. "An empty pill bottle with her name on it, her journal with an entry of every day and time Craig touched her and when she told you about it, and this paper with your name on it." Katrina turned the paper around so Ruth could see it. "All these things hanging out from underneath her pillow. This paper states that you are her legal guardian and that you took her to the abortion clinic to get a medical abortion to terminate her pregnancy, and this journal proves that you knew about Craig touching my baby."

"Oh my God! Ruth, is this true?" Betty asked, shocked by what was unfolding in her cafe.

"Here's the evidence!" Katrina said, handing the pills, journal and paper over to Betty. She looked at the paper and opened the journal. What Betty read weakened her stomach. What Katrina had said was true. *This just didn't seem like Ruth.*

"Ruth?" Betty called her name, but her friend continued to look away.

Malaysia saw the shame in her grandma eyes. Her situation was causing her Grandma to re-live the trauma again. Only this time, it was her who was being raped, not Ruth. Young Ruth was sitting in that chair, looking away and frighten to speak. Not old Ruth. Old Ruth couldn't protect young Ruth at this moment. Malaysia ran over to her grandma and hugged her.

"Ma, just leave Grandma alone," Malaysia said.

"Malaysia, move!" Katrina yelled.

Malaysia could tell her mother was pissed and wasn't playing. She stepped back, remembering how she shot Craig.

"Ms. Ruth, look at me! I need an explanation! He got her pregnant, and you took my child to have an abortion without my consent?! Who the hell do you think you are?!"

"Katrina, wait a minute," Betty said, stepping in between them. "Ruth answer her." But Ruth said nothing. She couldn't even look in their direction. She was gripped in a traumatic state and couldn't find her way out. She couldn't speak. She couldn't look anyone in the eyes. She could only look away and remain silent.

"So, she just going to look away?" Katrina asked, becoming enraged by Ruth's silence. "You just going to look away? You can't face me and tell me why you kept it to yourself? You supposed to be the big bad wolf, huffing and puffing, and blowing down everybody, but when it comes to this conversation, you tune out the song. Just because you can't face your past, doesn't mean my child should suffer like you did!" Ruth flung her head around and stood up to face Katrina.

"Little girl, shut yo ass up! What you know about suffering?" Ruth asked.

"Try two years old to your thirteen," Katrina replied. Betty was lost on what both ladies had suffered. She never knew about Ruth's abuse, nor did she know anything about Katrina being sexually assaulted at two years old.

Malaysia was aware of her grandmother's assault but had no idea of her mother's.

"Katrina… Ruth… I don't understand." Betty said. "Katrina what are you talking about?"

"She your friend, Auntie. You ask her what I'm talking about."

"I told Jason you weren't no good, and he sat up there telling you my business. Just get out my friend's shop," Ruth yelled, as she took a seat back at the center table, "and leave me alone!"

"I don't have to go anywhere," Katrina stated. "Yo friend, my aunt. Ms. Betty my blood, you water. Must I remind you? Carole was my mom. And you remember what happened the last time you stepped to my mother! Try her daughter."

"Mama, stop it," Malaysia cried. She moved her mother out the way and hugged her Grandma. "Grandma, it's okay."

Betty stood dumbstruck by the entire situation. Things were getting out of hand, and she had to stop it before it got worse.

"Katrina, stop it! You a woman of God. You don't act like this," Betty said.

"When it come to my child, Auntie, I lose all religion. She got to answer to this now! I need to know why?" Katrina asked, still demanding a response from Ruth.

"Okay, just hold on. Let me get her to talk." Betty walked over to Ruth, who still had Malaysia hugging her neck. "Ruth, I need you to say something. This don't look right. If you knew and didn't say anything—"

I got to tell the truth, Malaysia thought to herself. *I got to get there focus off my grandmother.* "Auntie Betty," Malaysia said. "I told Grandma not to say anything because I was ashamed. I didn't want people to judge me at the church or kids from my school to pick or act funny toward me. I didn't want the embarrassment. And Mama, I didn't want to tell you because I figured you would be mad at me."

"Mad at you?" Katrina asked, astonished.

"Yes, because I felt... if... I... would have told, it would have put you in a difficult position. Mama, I didn't want to ruin our image. I didn't want to make you choose between me and him. So, I took the abuse. I thought I was protecting us."

"Protecting us? I'm your mother. I protect you! You are my child. He just a man. You are my first and last love. No man can replace my love for you. Don't you ever sacrifice yourself for my happiness or our image! I don't care about that. What Craig did to you, was not okay. You didn't deserve that. I would never choose a man over you. I'm not cut from that type of cloth. You mean more to me than any man. Matter of fact, let me tell you something. Child, when God sent me you. I was young and didn't have a clue on life. Your father died and I was scared. I didn't know if the gang who killed him would come and kill me and you too. Not only that, but I didn't know how I was going to provide for you without your dad. And then I feared not knowing whether or not I would make a good mother or not. But the first time I laid eyes on you, I felt a joy that I never knew. You inspired me; you gave me hope," Katrina said wiping the tears that began to form in her eyes. "Oh, Malaysia, you saved my soul. I'll never forget the first time I heard you cry, my, how it shook my soul inside. You were too innocent to be born into this sin. You were so precious; I couldn't believe you were my blessing. I watched you crawl. I watched you walk. My heart skipped a beat the first time I heard you talk. As time flew, you just grew. And while I thought I was protecting you; you were being abused."

Katrina tears flowed heavy, like rain pouring from the sky. She wiped the remaining tears that hung onto her cheeks, like raindrops being held up by a leaf. She closed her eyes and took a big, deep, breath and released it.

"You know what? What's done in the dark, gonna always come to the light. I do believe there was a reason for it all." Katrina opened her eyes and looked at Malaysia. "For you to go through what I once went through. When it happened to me, I wasn't nothing but two." Malaysia placed her hands to her mouth and began to cry.

When Katrina was younger, her mother would let a girlfriend of hers watch Katrina while she went to work. One day, when her mother was coming in from work, she caught her friend performing cunnilingus on her daughter. She pulled her off her baby and stabbed her in the side three times. Carole never told anyone about what her friend did to her baby. She took jobs at daycares, where she could keep her eye on Katrina. She trusted no one around her baby. Even when she had a boyfriend, they could never spend time alone in her house with her daughter. The only person she trusted with her baby was Betty, her sister. Katrina didn't find out what happened to her until her mother was on her death bed.

"I was too small to even talk. I was molested by a woman, my mother's best friend, and I don't remember it at all. But I'm grateful that I don't have no memory and I'm sorry that you have all the memories. I don't want you to let this break you. And I'm sorry, if in anyway, by this happening, you felt as if I neglected you, by not being present during the times he hurt you. You are not alone in this fight, baby girl. You got God and me. And we're gonna fight the trauma and pain together."

Katrina removed Malaysia hands off her face and wiped her tears. She was starting to feel the spirit of God speak to her. "I remember when I first got saved. I think I was about your age. Aunt Betty came to your grandma's house and gave me my first Bible and took me to church. I remember catching the Holy Ghost and feeling the spirit run through my veins and speaking in tongues, Thank you, Lord! The same day, I met your father. My Lord! I was anointed by that man. Yes, Lord! Your father was praised in these streets as a King. He was a rebel but the Lord, he always knew. He had a stride that no line could form. He had a smile that out did the sun. A blessing and yet a curse."

Ruth closed her eyes to keep from revealing her tears, but they still slid through her closed eyelids.

"There are secrets we don't share 'cause they hurt. But Jason," Katrina turned to look at Ruth. "—he always knew. Your son, he knew about the abuse. But only God can make it right. Yes, Lord! And yo closet is why you can't sleep at night. But there's power in his name and if you believe in Christ then, Ms. Ruth, you need to surrender your pain today and ask him for a brand-new song, because we got a generational curse going on here. Hallelujah! Praise God!"

Katrina began fanning herself, as the spirit shot through her like a comet. She was ready to make her peace with Ruth.

"Ms. Ruth, before I came through that door, I was ready to whoop your behind, because in my mind, you were wrong for not telling me what was happening to my child. But God is good! God is great! God just told my spirit that you are mentally traumatized from your past and you gotta seek some help, to heal your soul. And I'm sorry for what happened to you. It's not your fault." Katrina turned her attention back to her daughter. "And baby girl, it most certainly wasn't your fault. Whatever help you need from this traumatizing situation, I'm going to make sure you get it. You're not alone like I said before You got me… you got your mother." Malaysia went and hugged her. "I love you, child," Katrina said. "Don't you ever keep a secret like that from me again. From now on, we tell each other everything, okay?"

Malaysia nodded. "I won't mama, keep anything from you. I promise."

Betty watched as tears filled Ruth's eyes, after observing Malaysia and her mother heal together. Ruth couldn't sit at the table any longer. She wanted to make peace with the situation, but she still hadn't made peace with her own past. She rose from the table, prepared to leave the café.

Malaysia went to her grandmother because she knew her grandmother had experienced it before, long before Malaysia's abuse began. Her grandma was her safe place. She didn't know her mother had experienced it too.

I should have taken it as a sign then, Katrina thought to herself, as she continued to hug her daughter. *Maybe that's why mama was so heavy on my heart earlier. She was trying to tell me about Malaysia. It's amazing how the dead communicate with us. Thank you, mama,* Katrina said to herself, as she continued to hug Malaysia.

* * *

As Betty was on her way home, she couldn't stop thinking about Malaysia, Ruth, and Katrina. She knew it was something sinister going on with Craig, but she never expected it to be this. *How long had the abuse been going on? How long had Malaysia been a victim to Craig's assaults?* It was a horrible image to imagine. Betty couldn't stomach, how a man, who's been in a child's life since a toddler, watch the child become a young lady, then up and decide to touch her. *Ruth had been touched too. All these damn secrets. Secrets never did nothing but hurt the person who was holding on to them.*

Betty started thinking about Katrina being molested at two years old by her mother's friend. Betty knew exactly who that friend was. She had wondered why her sister stopped dealing with the woman. She never knew her touching Katrina was the reason. As Betty approached her hidden and cozy lit home, located off of county road one-nineteen into the woods. Valarie's car was parked in her driveway. *What is she doing here? I have experienced enough drama for the day.* Betty cut off the engine and sat in the car looking at her cottage-style home. She was tired of trying to be a savior. She had no idea why Valarie was there, but she didn't feel like hearing anyone's problems. She had a lot to digest from earlier. She was at a point to where she was ready to let go of any and everything that drained her energy.

Betty opened the door and stepped out of the car. She noticed her rose garden surrounding both sides of her steps were in full bloom. There were Rainbow Niagara roses that were yellow and orange with pink stripes. Next to them were the Cha-Ching roses that were a glowing yellow along with the strike it rich rose, mixed in with red Georgia burns and Snowfaire. The rose garden made the entranceway to the front door look welcoming and bright. She walked up the steps and pulled back the screen to the door. She could hear Valarie and Stephanie talking.

Something is wrong! I don't feel like doing this.

Betty didn't want to walk into any more drama. Her ears have heard all it could bear. She just wanted to get away from all of it, but she knew she couldn't run from what was awaiting her inside of her home, just like she couldn't run from combat when fighting in the desert. She braced herself and opened the door to see Valarie sitting on the couch and Stephanie consoling her.

Betty's home was quaint and charming. It had the feel of a warm blanket after a cold winter day. The fireplace and the candles on the end tables and coffee table made the room feel relax and comfortable. There was a built-in bookshelf filled with cookbooks, self-help books, romance, drama and fantasy novels. Pictures of inspirational quotes and Bible scriptures filled her walls along with framed family photos of Betty's mother and father, Stan parents and sibling, Betty and Stan with their son, her sister Carole, Katrina and Jason, and Malaysia when she was a baby, James when he was incarcerated, and a photo of her, Ruth and their friend Maxine when they were children.

Succulent plants filled each corner of her home. Her coffee table had a big rose centerpiece, that she made with the roses from her garden and the Holy Bible underneath. Betty's home was the escape away from problems, not the escape to encounter them.

"Ms. Betty, your here," Stephanie said. She jumped up off the couch and walked over to Betty. "Ms. Betty, Valarie needs to talk to you. Like really talk to you." Betty looked over at Valarie, and she could see the distraught in her eyes. Betty wanted to send her away, but her heart just wouldn't allow it.

"Go fix us two espressos," Betty said. Stephanie went into the kitchen, while Betty went around the end table to sit beside Valarie.

She didn't know how to start the conversation. She still had Malaysia, Ruth, and Katrina on her mind.

"I'm HIV positive, Ms. Betty," Valarie said initiating the conversation. Betty eyes widen. She lowered her head to look away. The news sadden her heart. Betty slowly raised her head to look at Valarie, whose tears were streamed down her cheek. Betty placed her hand on Valarie's hand, and began to pat and rub it. "I've been carrying this secret for years, and now I'm at a point to where I don't want to hide it anymore. I told my son, Joshua and he cried. Locked himself into his room and asked me to go away. Then when I told James, earlier at the café, he just walked out on me. Didn't say a word. He broke my heart." Valarie began sobbing uncontrollably.

Betty removed her hand from Valarie to grab her some Kleenex that was on the coffee table next to her. She pulled a few and handed them to Valarie to dry her eyes.

"Ms. Betty, I don't think I can continue working at your café. Once people learn the truth about me, who's going to want me handling their coffee."

Stephanie came back into the living room. She sat both of their mugs on the table and stepped back into the kitchen.

"I'm stressed," Valarie said, "and my mental health is in more jeopardy than my physical health. I need a break from everything."

And that's exactly what Betty needed – a break from everything. She sympathized with Valarie on that. They both needed something to give them peace and tranquility, but quitting was too easy. She couldn't let her quit and nor could Betty quit being a savior.

"Well, take a break," Betty said. "But don't quit. It's nothing wrong with taking a break from life, a job, family, friends, a relationship. Some people don't know how to take a break. They think to have it all 'you gotta stay constantly grinding to build a dream. But what's a dream if the dreamer can't get no sleep. Take care of your mental health. Without it, you can't care for your physical or spiritual health. So, do what you must, honey. You'll always have a job at Betty's café. I don't care what people will say. I only care about what God will say." Betty picked up her mug and sipped the expresso. "That's how I been moving all my life. If God doesn't say it, then it doesn't matter." Valarie picked up her espresso and drunk it as well. "James came by the café looking for you. I guess this is what he wanted to speak with me about. Your condition."

"I guess so," Valarie said. "I didn't wanna tell him, and when I did, he left. Everything that has kept me bubbled in about my condition made sense again. For years, I had been so angry at myself because I couldn't understand why God would allow a person like me to have such an illness. I was faithful in all three of my relationships. I wasn't hoeing around. I was raised in the church, and I loved God. But when He sent me this condition, I hated him. How could he allow this to happen to me? His child! He was supposed to protect me and love me, but he had forsaken me."

"He never left you," James said, standing at the screen door. He startled Valarie and Betty the whole time they were talking. They didn't hear him creep up the stairs. Betty got up from the couch to let him in. James walked into the living room to see Valarie sitting there sad and helpless. He had been standing at the screen door listening to Valarie and Betty talk since Stephanie brought them their espresso's, but Valarie's cries were so loud that they didn't hear him or turn their head in the direction of the door to see him. Despite the condition that Valarie had, he still loved her. And in that moment, her condition didn't matter. "While you thought you were alone, He was always there. He loves you Valarie, and I love you. He gave you a curse, so I could come break it, and show you that, regardless of what your condition is, you can still be loved by someone who doesn't have a condition. I accept you, and all that comes with you. I love you, Valarie."

That was all she needed to hear. Those three words. *I accept you*, un-bubbled all the emotions that have kept her bubbled up all these years. She rose from the couch, walked over to him and reached for his hands.

"I love you too," she said. He pushed her hair out her face and kissed her. Betty smiled; she was proud to see there was a happy ending to their story after all.

"James," Betty said, interrupting their kiss. She walked over to them and took both of their hands. "Take her and get out of here. You two go and talk about this. Heal one another and comfort each other. Love each other. You don't need me to do that.

"You right, Ms. Betty," James said. "Valarie can we go somewhere and talk about all of this? I wasn't ready earlier and I'm sorry, but I'm ready now."

"Sure." She turned to face Betty. "Thank you for everything."

"No need to thank me," Betty said. "Thank the man upstairs. Now get out of here." Valarie hugged Betty and kissed her on the cheek.

"I love you," Valarie said.

"I love you too," Betty responded.

Valarie walked down the stairs to her car and James went to his.

"Y'all be safe out there," Betty yelled to them as they began to pull away from her driveway. Betty went back into her house and slammed and locked the door. She belched out a loud scream and grabbed the glass vase on the coffee table and shattered it on the floor. Stephanie ran into the living room and saw Betty standing with her back to the door in tears.

"Ms. Betty," Stephanie said, as she walked over to comfort Betty who had sunken to the floor. "What's wrong? What's the matter?"

Betty didn't respond. She just continued to cry, and gasp for air. She was having an attack. Stephanie cuddled her in her arms, hoping the affection she provided would help Betty calm down, but it didn't. Betty just continued to scream and gasp for air. Stephanie didn't know what to do. She didn't know what caused this frenzy and rage Betty was exhibiting.

God what should I do? I don't know what to do. Stephanie worried eyes roamed around the house until she saw the Lord's Prayer on the wall. *Pray,* Stephanie spirit told her. "Our Father," she cried, as she continued to cuddle an overbearing Betty. "Who art in Heaven hallowed be thy name. Thy kingdom come, thy will be done, on earth as it is in Heaven."

"Give us this day," Betty said, beating Stephanie to the word as she slowly calmed down, "our daily bread and forgive us our trespasses."

"As we forgive those who trespass against us." Stephanie joined back in on the prayer with Betty as they both continued on together. "Lead us not into temptation but deliver us from sin and evil. For thine is the kingdom, the power and the glory, forever and ever. Amen."

"Thank you, Stephanie," Betty said. She was finally able to speak.

"Ms. Betty," Stephanie asked, with her heart still racing. "What just happened? Where you having a panic attack."

"Something like that," Betty said, exhausted from the attack. "I suffer from PTSD. Sometimes certain thoughts and people can trigger it. I'm sorry I never told you girls about it. Lately, I been battling it alone since Stan died. He knew different ways to calm me, and the Lord's Prayer was one way, to get me out of that trance."

Stephanie took hold of Betty's hand. "Ms. Betty it's okay. I don't look at you different. You're a woman with great strength and a troubling past. I get the trauma."

Betty was grateful that Stephanie was there for her, but Betty was ready to let go of everyone's pain that she carried as her own. She was ready to shut down nice, kind and helping Betty, along with the café. Everything was affecting her mentally. She didn't want to get to the point, where she would have a mental break down daily, due to the stress and worrying about everyone's problem.

"Stephanie, I think I might close down the café," Betty said in a sad tone. Stephanie eyes grew big at the announcement.

"You can't do that, Ms. Betty. That café is our home. All the women are starting to get along now, thanks to you and your café."

Betty knew what it meant to the girls, but she wanted them to see what it was doing to her.

"Stephanie that café, the drama and stress is costing me my sanity. It's too much pain in that café."

"That's because a lot of healing took place there," she said in a high-pitched tone, angered by Betty's decision. "Me with my abusive husband. Nina with her regrets of an abortion. Jenny accepting the fact that her rape wasn't her fault or the child she gave away. Then Valarie, who had a whole mental break down today after telling James her secret. Your café is the confession room. It's a healing ground. You can't let it go. The women there need that place, and we need you.

"That's the problem," Betty snapped without trying. "I'm tired of being available. Every time there's a problem, every time there's an issue, I have to solve it. And I'm tired. I can't be everybody's mama. I ain't got but one son! And he don't even call on me or beg me, as much as a stranger."

Her words offended and shocked Stephanie. Her eyes cried without any tears. She didn't know Betty looked at her and the others as strangers. She removed her hands and gave Betty a salty and disappointed look. Stephanie wasn't liking this new Betty. This new Betty was careless and heartless with words.

Betty could see in Stephanie eyes she was hurt. She didn't mean for it to come out like that. Betty took back hold of her hand. "Stephanie. I'm not calling y'all strangers," she said in a soft and compassionate tone. "I'm just saying, my own flesh doesn't need me as much as y'all. And I'm always available to heal a soul. And no one is trying to heal my soul. I lost my sister, then my husband. I suffer from PTSD. I go to therapy because I am depressed and I still have to go to that café and take in y'all drama, y'all problems, y'all issues, and at the same time, I'm trying to heal me. Who the hell gonna heal Betty, but Betty. I'm fed up and I'm exhausted."

"Well, why don't you do what you just told Valarie to do," Stephanie quickly interrupted Betty. "Don't quit, just take a break. Me, Nina and Jenny can run it. We will do that for you. Ms. Betty, me and them women love you. We didn't know our problems were so much on you. Yet, you were so willing to help. But I guess that's also your weakness. The fact that you have a helper's heart, and you don't know when to stop."

Betty shed a tear, because this time, someone had finally read her right. "I been helping people all my live," she said, wiping away her tears. Stephanie placed her hand on Betty's shoulder.

"Well, maybe it's time you put that on pause and let someone help you. I don't mind being of service to someone who opened their home to this stranger," Stephanie said jokily, making Betty crack a smile. "Because I know what it's like to suffer in silence and no one hears you. Ms. Betty, I hear you."

Stephanie wrapped her arms around Betty as if they were a warm blanket covering a shivering friend. She made Betty feel like a teddy bear – good and loved. Betty leaned back and looked into Stephanie's warm and loving eyes. This felt like her child.

"You are the daughter; I wish I could've had," Betty said, wishing Stephanie were her biological seed.

"And you're the mother I never got to have. Like you say, there was a reason God brought me into your café."

Her word's made Betty's heart soar and her spirit fly high. She was paralyzed with happiness by this beautiful butterfly. It was coherent, very clear to see. Stephanie wasn't a stranger or and employee in Betty's Café. She was her family, her friend, her daughter that God had sent.

* * *

Jenny sat on the sofa in her dimly lit apartment, surrounded by unpacked boxes and a TV. It had been a month since her and her girlfriend Kristen had moved into their new place, and still they were living out of a box, ready to move again. Jenny held the acoustic guitar closer to her body as she closed her eyes and began strumming the strings. She was trying to get the melody for the song she performed for Ms. Ruth, and now would be the time, since downtown Birmingham was quiet and not bustling. At first she thought the song didn't have any potential but after witnessing the standing ovation that Ms. Ruth gave her, it inspired her to go home and work on the song some more.

"Hey, you," Kristen said coming from their bedroom. "What are you doing up here?" She plopped down on the couch beside Jenny, who opened her eyes to see her lover's shiny blue eyes, peach complexion skin, and wavey, shoulder-length hair. Kristen smiled at Jenny, making her blush and feel warm inside.

"I'm trying to figure out the tune for that song I wrote."

"You still working on that?" Kristen asked, nibbling on Jenny's neck. She took her tongue and gently licked the shell of her ear, teasing it with a gentle pat, making Jenny's g-spot tingle. Kristen then trailed her tongue down to Jenny's neck and sucked on it like she was a vampire. She removed the guitar from Jenny and placed it beside her on the sofa. Jenny was leaking like meatloaf in the oven between the legs. She couldn't wait for Kristen to lay her back and devour her meatloaf. "You wanna lay back and spread your legs," Kristen asked. Jenny nodded and laid back on the sofa with her legs set apart for Kristen. She bent over and lowered her mouth to Jenny's oven, stuck out her tongue, and crept down upon it for a taste.

KNOCK! KNOCK!

"Fuck, who's at the door," Kristen shouted. Jenny got up off the sofa to look through the peephole.

"It's my dad," Jenny said, afraid to open the door. Seeing her father was like seeing a ghost. She hadn't talked to him in months. It was a surprise to see him at her door.

"Jenny, I know you're in there. Please, open up. I need to talk to you. It's important." he said, yelling from the other side of the door. Jenny turned around to face Kristen, waiting on her approval as to what to do.

"He's your dad. Gone and let him in," Kristen responded.

Jenny opened the door. Her father was a tall slender man with short, dirty blonde, curly hair with freckles. He wore a pair of glasses, a dark blue-collar shirt with his name tag displayed as Mr. Hill with khaki pants.

"May I come in?" he asked. Jenny wanted to slam the door in his face but instead, she move out of the way and let him in. He walked into the apartment to see everything was stilled boxed up.

"You girls been here a month now, from what your Aunt Casey told me, and you still haven't unpacked yet. What have you two been doing?"

"Fucking!" Kristen murmured. Jenny bottom lip dropped in embarrassment.

"I beg your pardon," Mr. Hill replied.

"Kristen, give us a moment," Jenny said, giving her a horrid stare.

"Cool, I'll be at the bar. Just call me when he leaves." Kristen went out the door and slammed it, making Jenny jump in her stance. She didn't like Mr. Hill and Mr. Hill didn't like her. He didn't approve Jenny's sexuality, and Kristen disliked him for not approving.

"Jenny, this living situation of yours needs to change. You both been here a whole month, and everything is still in a box but your TV, couch, and bed." He pointed at their bedroom that was clearly visible. "You don't have to live like this. You're a beautiful girl. Why don't you find yourself a man, and not some woman pretending to be one?"

Jenny folded her arms and rolled her eyes at her dad. "I don't want a man, Dad. I want Kristen, and the reason all these things are still boxed up is because were moving again. She bought us a home in a really nice neighborhood in Chelsea. That's why everything is still boxed up."

He scrunched his nose and nodded his head. "You know I've always wanted what was best for you," he said, walking closer to Jenny.

"I couldn't tell," Jenny added, "You always bought me the best, but you never gave me your best."

"What! That's not true," he said in defense. "I worked hard to give you and your mom the life we had."

"And somewhere down the line, you couldn't figure out how to manage your time." Jenny sass. "You never gave us enough time, and now I'm trying to figure out why are you here, Dad." She threw up her hands. "What is it that you want?"

He put his hand in his pocket and looked down. "Jenny, I have cancer. Stage four cancer," he said, raising his head to see her astounded facial expression. "And I realize I sucked as a dad, and you're right, I never could manage my time. But honey," he walked closer to her and placed his hands on her shoulders. "I'm running out of time and I need you while I fight this thing."

She closed her eyes and widened her mouth. She removed his hands from her shoulders. She couldn't believe the audacity of her father, to prey on her with his illness when he was never there during her addiction. She exploded with anger inside.

"You need me," she respond furiously. "Oh My God!" She ran her hands through her thick stringy hair. "This is bullshit! She formed a fist with her hands, wanting to knock the hell out of him. "When mom died," she said, pointing her index finger at him, "I needed you. When you were letting Elizabeth treat me like shit and speak down to me about my sexuality, I needed you, Dad. When I went off to college and those boys raped me." She closed her eyes holding in the tears. "I needed you too, Dad," She opened her eyes to reveal their redness. "When I went to the abortion clinic, afraid to go through with the procedure and they told me adoption was an option, I needed you too, Dad. When I was in the hospital giving birth to my son and the adoption agency," she paused, placing her wrist up to her nose, letting her tears flow like a river on a stormy day. She wiped her eyes and looked back at her Dad "took him out my arms, when I wanted to keep him, I needed you too, Dad. When I was stripping and strung out on drugs and the only one that came to my aid was Kristen. Where were you, Dad?"

"Where was I?" he said loudly. "When you went to rehab, I paid for it, Jenny. I made sure you got the best care."

"You helped pay for it," Jenny screamed, "but you didn't see me through it. No flowers, no cards, no visits, not even a call. I died and you didn't come to my burial. You put a middle finger up to me and that's exactly what I'm going to do to you now." She walked to her apartment door and opened it. "Get the fuck out of my apartment."

"Jenny, wait. This conversation wasn't supposed to go like this."

"Just get out," she screamed at the top of her lungs, silencing her dad. "You're out of time here. Just leave!"

He swallowed his pride and walked out the door. Before exiting all the way, he stood in the doorway and faced Jenny. "Maybe one day you'll have a change of heart."

Jenny slammed the door in his face. She leaned up against the hard, thick apartment door, ruminating on what just happened. It felt good to release the pressure that had been weighing on her since she was an adolescent. She felt good and bad about how she handled the situation. A part of her felt sorry for him and the other half felt nothing. She wanted to be there, and then she didn't. She wanted him to feel the abandonment she felt while he was present in their home, but yet wasn't there. She wanted him to need her, like she once needed him. She decided she would be there for him, but just not within sight. *I need an espresso. This is going to be one long fucking night.*

* * *

Nina stood in the living room of her townhouse apartment, rambling through her chest of drawers, searching for her crystals and stones. She came across the amazonite, a greenish blue stone, that clears the air of toxic, negative energy. She placed it on top of the chest. She looked back down and saw the rose quartz. It was a medium-dark, pink crystal and it helped in giving and accepting all forms of love, including self-love. She held it in her hands and picked up the sunstone, which was an orangish-red color. It would helped root Nina in confidence, vitality, and leadership. The next crystal was the Chalcedony. It was a grayish-blue crystal, and its purpose was to bring the mind, body, and spirit into alignment. She placed what she had on the chest next to the amazonite. She closed the chest drawer and opened up the drawer next to it, where her hematite and howlite was. She grabbed them and placed them on top of the chest with the others. The hematite stone was a steel, gray to black color with thin, blood-red lines and silver crystals embedded. It helped Nina stay grounded and focused. The howlite was a white marble color, with dark veins running through the matrix that bore the resemblance of a spider web. This stone was a calming crystal that Nina most definitely was going to need for this spade game she was about to embark upon with her friends, Peaches, the transgender man turned woman, Danielle, her homegirl she used to work with at the strip club, and Jada her spiritual friend, who had gifted her all her stones and crystals.

They all sat at Nina's square glass table, discussing who were on teams, and who was going to shuffle the cards. All the ladies knew each other. They attended Miles' College together, which is where they met Nina. She placed the crystals underneath a stand that contained a round, royal blue, gold-trimmed plate. Nina reached for her sage that was also on the chest and burned it. She waved it around in the air, letting it cleanse the room of negativity before placing it on the plate. She reached for her phone that was on the chest and connected it to her Bluetooth speaker. Erykah Badu's, *Didn't Cha Know* blared through the speakers.

She had created a vibe in her apartment that was appeasing to her friends as she turned around to see them grooving to the tunes. Nina's townhouse had a funkadelic feel. It was big and spacious like a house and had low, dimmed lights and lava lamps on the end tables. She had gigantic canvases of afro art scattered throughout her home, along with paintings of lions, leopards, panthers, and snakes. She had a Divan Casa Dubai transitional fabric sectional sofa. One section of the sofa was royal blue, the other was burgundy, with multicolored pillow of brown, yellow, burgundy, and royal blue. Behind her couch was a beautiful waterfall canvas that lit up and made waterfall sounds. On her coffee table was a strength and growth feng and two crystal energy amethyst candles. In the corner of the home, near the window, was a Omera hand-crafted love seat with a wooden crate filled with spiritual awareness and psychology books. Eucalyptus plants surrounded the space and other parts of her home. Content with the atmosphere she created, Nina was ready to mix together some spirits for her and the ladies to sip. She walked into the kitchen and went straight to her glass, gold-trimmed cabinets. She opened the doors and began looking.

"Let's see," she said, "what do I need to make this drink?" Nina sang to herself, looking at the array of spirits that filled it.

"Bitch, hurry up, I'm parched," Peaches said, poking out her big full Mac lips with her mustache hoovering over them at Nina while shuffling the card.

"Hold on, Tramp," Nina said, rolling her neck and batting her eyes at Peaches. She turned her gaze back at the cabinet. "I'm trying to find these liquors for this drink."

"What all you need, Nina? Do you need me to go to the store?" Danielle asked with her squeaky voice. Her long silhouette nails clanked on the table.

"Nope! I got it," Nina said, grabbing the bottles that she needed for her mixed drink. She placed them on the counter next to the pitcher and removed the caps from all of them.

"What all you putting in there?" Jada asked with her strong Jamaican accent.

"Let's see," Nina said, looking at what all she had ready to mix. "I got four shots of espresso. Malibu rum, cognac and Cuervo. Lemonade, pineapple and orange juice with lemon and lime wedges, and a cherry on top. Bam! That's what I'm giving you hoes."

"Bitch! I ain't gonna be able to drive home tonight. Somebody call me a taxi," Peaches joked.

Nina began pouring the spirits into the pitcher and topped it off with the lemons, limes, and cherries. She tossed all her emptied bottles into the trash and placed the others back in her cabinets. She picked up the pitcher and walked to the table, setting it off to the side.

"Damn Nina, that look good, what you call that?" Jada asked as she reached across the table to grab the pitcher and pour it into her plastic cup.

"Espresso-Yourself," Nina said, grabbing the pitcher from Jada to pour the drink into her cup. Once finished, she pass the container to Danielle, who started examining the pitcher before pouring,

"This that shit they be selling at the poetry club, huh," Danielle asked Nina as she began pouring the mixture into her cup.

"Naw, girl. That's just some shit I came up with. Who deal?" Nina asked, gazing around the table. All the ladies looked stunning to her.

Peaches was a dark-skinned muscular woman, with long white curly streaked hair. She wore long eye lashes with green glittery eyeshadow. She had on a white t-shirt with green solid words that read, *Take A Picture Bitch!*

Danielle was short and caramel. She had her hair slicked back with a side ponytail, and her edges laid. She had light-brown, seductive eyes and medium-long eyelashes. Her lips were plump and cherry red with a solid silver studded piercing in her cheeks. She wore a white lace halter top that revealed her monogrammed necklace and a rose tattoo that spread across her chest. A pair of big hoop earrings completed her ensemble.

Jada was tall and slender and had coca brown skin. She wore a yellow and green head scarf and no makeup, but her skin had a radiant glow. Her eyes were slanted, and her lips were thin and tight. She wore a strapless dress that matched her scarf and a crystal bracelet and earring set. All the women had their own style and spoke their mind like Nina.

"You, bitch," Peaches answered Nina's question, slamming the cards down in front of Nina.

She grabbed the deck and began to deal. Her and Jada were on teams, while Peaches and Danielle formed the other team.

"Nina, where Queenie?" Jada asked, reaching into her handbag that hung on the back of her chair.

"She staying over at a friend. You wanna fire it up go ahead," Nina said, passing out the cards and giving Jada permission to smoke in her home, which she didn't mind, as long as her daughter wasn't around.

Jada took out the blunt and lit it. She placed it between her lips and began to inhale and exhale. She blew the smoke in Nina's direction, teasing her to want a taste.

Nina finished passing out the cards and gathered hers, while looking across the table at Jada. She was tempted to hit the blunt. The aroma of the weed was strong and sweet. The scent lingered through Nina's nose into her mouth, making her lick her lips.

"You want some, don't you," Jada said, watching Nina try and fight the urge.

"Jada stop teasing me. You know I stopped smoking," Nina said, placing her card down on the table. "But it does smell good, tho." She fell victim to the blunt.

"This that California Kush," Jada said, reaching across the table to hand it to Nina. She didn't want to, but she wanted to. She took the offered blunt and hit it.

"That tastes nice," Nina said. "Real nice."

"Well, bitch, don't babysit it," Peaches said, placing her card down on the table, "I wanna hit it too. Pass the peas like they used to do. I say pass the peas like they used to do," she sung playfully.

"Here, you fool," Nina said, passing the blunt to Peaches and picking up her cup for a sip, while studying the cards in her hand.

"So, Nina," Danielle said as Jada placed her cards on the table. "How do you like it at the coffee shop? I see you haven't quit yet," she added.

"It's cool, laid back. It can get hectic early in the morning, but other than that, it's chill. I work with a lot of emotional-ass women, but I'm used to that. That's how I met y'all asses. Shaking my ass and titties," Nina sung jokingly as Danielle played, and Jada grabbed their book. Nina played her hand and focused her eyes on Peaches who was next to play.

"Girl, yes!" Peaches said, placing her card down. "Them was the good old days."

"I know right. I miss them days too," Nina said, watching Jada play.

"If you miss them so much why won't you come back," Danielle asked, placing her card down, and grabbed her and Peaches' book.

"It ain't for me no more," Nina said, playing her next card, and reaching to get the blunt from Jada. "I'm into poetry now, and I'm thinking about starting a counseling program to help girls who done had an abortion cope." Nina placed the blunt in her mouth for a hit

"You know what I forgot you were a psychology major," Peaches said, playing her card. "Go ahead, bitch. I'll support you, boo. Do that shit. Show these hoes how a boss move."

Danielle rolled her eyes at Peaches, and focused her attention back on Nina, while Jada played her card. "Whatever. So, what, you all Angela Davis now," Danielle asked, placing her card down for Nina to collect her book.

"Bitch, Angela Davis was fighting against injustice and corruption of the prison system. Get your history facts right," Nina corrected. She slapped her card on the table and passed the blunt to Peaches, who had quickly played her card.

"Well, why you out playing soul sister, don't forget that you came from the pole and stripping is your life," Danielle said, watching Jada play. Nina quickly turned her head to look at Danielle with a raised eyebrow

"No, bitch," Nina said, watching Danielle play, and Peaches take her book, "stripping is yo life. The pole was just my starting line; it ain't my finish line. Like I said, I'm starting a counseling service for women and girls, who had an abortion, and still suffer from it. And I would like your support, or you can just kick rocks out my door," Nina said, slamming her card down and giving Danielle the stank eye.

"Wait a minute," Peaches said, placing her card down, and passing the blunt to Jada. "I thought you hoes were playing. Y'all serious right now."

"I'm not," Danielle said. "That's Nina getting smart with me." She threw her card down behind Jada as Nina collected her book.

"You damn right, because I'm sick of you always trying to bring me back to the club when I'm rising high. I'm good where I'm at, Danielle. I promise. And I would like it if you would stop criticizing me for working at the Café and the poetry club. Come out and support me! Peaches come to the café all the time for a latté, and Jada comes to me and Harp's shows. You should come watch me perform on stage with my clothes on. I think you'll like me with my clothes on versus me on the pole naked." Nina slammed her card down and waited for Peaches to play. Nina and Danielle sat in silence as Peaches and Jada took their turn. Nina stared at Danielle, who had played and took her book.

"You right," Danielle said, watching Nina play. "I need to be more supportive of you. I just miss you at the club. It don't seem right with you gone." Danielle put down her card after Peaches and Jada played. Peaches took her book, while Nina was distracted by Danielle. "I promise to start being more supportive," Danielle said as she placed her card down again after everyone. Nina took her book and flashed a 'thank you smile' at Danielle.

"See, this why I like fucking with y'all," Peaches said, watching Nina play. "'Cause y'all keep it real with no hard feelings. I love it." Peaches pretended to swipe away fake tears.

"Peaches, you funny," Jada laughed, putting out the blunt, while playing her hand. "So, Nina, where is Harp's fine sexy ass?" Jada asked, taking her book after Danielle played.

"I don't know. Probably laid up with some woman," Nina responded, eyeing her last few cards in her hand after she made her play.

"Bitch, how do you fuck Harp, knowing he be sleeping with other women?" Peaches asked, placing her card down.

"I wonder that too, Peach," Jada said, "Nina do you make him use a rubber?"

"Hell, yeah," Nina said, watching Danielle play. "I ain't letting Harp hit this raw." Everyone paused and looked at Nina.

"Bitch, quit lying," Peaches said, snatching her book. "You know you have at least once. Let him put that meat in there raw."

"Or more than one time," Danielle added, sipping her drink.

"Come on, Nina, tell the truth. Has he?" Jada asked.

"I can't stand y'all tricks," Nina said playing her hand with a smirk, after being exposed.

"I knew it," Peaches said, playing her hand, followed by Jada and Danielle playing theirs. "Y'all see how she be trying to play us? Like that man ain't poking it raw," Peaches added before taking her book.

"Nina, you my girl," Jada said, "and I don't try to get in your business, but you can do better than Harp. I know he fine, but damn, is he really worth the energy?" Jada grabbed her book waiting for Nina to respond.

"He's not, but I just like, what I like," Nina said, taking her book, beating Peaches and Danielle seven to six.

"But Nina," Peaches said. "You liking what you like, be having you sitting up here, looking like spoiled milk. Just all soured up. You too noble to be sleeping with servants and peasants. Get yourself a King; one who will treat you like a Queen."

"Well, I haven't met a man that's on the level with Harp. Fine, educated, and financially stable. With his own house, car and business, plus no baby mamas. And can blow my back out. I'm good," Nina said, turning up her cup.

"Um, must be nice to be crazy about a dick you don't want," Peaches said, turning her drink while flashing her eyes.

"Now, Peaches. I been sparing you all night. Why you got to go there." Nina laughed.

"I'm just saying. You sound like you in love with the man. And yet, you don't want him. What that about suga?"

"First of all," Nina said, leaning closer to Peaches, "y'all know my past. Every nigga I done ever loved ain't done shit but hurt me. I'm not letting that happen again."

"But you the one that like taking out the trash, Nina. Damn. Quit playing the dumpster man. You going around collecting trash like you don't know your worth."

"Oh, I know my worth. Hey, Peach," Nina said, pointing her finger at her friend, "the pot can't call the kettle black, when you sleeping with down low brothers."

"Well, damn," Peaches said, acting as if she was going to pass out.

"Y'all both in the same boat," Jada said, laughing with Danielle joining in.

"Don't play," Nina said.

"Well, maybe," Peaches said, trying to be serious, "we both need to work on that. Me with my hidden lovers. And you with your toxic men." Nina agreed and they both bumped fists and began preparing for the next card game.

* * *

CHAPTER 5
~Friendship - A Gift From God~

Ding Dong, chimed the main entrance bell.

Someone had entered the café. Betty stood behind the counter with her glasses hanging onto her nose, looking at her sales for the month on the register before she closed for the day. Betty could hear the clacking of heals, but she didn't look up to see who it was.

"Good morning," Betty said, finally raising her eyes from her sales report on her computer.

"Hello, Betty," the woman said. Betty turned her attention away from the screen to face the lady whose voice sounded familiar.

"Do I know you?" Betty asked. She couldn't see the woman's face.

"You don't remember me?" the lady asked. Betty pulled her glasses up and walked from behind the counter to get a closer look at the woman. There was something familiar about her, and Betty studied her features hard until recognition burned bright within her.

"Maxine!" Betty shouted with excitement. Maxine was Betty's childhood friend from back in the day. She was in town for a leadership conference and decided to pay Betty a visit. Her, Ruth, and

Maxine were like the golden girls – Betty was Dorothy, Ruth was Blanch with a hint of Sophia, and Maxine was their Rose, up until her and Ruth fell out over Ruth neglecting her sons and her nasty attitude in their young adult years. But Betty and Maxine remained good friends throughout the years. Betty went over to hug her. "Girl, I haven't seen you since we were young women!" Betty stepped back to check Maxine out. "You look good," Betty said.

Maxine was a dark-skinned, full-figured woman dressed in a dark brown sweater dress. Her hair was gray and styled in a bun. She wore light make-up and white shiny pearl earrings with a matching neckless.

"Thank you," Maxine said, "so do you!"

"Well, what can I say? This black just won't crack," Betty responded jokingly.

"It's like a bottle of fine wine. It just gets better with time," Maxine returned.

"Ain't that the truth? Have a seat and let me get you something to drink." Maxine took a seat at the center table, while Betty went behind the counter.

"You want coffee?" Betty asked.

"Yes, I'll take a cup," Maxine said, looking around Betty's Café, admiring how nicely decorated it was. "And you don't have to add anything to it. Just give it to me black, like an evil soul."

"Alright then." Betty poured the coffee into the mugs. "I think I'll take mine the same way." Betty carried the mugs of steaming hot coffee to their table and set one in front of Maxine. "Here you go. It's so good to see you! How life been treating you?"

"Life been life," Maxine said. "It done took me up and brought me down, but that's just life. I think at sixty years old, me and life are finally starting to see eye to eye. It ain't been a ball that life done threw, I couldn't catch and strike it out. Sickle cell, high blood pressure, cancer, diabetes, bi-polar disorder, anxiety, depression, losing my parents and son; and I'm still flying. My wings aren't broken. There was a purpose to it all. I had to lose, so I could grow. I had to be tested, so I could have my testimony. And I'm flying. Friend, I'm still flying."

"Maxine, I didn't know you had all that going on with you," Betty said. Maxine wrapped her fingers around her mug and nodded. "And I'm so sorry about your losses." Betty reached out to touch Maxine's hand. "We got to reach out to each other more. At the end of the day, you are still my friend."

"Thank you, Betty," Maxine said. "That means a lot coming from you. So, how life been treating you?"

Betty removed her hand from Maxine's. "Life done bruised, scorned and surprised me," Betty said. "At sixty years old, I can say I'm as healthy as a mule, but my heart still got some healing to do. Last year, I lost my one and only sister, Carole. She was sick and didn't even know it. Her body attacked her, and she died from Lupus and didn't even know she had it. Six months later, my husband, Stan, died. He had Stage 4 colon cancer. He had been bleeding from his anus and was too ashamed to tell me. He thought it was due to constipation and straining while using the bathroom. Then he said, he thought he had hemorrhoids, not knowing he had colon cancer all along. That's why I stay on my son so much now about getting a colonoscopy. Men don't believe in going to the doctor until it's too late. Three years of the signs and he ignored them, 'cause he didn't want to know."

"But it happens, Betty," Maxine said. "I was like that when I first got the signs that I was a diabetic. I didn't want to accept it. I watched what it did to my parents. My father had both his legs amputated and mama had to get her toes cut off. I didn't want to go through what they went through. It was hard on me and my siblings to watch them suffer. We prayed for their healing to only watch them get worse. No child wants to see their hero unable to fight. No child wants to bury their parents. Neither does a parent want to bury their child. It's hard Betty, but you're strong. Look at you." Maxine looked around her cafe, while Betty continued drinking her coffee. "You are bless, my friend."

Betty nodded her head. "That I am. This coffee shop is a safe haven. Since I been here, there ain't been nothing but coffee and healed souls that leave out that door once they enter. It's amazing what a cup of coffee can do to the spirit, once you sip it. It also amazes me how healing can come from a place like this and not a church. I love it here. I love to see my customers line up at that counter early in the morning just to start their day with a cup of my coffee; just so they can stay woke. I also love to see the older men and women come in and gather at this table and speak their minds over a cup a coffee. Ain't nobody biting their tongue. Everyone is expressing their truth and not giving a damn who it offends or how they feel, right here in Betty's Café. I sell treats and I warm hearts. I serve magic in my shop. Ain't no better healing than conversation and a cup of coffee.

"I must agree," Maxine said. "They are a special combination."

"Betty! Betty," Ruth shouted from outside the café window.

Ding Dong, chimed the main entrance bell.

Ruth entered and headed toward the table. "We need to talk." Ruth announced. "Tell this customer she got to go because we need to talk."

Betty couldn't believe Ruth, barging into her café, being disrespectful and a tyrant in front of Maxine. This deeply unsettled and embarrassed Betty.

"Well, it's nice to see you, too, Ruth," Maxine said. Ruth looked her up and down. She couldn't figure out who she was.

"Who is you?" Ruth asked.

"You don't remember me either?" Maxine returned. Ruth looked at Betty. "Betty, who this young old heiffa?"

"Maxine," Betty said through clenched teeth. The gall of Ruth's abrupt actions irritated Betty.

"Maxine?" Ruth chuckled. "Girl, I thought she was dead!" Ruth leaned down to whisper to Betty. "She don't look dead."

Ruth knew Maxine wasn't dead. She discovered that back when Maxine was in the hospital fighting for her life. Maxine had slipped into a diabetic coma, and there were rumors spreading that she had passed. Ruth just wanted to pick and make Maxine feel uncomfortable.

"And neither do you," Maxine said, overlooking Ruth's attempt to hurt her. She wanted to be the bigger person, since she was the one who ended their friendship. She wanted to approach Ruth with love, not match hate with hate. "So, are you going to hug me?" Maxine stood from her chair and widened her arms for a hug from Ruth. "Or you just gonna stand there?"

"I would hug you," Ruth said, "but it wouldn't be real. It would be fake. Just like that piece sitting on top of your head."

Maxine dropped her arms. She'd never been so humiliated. Ruth's disdain made Maxine recall why her and Ruth stopped being friends in the first place – Ruth never knew how to be a friend.

Betty caught the slight glimpse of pain that flashed through Maxine's eyes before her old friend masked it with a gentle smile. Maxine can pretend that Ruth's words and actions weren't hurtful, but Betty would be damned if she did. "Ruth, I am sick of you," she said, springing from the table. Ruth's energy was exactly what Betty was trying to avoid. Betty was fed up with Ruth and her nasty ways. And here she was picking with Maxine about being dead, knowing Maxine almost did die. It was the boiling point. "You will not keep coming in my café like it's your home and disrespecting my employees or my customers! If you can't respect what I got going on here, then you need to leave!" Betty pointed in the direction of the door.

"Girl, to hell with you!" Ruth shouted. "I been coming in your damn café like this since you opened. Now you want to say something 'cause Maxine here?"

"This ain't got nothing to do with Maxine. This is about you," Betty said. "I take a lot of mess from you because you are my friend. We been friends since kindergarten, and you still act like we're in kindergarten. Yelling, shouting, screaming, using profanity in front of my customers. No respect for my business. Are you even really my friend?"

It wounded Ruth to hear Betty question their friendship. Throughout the years, Ruth was the only close and near friend Betty had. Maxine wasn't there to comfort Betty when Stan and Carole pass, nor was she there when Betty was laid in bed depressed and wouldn't feed herself after losing Stan. Ruth was always there to console and comfort Betty. Katrina and Betty's son didn't even do that. Didn't no one want to be around a grief-stricken Betty but Ruth, and her questioning their friendship burned a hole through Ruth's soul.

"Well," Ruth said, bracing herself to speak, "since you had to ask, I really can't say! But how dare you, Betty, question my friendship after all I did for you after Stan." Ruth pointed an accusatory finger at Betty. "And now you wanna cut me, in front of this wench. I can't be who you want me to be. I can only be me! So, don't you EVER question my friendship! Don't neither one of your old asses question my friendship! I been nothing but a good friend to both of ya!"

"You just don't change," Maxine said. "You are still the same mean, selfish, 'can't tell you nothing' Ruth."

"And this coming from the walking dead," Ruth insulted her again.

Maxine gave Ruth a gentle smile, while bruising on the inside of how cruel she was being to her – still joking with her about being dead.

"You right," Maxine said. "My spirit was dead for a long time, then God came and resurrected my soul, and now I go out into the world; I minister and teach the word of God and help heal people who can't find their souls."

Ruth took a seat at the center table, blocking out what Maxine had to say. She didn't come to the café to hear about Maxine's life and ministry. She wanted to talk with Betty and make things right with her. Out of all the things she had lost in the previous day, Betty was the one thing she couldn't stand to lose.

"Amber Ruth Wilcox," Maxine said. "There's something I want to say to you."

Ruth's head was turned in the other direction. She had tuned Maxine out to the point she didn't even hear her call her by her government name. Ruth had Betty on her mind and was trying to figure out how to approach James and Katrina. Only Betty could help her sort this out. Maxine's talking was white noise.

"Ruth, look at me," Maxine shouted. Ruth jumped slightly but slowly rolled her eyes in Maxine's direction. "I'm trying to tell you something, will you listen to me please." Ruth really didn't want to listen, but what was she losing by letting Maxine say whatever it was she needed to say. She was already feeling like she had just came and stole Betty away. What more damage could her words do? Ruth gave her a hand signal to talk.

"When I lost your friendship, I felt as if I had lost a gift from God. For years, I was trying to figure out how to approach you and tell you, I miss you, my friend. And when I tried, you made it clear that some things must come to an end." Ruth nodded her head agreeing with Maxine. "Whether it's living or dead. The season had come, time had passed. Let it go. But even though I let go of the friendship, it never stopped me from asking about you," Maxine continued.

Ruth didn't want to allow her heart to feel that, but it did. She used to ask about Maxine too.

"I made it my business when I spoke to Betty to ask about you. It just put my mind at ease, knowing you were okay. And then the day James got busted, my son, Kevin, went into a diabetic coma, like I once did. But he didn't make it. He died."

Ruth closed her eyes and tried to suppress the pain she felt after losing Jason to the streets and letting the streets put James behind bars.

"I could feel your pain a thousand miles away. I lost a son that I would never see again. And you lost a son that you couldn't even touch; but had to see through a glass. So, I prayed for you, Ruth. I prayed that God would allow you to hold James again since I would never hold mines. And in these days that we are living in, you never know when it's your time to go."

Ruth opened her eyes and nodded at Maxine. *She was right. Life is too short to let unnecessary shit overrule you.*

"I want you to know that, even though you were here, and I was there, you've always been my friend in my heart. I couldn't let our friendship go, even if I wanted to. Out of all the gifts God has given me, our friendship – me, you, and Betty – is by far the greatest gift from God. Someone to say, you are my friend; to have someone who you can laugh with, cry with, share your secrets, your dreams, and fears. That's priceless. Just to have a sister who you don't share a mother or father with, just the spirit of God, is the greatest feeling a person can have. And I can't think of a better way to tell you this, but I miss our friendship, old friend. Can I please hug you?"

Ruth was hesitant about hugging Maxine. It had been years since they had seen and spoken to each other. The ending to their friendship was harsh. Both said things that they later regretted. But for years they had used Betty as a device to see how the other was doing. Although

Ruth began to slack in doing so; Maxine never let up and pride at this moment was causing Ruth to not let in. That same stubborn pride cost her everything, her son, granddaughter, and Betty. She needed to kill her pride and stone it in the heart. Ruth stood from her seat. She twisted her mouth and bit her bottom lip and locked eyes with Maxine.

"Maxine," Ruth said. "I want you to know something. As cold as my heart is, I always held on to our friendship. Betty can testify. When I got the news you were dead, I flew my car over to Betty's house, so she could call you, and I could hear your voice. She tried to give me the phone to speak to you, but I turned away, I didn't want to admit that I still cared. I got pride like a shield. I block everything but never let anything in. It's not something that's going to happen overnight, but I plan to work on it. And I'm sorry about your lost. Kevin was a sweet boy. Jason loved him like a brother, and I thank you for the prayers. If you don't mind, keep doing that for me. I'm at a point in my life where I desperately need it more than ever. But with all that said, I'm willing to put this grudge to an end and start over being your friend. Now I haven't changed too much from back then. I'm still loud, I still cuss, but most importantly, I speak my mind, depending on the situation," Ruth said, casting a look in Betty's direction. "Which is why I came here to speak to you." Ruth took a deep breath. "About yesterday, I'm sorry for being pissed at you, Betty. For putting on my shoes and walking a walk, I could never really walk, and that's being a mother and grandmother. I'll admit, I couldn't speak on it then, but I can now. I knew that Craig was messing with Malaysia, and I was trying to teach her how to cope, like I used to cope, when my mother's husband would mess with me."

"So that's what Katrina meant when she said Jason knew," Betty said.

"And so do you," Ruth said. "Now you know why all those times we were outside playing, I never wanted to go home. Mama knew he was raping me. Sometimes she would pull up a chair with a glass of wine and her cigarettes and watch, like she was enjoying it."

"Oh my God, Ruth," Maxine said, taking a seat at the table.

"I figured if she couldn't protect me then no one could," Ruth said. "I would ask her to make him stop. I begged her. And you know what she did? She turned her head and told me to go clean myself up and get to bed."

Betty shook her head. "Ruth, you should have told us," Betty said.

"Hell, I was ashamed. Embarrassed. You two had the perfect life, while I had to be raised by wolves in sheep's clothing."

"Perfect?" Betty questioned. "My life wasn't perfect. My daddy was abusive to my mother. But if we would have known then, we could have told someone who could have helped you."

"Who, Betty?" Ruth asked, placing her hands on her hip. "Who was going to believe us? Back then the creed was, 'what happens in this house, stays in this house.' I couldn't go to my mama's sisters and brothers and tell them their sister's husband was fucking me, and she was watching. They wouldn't believe that. The first lady of the church's husband, the pastor, was sleeping with her daughter. They were both people of God in the public eye, but once the curtains closed, they were children of Lucifer. No one would believe me."

"But you don't know because you didn't tell, Ruth." Ruth's confession angered Betty. It took her back to Malaysia and Katrina. And the thought of them being abused caused Betty to snap. "Y'all got to stop this. Quit biting your tongue when somebody touches you because you are afraid or ashamed what people might say. If you don't tell, it won't stop. You still should have told someone, Ruth. You shouldn't have kept that bottled up all these years, and not said nothing till now. What's the point in our friendship if you can't share your secrets? You knew mine."

"Well, not all secrets are meant to be shared among friends," Ruth said, "only with God. This was one of those secrets."

"Well, why share it now?" Betty asked. Ruth lowered her head.

"She feels guilty," Maxine added. "For teaching her grandchild how to cope like she once did."

"I'm not a bad person," Ruth said, looking up at them with tears in her eyes. "I'm bittersweet. I was trying to protect Malaysia from people."

"Ain't no protecting her from people," Maxine said. "Good and evil is everywhere. The only protection you can give her is prayer. That's the only weapon she needs for people."

"I agree," Betty said.

"You right," Ruth agreed reluctantly, "but until you been a victim of rape you just wouldn't understand. It confuses you. When the person doing it, done watch you grow up. Not only that, but your mama, who supposed to be your protector, knows and does nothing."

"I get what you are saying," Maxine said. "I never had to go through that, and I hate that you did."

Betty went behind the counter to fix her, Ruth, and Maxine a mug of coffee. Ruth's story shot bullets through her. Betty's stomach churned at the thought of Ruth's stepfather touching her, and Craig sleeping with Malaysia. It was an awful image on display in her mind. She wished there were something she could have done to save both of them, but there wasn't. She hated the feeling of knowing that she was alive and well, but couldn't save neither of them, from either of the men. But this is what Betty was trying to escape from, being the savior. She said she was gonna let it all go, but it was like a drug, and she was the junkie. Problems were just calling her name and she desperately fiend to be the solver. She finished preparing the coffee and set the mugs on the serving tray. She walked cautiously back to her friends and carefully placed the tray on the table.

"Ruth! Come have you a coffee and a seat." Betty sat and grabbed her mug to drink.

Ruth pulled out a chair and took a seat at the table. She reached for a cup, but Maxine grabbed it first.

"Go ahead, Ruth," Maxine said, "you can have it"

"Don't be nice to me because of what you know about me," Ruth said in a sassy tone. "Go ahead and get it."

"No, Ruth, I want you to have it."

Ruth didn't want to be the crippled person at the table who everyone was being nice too. She didn't want them treating her with kid gloves; she wanted the same treatment she always received. That way, she wouldn't feel strange or regretful of her choice to share.

Betty placed her mug down on the table. "I'm sorry for how I acted earlier as you confessed. It just broke my heart to know all of that happened to you and no one was there to help you, not even your mother. How old were you when it started?" Betty asked.

"Thirteen," Ruth said. "My mother had run off behind this man and left me to be raised by Big Mama when I was three. I didn't even know her until I turned thirteen. She came and visited us on my birthday. Big mama was pissed. She told Big Mama that she was moving back home, and her husband was going to be pastor at this church, and she needed me to complete her Christian family. Big mama told her, '*hell no. You abandoned this girl at three, then want to wait till she almost a woman to raise her. Get out! She my child! The only way you get her is if I die.*' She spoke too soon. Two days later, she had a stroke and died, and I was living with my mama and her husband. At first, I thought me and mama was going to build a relationship and get to know each other, since I knew nothing of her, but instead, she put me off on him. She was so busy trying to be this important figure at the church that she didn't even try to be an important figure to me."

"I knew after your thirteenth birthday something was wrong," Maxine said. "You know how you could just sense a problem? I felt it, but I just never asked because, I figured if something were wrong, you would say something."

"But I didn't know who to talk to about it," Ruth said. "Like I was confused. Like what the hell. Why? Why was this happening to me? Did all adults do this or was it just me? I went through a real psychological break down, and the day she pulled up a chair and watched, I thought I was going to die. She really didn't care about me. She broke my heart."

"Do you still communicate with your mother?" Maxine asked.

"Not since I moved out," Ruth answered. "I see her out in town, and I don't even look her way. She could be on fire, and I wouldn't piss on her to put her out."

"So, wait," Betty said, remembering when Ruth moved out her mother's home. "You moved when you were pregnant with Jason. So…"

"My mother's husband is his father," Ruth said.

"Wow… and Jason knew?" Betty asked.

"I told him," Ruth said. "And I guess when he was dating, Katrina, he told her, and I told Malaysia way before she came to me about Craig touching her." Ruth grabbed her mug and began to sip.

"You know it's sad when things like this is done by people of the church," Betty said. "Especially the leaders of the church."

Ruth placed her mug down on the table. "That's why I didn't want to say nothing then," Ruth explained. "Just like Malaysia didn't want to say nothing. It's hard to believe when the person doing it is such a prominent person in the community, especially the church."

"Well, Ruth," Maxine said. "Today is a new day. And your past is your past. It's time to forgive, but never forget, and move forward with your life. My friend, this been troubling you for a while and then here it comes, back into your life, but this time for your granddaughter. It's time to let go, and let God take control. It's time for you to ask Father God to show you the way and order your steps."

"It's time to make peace with this, Ruth," Betty said, "and yourself. Release those skeletons out of your closet."

"Well, before I do that, let me make peace with you," Ruth said. "I'm sorry for jumping down your throat. I guess some people don't know when they have a good friend. I couldn't think of anyone who could put up with me as long as you have. Hell, even Maxine got the hell away because of my ways. But you a good friend, Betty, you always have been, and I thank you for that. As Maxine said earlier, friendship is a gift from God. I have been truly blessed to have you in my life for fifty-five years. Can't too many people say that, but I love you, Betty."

"I love you, too, girl," Betty said, standing up from her chair. "Get over here." She opened her arms. Ruth rose up out her chair and went to hug Betty. "You will always be my friend. I love you, Ruth."

"I love you too, Betty," Ruth said.

"God is truly working here today," Maxine said, fanning her eyes from the tears she shed. Betty and Ruth stepped away from each other. Betty turned to Maxine. "Girl, I told you," Betty said. "This place ain't nothing but a healing ground!"

"Girl," Maxine said. "Ain't nothing wrong with that. Everyone needs a good healing, and I feel we all have accomplished that today."

"I know I did," Ruth said. "It feels good to get that out after forty-seven years."

"That's a long time to carry a storm," Maxine replied.

"But being here with you girls," Ruth said, "brought the sunshine back. Now I just got to get everything back in order. Which reminds me, Maxine, you remember that song you used to sing back in church, the one that made all the old folks pass out?"

"You talking about *Order My Steps*?" Maxine questioned.

"Yeah, that's the one!" Ruth said.

"You always had a nice voice, Maxine," Betty said.

"Can you sing it for me?" Ruth asked.

"Sure," Maxine said. "Anything for you, dear friend."

Maxine sung *Order My Steps*, and it was angelic as Mimi Redd herself, bringing tears to both Betty and Ruth's eyes. Once she finished the song, Betty and Ruth stood up and gave her a hug. This moment was a flame that Betty had been waiting to rekindled. It was long over do for her friends to be in the same room together, trying to make their friendship work. She knew it would take time, but it overjoyed her heart to see them trying. Betty's friendship with these women meant everything to her. It was a gift she treasured and would always lock and keep.

* * *

Valarie sat in the swing on her front porch, watching the sun set and the close-knit houses that surrounded hers. She was thinking about her next step in life since Betty, James, Joshua, Jenny, and Stephanie knew her secret. She took out an FMLA (Family Medical Leave Act) at her other jobs to give herself a mental break, so she could adjust to her secret being out amongst those who knew her. James was at work, and Joshua was still locked away in his room. She wanted to have a talk with her son and explain her reason for keeping her illness from him, but he wouldn't open the door. He wouldn't respond. As she rocked back and forth in the swing, watching the cars ride up and down her suburban street, she heard the wooden floors in her home creaking. Joshua was at the screen door, looking at his neighbor's house across the street.

He gazed at his mother, who patted the cushion next to her, signaling Joshua to sit. He exited the house through the white border screen door and took a seat beside his mother. He sat hunched over with his hands clasped together, staring out into the woods off to the side of the porch.

Valarie could tell he had questions that needed answers, but he didn't say anything. He just sat quietly; his eyes focusing on nothing in particular in the woods. The silence killed her soul. She just wanted him to look at her, say something to her so she wouldn't feel so invisible to him. "Just ask me, Joshua," she said. He turned his gaze from the woods to his mom. "Ask me whatever you want."

"Did my dad give this to you?" he asked, looking through the soul of her eyes.

"Son, I honestly don't know, because you don't have it. Just me. The whole time I was pregnant with you, my blood work was good. Then two days after I had you, they come and told me that my white cell count had dropped." Tears began to fall from his eyes.

"Did they do something to you, Mama?" His voice grew thick and heavy with emotion. "Something that you didn't know about. Like maybe a blood transfusion or something. 'Cause it's not making sense to me how. You carried me without it, and then, suddenly you have it and I don't." Joshua shook, his head in confusion.

"Son, I been trying to make sense of this for years. When I had you, I know they did put me to sleep, but they said they didn't give me anything or do anything to me."

"You need to get a lawyer, Mama. You need to find out whether or not they were telling you the truth."

"And where am I supposed to get the money to get a lawyer? Everything I make goes into this house and us."

"Ask the guy you talk to. He seems pretty cool. I can even get a job and help."

"No!" She pointed her finger at him. "You gonna go to school and play ball."

"Mama," Joshua shouted. "I don't wanna play ball. I wanna be here and take care of you, Mama! I can't lose you."

"Joshua," she cried. She placed her arms around him and held him close to her heart.

"I can't lose you, Mama. You're the only person who means anything in my life. I love you. You're my friend, my confidant and my biggest supporter. I can't lose you."

Joshua words stung Valarie like a wasp, bringing her heart down to her knees and sucking her soul out like a whirlwind. She could feel her baby exploding like fireworks inside as she held him in are her arms and he cried. Valarie wished she could take his pain away, but she knew she couldn't. Releasing her secret allowed her to breathe, but it slowly suffocated her son. She didn't know what was in store for them. She didn't know how their new story was about to begin.

* * *

James headed out the door of his home to go and see Valarie. As he turned around and headed down his stairs, he saw his mother, Ruth, leaned up on his car, smoking a cigarette.

"I didn't come for war. I come for peace," Ruth said, flicking the cigarette to the ground.

"Make it quick. I got somewhere to be," James said, looking at his watch.

"Well, I know it ain't work. Hell, I just followed you from the café, when you made your last delivery across the street at Colemans. So, you can hear me out." James folded his arms and huffed at Ruth. "You hate me, and I can't blame you for that, I wasn't a good mother, and I'm sorry for that. Your daddy had me thinking he was a different kind of man, and he wasn't. Your father did a lot of shady things to me that you were too young to remember. And when he left me for broke, he made me retrack to an old way of living." Tears fell from Ruth eyes. *In order for our relationship to work, I have to tell it all.* "I was raped, James, by my stepfather. Thirteen years old, and my mother sat back and watched. My stepfather is Jason's daddy."

Ruth's confession made James ears bleed and his eyes turned fire red. He stumbled to sit on his front steps, taking in what he had heard. He began pounding his fist into his hands. He took in deep, repetitive breaths – in and out. When he found no relief in punching his hand, he began to hit his knees. This news hurt, worse than Valarie's news. James focused his dark eyes back to his mother, who had swiped away all her tears. Ruth went and sat beside him and placed her hand on his knee.

"I used to sell my body before I had you. I would leave Jason alone or with my friend Maxine, just so I could let a man do whatever he wanted to with me, and I never felt nothing, not even pleasure. It was like laying there letting my stepfather rape me over and over again. That was the mind set I would use when selling my body for money. When I met your dad, I tried to put all that behind me. I tried to be a good wife, a good mother, and then he cheated and left me." Ruth bit her bottom lip and looked afar. "The little job that I had at the time didn't fulfill the debt that your father created. I had to go back to the streets, sell drugs, sell my body, and abandon you boys. And I wanna say James, I'm sorry that you got the worse part of me, and Jason for a short period of time was able to have the good part of me, before I had gone astray again. When it was just me and him, he would see me leave him and go off with men, and he would ask me, 'Mama, what happened to you? Why do you let men hurt you?' When I told him what had happened to me as a young girl, all he ever did was love on me from that point on. He grew up to be the man of the house at a young age, and when he knew I was coming in from flipping a trick, he would have me a meal and bathwater waiting on me. I knew your brother loved me. He was the first man to accept me and know my past."

"That's why you couldn't love," James replied.

"But I wanna learn how." Ruth made James feel the hope through her eyes. "My past had shackles on me, and after all these years, I'm finally getting to a hammer and knocking all the nails out. I'm going to get some help. I'm seeking counseling. I want you to come with me. I want us to start over and get a chance at something we never had."

James held his hands together and thought on it. Ruth in her mind, prayed he would say yes. "I'm not gonna say no and I'm not gonna say yes, Mama. Just give me some time. That was a lot that you revealed. Give me a few days, and I'll reach out to you."

Ruth smiled at James; she knew he was a man of his word. She moved her hand from his knee and patted his shoulder, letting him know that whatever decision he made was understood. Ruth slowly rose from his step and began walking to her car.

James remained seated and watched his mom for a moment. "Hey, Mama," he shouted out to her.

Ruth turned around to see him walking to her. He grabbed his mother and hugged her. She cautiously wrapped her arms around him, not used to the love she was receiving from him.

"I'll go with you, Mama," James said. "Whatever you need, I'll do it. I love you, Mama, and I'm sorry about what that fool did to you."

A rush of emotions filled Ruth, causing her eyes to flood with tears as she held her baby boy as if she had just given birth to him again. This was a moment of a lifetime, and she knew somewhere in heaven, Jason was overjoyed to see his mother and brother close and that new door opened.

* * *

Where are they? Stephanie was downtown at Restaurant El Barrio, waiting on Nina and Jenny. She was about to break the news to them about Betty taking a break from the café. Nina approached the table.

"What up, girl? Am I late?" Nina asked. Stephanie looked at her phone.

"Actually, you're on time. Now we're just waiting on Jenny.

"What about Valarie?" Nina asked. "Is she not meeting us here today?"

"No, not today. She had something important to do."

Jenny entered the restaurant and rushed to the table like she was late for work at the café. "Hey, Stephanie, Nina. Sorry I'm running late."

Stephanie raised her hands in forgiveness. "It's okay," Stephanie said, "you really aren't late."

Jenny sigh, relieved to hear she was on time.

"So, what's this meeting about?" Nina asked, trying to read Stephanie's worried expression.

"Well, Ms. Betty was supposed to do this, but she had a friend come into town, and she asked me to do it, so she could spend time with her friend before she leaves. Ms. Betty is taking a six-month break from the café, and she wants me to take her place till she gets back."

Nina and Jenny's facial expressions conveyed they weren't pleased with the news.

"At first, Ms. Betty was going to just close it, because all the drama was causing her to come home and have a mental breakdown. And I begged her not to close it, because it's our home. We were so distant at first, but I feel the café and the issues we've resolved there together has brought us closer, like sister's and friends. But I don't want to accept the role, unless I know you both are cool with me having it."

Nina and Jenny sat silent with their eyes focused on Stephanie.

"I think you'll be great." Jenny said. "After all you've been through. This will be a good start for you, and you're right, the café is our home. We've put out and overcome so much there. Thank you for saving it, and I'm going to miss Ms. Betty."

"Me too," Nina said, looking sad. "Ms. Betty is my girl, but I know it's gotta be a lot on the heart and the brain to sit there and be an ear and a shoulder to everyone's pain and yet still try to be all that for herself. She's one of a kind."

"Yes she is," Stephanie added, "I'm still grateful for her opening up her home to me. My own family wouldn't even do that, but she did."

"And glory be to her for that," Nina said.

"You guys wanna hear something funny," Jenny asked. They turned their heads to look at her. "My dad came and saw me yesterday, and he told me he had cancer."

Nina and Stephanie both look sad. They both hated to hear that kind of news.

"I'm sorry about your father," Stephanie said.

"Me too," Nina added. "Cancer taking everybody."

"And it can take him," Jenny announced without remorse.

Stephanie and Nina's eyes bucked at Jenny's remark. "Aw, Jenny you don't mean that," Stephanie said.

"No, I really do. Why should I be forgiving? Why should I erase how he abandoned me during my addiction and treatment, but be there for his? The sad thing is, I am forgiving, and I am going to be there for his treatments. Just not where he can see me."

Nina turned her head in shock at sweet loving Jenny, turning into 'paybacks a bitch' Jenny. The table was too quiet, so Nina threw out her flaw. "Well, you want to know what I discovered about myself yesterday?"

"What?" Jenny and Stephanie asked.

"I'm attracted to toxic men," Nina admitted with a gleeful smile. Jenny laughed, while Stephanie smiled and shook her head.

"Ain't we all," Stephanie joked.

"Well, not like me. I date men, knowing they ain't about shit, and I allow myself to crumble like bread in their hands once they're done with me. And I keep repeating this cycle over and over, and I think I'm about to do it again. I think I'm falling for my FWB."

"FWB!" Stephanie looked confused.

"Friend with benefits," Jenny laughed at Stephanie not knowing the abbreviation.

"Yeah, I didn't know about that term." Stephanie shook her head.

"I'm heading right back down Toxic Road. See, this is why we need Ms. Betty."

"Or Ruth," Jenny added.

"All hell naw'! Not Ms. Ruth! Somebody got to talk some sense into us," Nina said, eyeing Stephanie and Jenny. "And who to do it like the old lady gang? Dang." Nina's expression turned sad again. "I'm going to miss them at the café." A tear slipped from Nina and trailed down her face to hang precariously on her chin.

"Me too," Jenny said, letting Nina emotions consume her.

"Hey, y'all. Let's remember," Stephanie said, reaching out for both of them, "this is only temporarily. Ms. Betty is still going to be around, just less in the café during working hours. And when she there after hours, we can't unload our problems on her. We got to give her this space and peace, so she can come back to us whole and restored."

"I think you going to be the next Betty," Nina said, sensing it in Stephanie's demeanor. "Helping people, healing people. It's already in you. Good luck with this, boo."

Nina's words struck in Stephanie like lightning. She didn't want the role of Betty. She wasn't even built like Betty. Stephanie just wanted to help Ms. Betty and the other ladies keep their secondary home. They all had gone through and seen so much together there that she didn't want to let it go. Nor did she want the headache of trying to play and be everybody's mother. At this point she was unsure of her decision to manage the café.

* * *

Katrina stood over Jason's grave, reminiscing and staring at the picture on his tomb. She canceled her scheduled program to spend time with her daughter and handle some family business. A police car drove up to the gravesite and parked. Katrina sighed and returned her attention to Jason's tombstone. She didn't come to the grave site to see Jason. She came to meet with Jake. Katrina looked back to see him wobble out his car and make his way to her.

"Did they do it? Katrina asked, studying Jake with her eyes.

"You shouldn't see any more news reporters hanging outside your house." She nodded her head, happy with him taking care of that for her.

"What about Craig? When is the crew going to handle that."

Jake rubbed his chin. "Just give it some time. When he goes inside, we already got it set up. You'll hear about it on the news."

Katrina folded her arms, unhappy with the fact they were trying to play God. "This doesn't feel right," Katrina said, shaking her head. "I feel like a gangster out here talking this business with you. I don't feel like a woman of God. This whole situation feels evil. Just tell the crew to spare him."

Jake's eyes bulged in shock. "Really, Katrina," he said, folding his arms. "Yesterday you said he had to die."

"I know what I said. And I said it out of rage and anger. But I don't wanna be the reason why he's dead. Let God decide his fate."

Jake chuckled at Katrina. "God already did, and God said kill him."

Katrina threw up her hands disagreeing with Jake. "No, you said kill him," she said, pointing her finger at Jake. "That's not God's way and I won't be a part of this." She turned to walk away, wanting to forget she had this conversation with Jake.

"What if I said it's Jason's way," Jake yelled out to her. She swiveled around and gave him a 'you kidding' look. She walked back over to him.

"You can't speak for no dead man," Katrina said angrily at Jake.

"What about a resurrected man." Katrina was bewildered by his remark.

"What do you mean, by a resurrected man. Jason is dead!"

"But just like you and me. He's a spirit and his spirit lives on."

Katrina gave Jake an evil glare, and he raised his hand to make it known that he meant no harm in his words.

"Katrina we are not enemies. We're friends, and what's going to happen to Craig is not my call. The order was made before you called 911," he said. His smile was sinister and caused chills to run down

Katrina's spine. She watched as he walked away to his car. His words, his smile, all this created a ball of confusion in Katrina's head.

"Then whose call is it," Katrina called out to Jake. She tried to hurry and follow him to his car. "Whose call is it?" she yelled out again.

Jake had made it inside his car, and Katrina was right there behind him. She began beating on his driver's side window. "Whose call is it, Jake?" But he only ignored her and pulled off, leaving Katrina standing there.

Jake's words left Katrina's mind spinning. *Whose calling the shots for the crew now?* She knew it couldn't be Jason. He was dead. But it was someone who Jake didn't want to reveal. They were going to make sure Craig was killed, and there was nothing she could do about it. Again, she wondered, *who in the hell was calling shots and the leader of the crew?*

The End.

AUTHOR PAGE

Angel Averette-Powell is the founder & CEO of Crown Yourself
Production Publishing. CYPP is a company that produce theatrical
works, and publish books, poems and other creative works. The author
is an Alabama native, mother, wife, and writer, whose been writing
since she was 15, but allowed fear to stop her from chasing her
purpose. Now Mrs. Powell is no longer letting fear hold her back. She
is ready to change lives with her writing.

**Follow The Author on the following social media platforms for
upcoming book signing events.**

Facebook: Crown Yourself Production Publishing

YouTube: Crown Yourself TV

Instagram: author_ angelaverettepowell

Email: crownyourself.pp@gmail.com

www.ingramcontent.com/pod-product-compliance
Lightning Source LLC
Chambersburg PA
CBHW061521020726
47502CB00006B/2167